IN THE DARK

Claire Allan is a former journalist from Derry in Northern Ireland, where she still lives with her husband, two teenage children, two cats and a dog who thinks she is a human child. In her eighteen years as a journalist, she covered a wide range of stories from attempted murders to court sessions, to the Saville Inquiry into the events of Bloody Sunday and countless human interest features. Claire has been writing crime fiction since 2018. *In the Dark* is her seventh thriller. She has also worked as a story consultant on forthcoming BBC drama *Blue Lights* and is currently working on a TV adaptation of her novel *The Liar's Daughter*.

When she's not writing, she'll more than likely be found dog walking or on Twitter @claireallan.

D0231532

Also by Claire Allan:

Her Name Was Rose
Apple of My Eye
Forget Me Not
The Liar's Daughter
Ask No Questions
The Nurse

IN THE
DARK

CLAIRE ALLAN

avon.

Published by AVON
A division of HarperCollins*Publishers* Ltd
1 London Bridge Street
London SE1 9GF

www.harpercollins.co.uk

HarperCollins*Publishers*
Macken House, 39/40 Mayor Street Upper,
Dublin 1, D01 C9W8
Ireland

This paperback edition 2023

3

First published in Great Britain by HarperCollins*Publishers* 2023

Copyright © Claire Allan 2023

Claire Allan asserts the moral right to be identified as the author of this work.

A catalogue copy of this book is available from the British Library.

ISBN: 978-0-00-852458-6

This novel is entirely a work of fiction. The names, characters and incidents portrayed in it are the work of the author's imagination. Any resemblance to actual persons, living or dead, events or localities is entirely coincidental.

Set in Bembo Std by Palimpsest Book Production Limited,
Falkirk, Stirlingshire

Printed and Bound in the UK using
100% Renewable Electricity at CPI Group (UK) Ltd

All rights reserved. No part of this text may be reproduced, transmitted, downloaded, decompiled, reverse engineered, or stored in or introduced into any information storage and retrieval system, in any form or by any means, whether electronic or mechanical, without the express written permission of the publishers.

MIX
Paper | Supporting
responsible forestry
FSC™ C007454

This book is produced from independently certified FSC™ paper
to ensure responsible forest management.

For more information visit: www.harpercollins.co.uk/green

Acknowledgements

This book was a journey – and one that challenged me as a writer and reminded me I am always, always learning.

I want to thank, from the very bottom of my heart, my editor Thorne Ryan for being such a gentle and wise teacher and for helping me to see both the wood and the trees in a book I think we both should be very proud of. It's always terrifying to work with a new editor, but you made it easy and have been so reassuring throughout.

Thanks to all the team at Avon Books for their passion, their creativity and all that invisible hard work that goes on behind the scenes to get a book to print and onto the shelves. You are all incredible people to work with.

Thank you to Helena Newton for a beady eyed copy edit!

Thanks also to the team at HarperCollins Ireland who fly the flag closer to home and do such a great job.

As always, I must thank my agent Ger Nichol who continues to be the best cheerleader an author could ask for. This year, more than any other, you have gone above and beyond when you would have been justified in taking time out to mind yourself. It is always appreciated, Ger.

Thanks to my husband for gifting me with a room of my own to write in after all these years and for supporting my dream to continue making things up for a living. Thanks, of course, to my children for their patience, especially at deadline time. I love you so much and my office door is open – most of the time.

To my family and friends for just being amazing. My parents, my siblings, nieces and nephews – I love you so much and am very lucky to have such a supportive crew.

And my friends, in particular Fiona (aka Tony), Julie-Anne, Marie-Louise, Vicki and Erin for just being class. And to the Waves Crew, led by the formidable Serena Terry, for all the therapy.

To my Twitter crew – you made me laugh every day even when I was feeling really menopausal and grumpy and sure I'd never write again. Thank you.

To my fellow authors – who understand the madness that comes with this process – thanks for listening and assuring me I'm not alone. In particular: my soul sister Fionnuala Kearney who I adore with my whole heart, Sharon Dempsey, CJ Cooke, Louise Beech, Helen Fields, Anna McPartlin (for the best voice message ever!), Brian McGilloway and John Marrs. Thank you to Marian Keyes for your ongoing fabulous-ness and just how much you champion other writers.

To the booksellers – thank you to you all and particularly to the independent book sellers who go above and beyond. Special mention to Lesley at Bridge Books, Jenni at Little Acorns, David at No Alibis and Bob at Gutter Books. And thank you also to the Library staff, especially those at Libraries NI.

The character of Jacqueline 'Jacqs' McLaughlin is named after someone really special – the lovely mammy of Rachel, who became the proud new owner of our former home in early 2022. I promised Jacqueline on the day they viewed our house that I would use her name, and I keep my word. Amid the massive stress of a house move, you and Rachel made it so much easier. I hope you enjoy your namesake!

And finally, to my readers. There is not a single one of you I take for granted. Without you, I would not be living my dream. Thank you for reading, sharing, getting in touch, reviewing, and just choosing my book when there are so many out there to choose from.

For the women who held my hand
and reminded me to just breathe
when I walked into the waves during a very stormy year.

'Be with me always – take any form – drive me mad! only do not leave me in this abyss, where I cannot find you! Oh, God! it is unutterable! I cannot *live* without my life! I cannot *live* without my soul!' – *Emily Brontë*, Wuthering Heights

'If anyone injures his neighbour, whatever he has done must be done to him: fracture for fracture, eye for eye, tooth for tooth.' – *Leviticus 24:17–21*

Prologue

The process of exacting the perfect revenge is best viewed as a marathon and not a sprint.

If you're wise you play the long game. You make people think they're safe. You make them think that the worst has passed. That they've got away with it. You wait until life returns to normal. You wait until they are comfortable in the mundanity of their everyday existence.

Yes, you sow the seeds, of course. You set the wheels in motion. If you do it right, you create a drip, drip, drip effect until it all comes together. Until your revenge feels as if it has grown organically, and was always going to happen. Get it right, it can be a thing of beauty. Justice is, after all, always beautiful – even if you can't see it at the time.

The plan isn't the difficult part. Just remember the five P's: Proper Planning Prevents Poor Performance. It's a motto that was taught to me in school that works well in all aspects of life. I've never understood how people can enjoy the doing more than the planning stage. The planning stage is such fun. It's when you can let your imagination run wild. Where you can play with scenarios in your head. Where you can play with people – test them. Push them. Confuse them.

It's where you can take your time to work out exactly how to make the punishment fit the crime.

Ask yourself: what do they truly deserve? Ask yourself if you'll be able to live with what happens next. That one's important. Because you don't have to be a bad person to want revenge. Wanting revenge doesn't make you evil. Or wrong. It's a natural reaction. It's what you're owed. No one but you will have to look yourself in the mirror for the rest of your days.

No. The hard part is patience. It's taking that hurt, and pain and grief, and sitting with it until the time is right.

You must make sure it's all perfect, because once the right time comes and everything is in place – once you light the fuse – you won't be able stop it. You won't be able to extinguish it. You just get to enjoy it, and it will be all the sweeter for the wait.

And what makes it so enjoyable? Knowing, without a shadow of a doubt, that they brought it on themselves.

This is what I've been telling myself all along. I've sat and watched and considered everything, trying to keep a cool head. That's how I've coped – by viewing this all as part of a wider plan. As a marathon and not a sprint. It's how I've allowed myself to keep going. It has given me a purpose. We all need something to get us out of bed in the morning. Especially after the unthinkable happens.

Chapter One

Nora

We'd agreed to meet in the hotel lobby – a brightly lit, elegant space with views over the city centre. I knew I didn't want this Izzy person in my home – and Brendan was absolutely and resolutely opposed to that, too. But maybe I should've chosen somewhere quieter, somewhere more private. People will no doubt stare when I walk in. They always do. I've gotten used to that. How a room falls quiet when I enter it. I've gotten used to the nudges and the whispers. To people lowering their heads in case, God forbid, they make eye contact with me and are forced into any kind of awkward conversation.

There's not much they can say, after all. 'Hi, Nora. Any word on your missing child yet?' or 'Hi, Nora. Tell me this much: did you kill her and hide her body? I won't tell anyone, swear!'

People used up all their platitudes years ago. How it was awful. How they couldn't imagine. How God is good. (Ha! Any god who puts a mother through this is categorically and emphatically not good!) I've been advised to pray to St Anthony. I've had hundreds of novenas said in Daisy's name. Thoughts and prayers go nowhere when it's your child who's missing. It's all just meaningless mumbo jumbo. Thoughts and prayers are just words strung together by people who mean well but ultimately don't have to live through a moment of this hell. I've long since rejected any notion that religion can provide a comfort at this time, or at any time for that matter.

Over time, the platitudes were replaced by awkward silences. It was different, you see, when it was all fresh. When everyone was hoping they would be the one to play the hero and solve the case and we'd have a tearful reunion.

People get bored if things move too slowly. They give up if things don't move at all. There have been countless missing children since who have stolen the public's attention and sympathy. I don't begrudge those children that. I'm not a monster. Or, at least, I don't think I'm a monster. (That's a little gallows humour − the kind of thing I'm allowed to think but never say. I'm not allowed to joke at all anymore it seems. God forbid I'd laugh. It wouldn't look right. No one understands how I can laugh at all; least of all me.)

All these thoughts tumble and crash in my head and I push them away as I spot a young woman with short dark spiky hair and a pair of large red-rimmed glasses looking around her. I recognise her from her Twitter profile picture. She looks exactly how you would expect a TV producer to look. All stylish, baggy clothes that hang off her petite frame, and minimal make-up. She probably has a skincare routine; a proper one. More than the quick wipe with a face cloth I indulge in while showering followed by a dab of supermarket-branded moisturiser.

'Nora?' she asks, in a soft Home Counties accent.

'Izzy?' I ask back and she nods.

'Thanks so much for coming,' she says. 'I know this can't be easy for you.'

'No,' I say, as I sit down grasping my bag to my stomach tightly. 'It's not easy. But that doesn't mean I don't have to do it.'

'I can imagine,' she says, her voice warm and soothing. She

seems lovely and I'd like to believe she really is. But I've long learned that most people just want to take advantage of what happened to us so they can benefit themselves. So I just nod as a waitress arrives with a tray bearing a pot of tea and two cups, as well as a plate of scones.

'I hope this is okay with you? I can order you a coffee, or a soft drink?'

I suppose it's too early for a proper drink, I think. That would really get tongues wagging. 'This is fine,' I tell her. 'Honestly.' As my stomach grumbles I realise I've not eaten yet this morning and this scone is just what I need.

Izzy proceeds to attempt a little small talk as she pours the tea, but I don't have the mental energy for it. Not now. 'Look,' I tell her, after I've washed down a bite of rich fruit scone with a large gulp of tea. 'All I'm interested in is finding out what happened to my daughter. I want to find out if she's still alive somewhere.' It feels like a rehearsed line, even though it isn't.

'Do *you* think she's still alive?' Izzy asks cutting right to the heart of the matter and the familiar tightness in my chest grows stronger.

'I don't know,' I say. 'I wish I did. I wish I had some of that mother's instinct that they talk about, but I don't. I don't know if she's dead. I don't know if she was kidnapped. At times I've thought I'd rather her dead than kidnapped and out there in a place no one is keeping her safe. I know that sounds awful, but what if she was trafficked somewhere . . .' I let the sentence hang. There's no need to colour in between the lines on this one.

'I can understand that,' Izzy says, placing her teacup back on the saucer with a gentle clink. 'Hopefully if we shine another light on it, something might show up. It's a long shot, I know.' She shifts a little in her seat, dropping her gaze for a moment. There is a beat before she speaks again.

'Look, I'm going to be honest with you here. I've not been telling you the full story.'

The tightness squeezes even more. What is she going to say next? I lift my teacup to my mouth, but it's shaking so much I change my mind and rest it back on its saucer on the table.

'I want you to be a part of this. If I want the best chance at all of it being picked up – it has to be you. But if you feel you can't or don't want to be a part of it, I'm still going to make the documentary anyway. We will be telling a story, and we already have a number of interviews lined up. We're scheduled to be here for the next fortnight, and we start filming in two days. You agreeing to get involved is the best way to get attention for this film, and maybe the best way to right some of the wrongs that have been said or written about you is to have your involvement. People are voyeurs at heart. They want to see grief. I know that sounds cold, but I'm not here to bullshit you. But if you feel you can't be involved, we have many people who have already agreed to talk to us.'

I wasn't expecting her candidness or for her to tell me they were ready to roll. The emails she had sent said plans were at 'an advanced stage' – but this is one step beyond that, isn't it? She's in production. This isn't a case of her asking my permission to make the documentary – it's throwing me a lifeline. Either I grab it, or I drown in its wake.

She is essentially telling me that she wants me to cut a metaphorical vein wide open on film and bleed for everyone to see. If I say no, will this documentary be a hatchet job? Will these interviewees she has lined up be people who have any real insight, or will they be the usual faces who spout their theories without any real authority? Most other documentary makers have erred on the side of the neighbourhood gossip approach to 'evidence' gathering. Just who does she have lined up to speak with when she starts filming in just two days' time?

What side is Izzy Devine on?

'Do you think I hurt my own child?' I ask, my eyes directly on hers. Even if she's a good liar I figure I'll be able to see something in her expression that screams of her true feelings. There will be a pause. A blink. A swallow of the truth before the answer she thinks I'll want to hear comes out. There's always a tell.

'You want an honest answer?' Izzy answers, unblinking.

'I wouldn't have asked if I didn't,' I say even though I'm scared of what she might say. If she's brave enough to say yes, then I know I'll have to do everything I can to convince her she's wrong.

'Okay,' she says, sliding her glasses back up the bridge of her nose. 'I don't really know what to think. It seems so improbable to me that a person can have no memory of something so cataclysmic. I know shock plays a part, but it's been seven years. Then again, I don't think anyone is that good an actress to be able to pull that particular lie off so consistently, and to confound the psychiatric profession too. But I don't understand how a person, especially a child, can just vanish from the face of the earth. People don't really vanish, do they? There is no Bermuda Triangle in the general Derry area,' she says with a hint of a conciliatory smile. 'Yet, all those searches, fingertip examinations of the woods and surrounding areas and there was no body found? No trace of Daisy at all? It doesn't make any sense. I mean, the only place any blood at all was found was in your house . . .'

She lets it hang. This is the 'evidence' that so many of my haters cling to. 'But the blood . . .' is a constant refrain from people who clearly have never lived with an adventure-seeking four-year-old. They treat it with the same reverence that they would a signed confession.

Blood droplets, minuscule, barely visible, were found on the tiled floor in the hall. Tiny pinpricks of red that matched my daughter's blood type.

'The only thing the blood in our home has ever proved is that Daisy lived there,' I snap back, feeling the nails on my right hand pressing into my palm. I must relax. I can see why so many people like to cling to something as tangible as blood spots. Especially in light of a dearth of other evidence.

'She was four. She was always running. Never stopped for a second. Was always speeding this way and that. She'd fallen in the garden that morning and had limped through the hall to the kitchen where I put a plaster on her knee and kissed it better.'

I remember so vividly the trickle of blood running down the pale skin of her leg, soaking into her white ruffled ankle sock. She had been so brave – telling me in a sniffly voice that it was 'just an ouchie' and she'd fallen while chasing a butterfly. Her tears had dried as she'd told me about its soft colours and how it looked as if it was dancing in the air.

'I know your explanation,' Izzy replies, her voice an unwelcome intrusion on my memories. 'I think I've read every interview and every word written about the case. You wanted an honest answer, so that's what I'm giving you. I told you, I'm not here to bullshit you. I don't know who to believe.'

'So if you don't know whether to believe I'm telling the truth or not, why should I trust you? I've been burned before – you know that. You know that's why I don't talk to the media anymore except through a spokesperson. It's served me well. Tell me, Izzy, why should I change – just for you, someone who doesn't know if I'm lying or not?' I try to keep my voice calm, try to hide all trace of emotion, but inside my stomach is in knots. I want this woman to believe me. If I'm being honest with myself I want her to sit across this sofa from me and tell me she has my back and her documentary will fall very firmly in the Nora Logue camp. I'm not sure I, or my family, could survive another hatchet job. Another journalist who makes, then breaks, promises. I'm not sure I want to take the risk of this all blowing up in my face yet again.

'Look,' she says, and she leans in a little closer, 'we're on the same side of this, Nora. We both want truth and justice. We both want to know what happened that day.'

'So you don't think I'm trying to hide some deep, dark secret?' I ask.

She gives a little shrug. 'I don't think you'd have come to speak to me at all if you were consciously trying to hide something, dark or otherwise. Whatever the truth is, I'm inclined to believe you genuinely either don't know or don't remember. Either way, getting nearer to the truth is going to help us both. Even if that truth is something dark.'

A shudder pulses through my body. Izzy sips from her cup of tea while I contemplate all that she has said. Are we really on the same side? The side of truth and justice? It sounds like a cheesy soundbite. But it isn't. It's the truth. That's what I want. Truth and justice will equal the ability to move on instead of existing in this limbo land. I'm so tired of it at this stage. So very, very tired. My life came to a brutal halt that day. It's no way to exist. The missing her is bad enough; the not being able to remember when I last saw her, what happened, if she was hurt . . . My mind has filled in the blanks in a thousand unimaginable ways.

'So,' I say. 'You say you want to find the truth . . .'

'I want *us* to find the truth,' she says, looking me straight in the eye, her voice steady.

'So, you want *us* to find the truth,' I repeat and she nods. 'And you're making this documentary with or without me?'

She nods again. 'Yes, I am. I think there's an appetite for your story to be re-examined again with new eyes. Putting you front and centre of telling that story is more likely to bring as many pairs of eyes as possible to the hunt for Daisy. We've already been overwhelmed with interest.'

'Interest from who and from where?' Is it just gossipmongers or people who might actually be able to help?

She sits back in her seat, getting comfortable. 'You've seen *Making a Murderer*, *Tiger King* or *Don't Fuck With Cats*? Or heard of them at least?' she asks. 'Of course those are only some examples but . . .'

I nod. I have heard of those true crime documentary series; I've not watched them. I don't have the stomach to watch someone's real pain dissected in the name of entertainment. It's too close to home. But I've not been living under a rock and we do have a Netflix subscription. I have heard people talk about these shows, in the way some people used to talk about soap operas or celebrity gossip. I do keep abreast of current affairs, even if I try and limit my time on social media and stick to sites I know are safe. Places I won't be upset unduly by all the horror in the world.

'So obviously you know there is a huge appetite for true crime content at the moment. And that central to uncovering new leads, and even vital evidence in all these cases has been the dedication of the true crime community.'

I bristle. I don't have much time for the true crime community. I've seen how these forums have combed through every aspect of my life, ripped it apart and forced the pieces back together, creating some sort of Frankenstein's monster version of their perceived truth.

When Izzy says she has interviewees lined up and is ready to make her film, is she going to be relying on internet nutjobs and their insane theories? What Brendan calls the real-life equivalent of Scooby-Doo's gang? Are these the people she wants me to interact with? To sit alongside while I tear myself into pieces for the camera?

I'm guessing she senses my discomfort because she starts to speak.

'I get that people are cynical of true crime enthusiasts and I'm not going to tell you that there aren't crazies all over the internet. But some of the users of these forums are incredible and, from your perspective, they could be pretty invaluable. There's one forum in particular I have been dipping in and out of for years – long enough to get a measure of the users and how they approach their research.'

'I'm not sure how that's supposed to impress me,' I tell her. 'Everyone and their mother has an opinion on what did or didn't happen. These forums are just a way for these people to gather together and convince themselves they have it all sussed. But no one has it sussed. No one has cracked it or worked out why my brain won't let go of its secrets. All these experts and no answers, why should someone sitting at home be any better at this?' I know my voice is louder now, and there's an edge to it, but is this really what Izzy Devine is bringing to the table? Is that what I'm supposed to put my trust in?

'They aren't like that, Nora,' Izzy continues, her enthusiasm growing now despite the pissiness of my tone, and I can tell she is all in. 'And that one I use, well, I've seen enough of how they operate to know without a doubt this is not just some ghoulish gossip site filled with weirdos sitting at home thinking they're the next Columbo. There are ex-police on there. Journalists. Forensic analysts. There's a profiler who has started looking over your case already. A forensics guy. Research experts who are collating all the media coverage, all the statements in evidence. We've asked for access to police files. These people are fascinated with your case.'

'My daughter,' I remind her. 'We're talking about my daughter. A real human being, not just "a case".' I know I sound prickly – but that's because I *am* prickly about it. We are not names

13

on a screen or an unsolved mystery simply existing for people to pull apart and try and fit back together again like some macabre jigsaw puzzle.

'Of course,' she says, and has the decency to look contrite. 'I'm sorry. Your daughter. We can't really begin to understand how difficult this is for you.'

I pause. She's right, of course; there is no way she can know how awful this is. Or how many times people have promised help – that they will be the ones who will make the difference – only to let us down. It's true what they say – it's the hope that kills you in the end.

'Over the years I've seen a lot of well-intentioned people turn out to have little to offer but vivid imaginations,' I say. 'I'm sure you can imagine some of the horror stories I've read about myself online. Some of the hate. And that's without mentioning the death threats, the hate mail, the bricks through my window, the pure bile . . .'

Part of the reason Brendan doesn't like me going anywhere near the internet is that I can only take so much of what comes my way. Avoiding what is said online is a healthy choice. When I have dared to look, I've rarely read anything nice about myself.

'If all you read is people telling you over and over and over again how evil, neglectful and horrific you are, that narrative starts to creep into the shadows of your psyche. You start to believe it,' I tell her. 'Even though I can't imagine myself ever being the person they paint me as. I might not remember that day, but I remember her. I remember how we were together. How we gelled as mother and daughter. Invincible. Or so I thought. What could have changed in the space of an afternoon to turn that on its head? And yet – because I can't remember, I can't let go of my own doubt, never mind anyone else's.'

Izzy nods sympathetically. Does the head tilt that signifies she's listening, but I wonder how much she really, truly understands?

'Look,' I tell her, 'I appreciate that in a few high-profile cases these wannabe detectives are able to see something or pick something apart in a way that hasn't been done before, but this case had an entire police force behind it. A massive search operation. People combed those woods and the surrounding areas. The eyes of the world were on us. I don't think . . .'

Izzy nods. 'I understand your cynicism. I totally get it and of course this is more than just playing Inspector Morse for you. This is your child. Your beautiful girl. And it's your reputation, and your self-belief. But don't underestimate the ability of the true crime community to have empathy for what you have been through, or to have the passion to dig deep. Unlike the police, they aren't under pressure to move on to the next case. They aren't answering to a management team. They give their time to things like this because they genuinely believe they can make a difference. I know these people. They're invested. They have the time and energy to re-examine things forensically – to look at the big picture as well as the micro details.'

'Daisy's case is still open,' I say, but even I know that while the investigation is in fact still ongoing it has nowhere near the manpower it once had behind it. The police have, they have told me, exhausted all current avenues. While they are of course open to new leads, and while once a year they release a new appeal for information, in real terms their search for the truth has stagnated.

'I'm aware,' she says. 'And I've been trying to get Detective Inspector Bradley to talk to me about it, but he doesn't seem too keen to chat. He seems to be a very busy man. Always in some meeting or dealing with some current investigation.'

She's subtle at making her point, but I know what she is saying. DI David Bradley, the senior investigating officer in

Daisy's case, has bigger fish to fry these days. Cases that he stands a chance of solving. Still, it pulls at me that he hasn't made himself available to talk about the case. He has always been proactive in terms of securing media coverage relating to the search for Daisy. Maybe he has given up on us too. Or maybe he knows something about Izzy Devine that I don't.

Regardless, the upshot is that if even the token efforts now to find Daisy are grinding to a halt, where does that leave us? In some awful in-between place not knowing the truth?

I don't know what to say. Desperation that we are being left behind starts to claw at me. I can't allow that to happen. What kind of a mother would it make me to just let this fade into the background? How could I live with myself? How can I allow my child to become a faded picture, which looks dated, old, forgotten.

Heat prickles at the back of my neck and nausea swirls in my stomach. With all my cards on the table here, I'm not sure I have any real choice but to get involved. Some control has to be better than none, surely? And Izzy seems so enthusiastic. Maybe she's right that fresh eyes might pull something new from the abyss.

'Can I get a glass of water?' I stutter and Izzy nods, raising her hand at a passing waiter and asking him to bring two glasses of iced water. I am regretting the half a scone that I have eaten as it sits like a lead weight in the pit of my stomach.

'I know this is scary,' Izzy says. I assume she can guess my discomfort by the way I'm rubbing and scratching at my wrist. At the daisy tattoo. It's a nervous habit. Sometimes I need to feel my skin burn, or tear. I don't always realise I'm doing it.

'I know it's a big ask,' she continues, 'but on the flip side it's a great opportunity to have fresh eyes examine things in a different way. People aren't perfect. The police are far from perfect and while I have no doubt they've done what they can, things do get overlooked. You never know what we might turn up.'

Maybe, I think, as a glass of iced water is put in front of me, condensation already misting on the outside, I'm more scared of what they might find than I am of this void. There is a twisted comfort in not knowing the full story – I can believe what I want. That she is okay. That she is being looked after and loved. No one can tell me, categorically, that's not the case.

I don't know how I will feel if I find out the worst has happened. I shiver, my mind racing with thoughts. It's over-whelming.

This documentary is happening now. Right now. I don't have time to mull this over. I don't have time to discuss it with Brendan any more. (I already know where he stands and I don't think anything that has been said will change his mind. If anything the involvement of the true crime community is only likely to harden his stance.) It's up to me to make the call.

'Look, I know this is not work for you. This is not a passion project. This is your life, and the life of your daughter,' Izzy says. 'But I want to reassure you that it is very much a passion project for me. I was twenty-four when Daisy went missing. Working in a local newspaper in the Home Counties covering the most mundane of weekly fixtures,' she says. 'I'm not sure why; maybe it's because my mum grew up here, or because I used to holiday here when I was a child, or maybe because it all just seemed so awful, but I was so drawn to your story from the very outset. I've been watching it ever since. I'm not going to make any promises about what this will or won't achieve. I can't even promise that it will definitely be picked up by a streamer or channel. But I will tell you that it's my intention to tell your story to the very best of my ability.'

I nod, the itch on my wrist easing a little.

'Obviously, that's stronger with you on board,' she says. 'It could even be that my simply coming at this behind a camera lens puts a degree of pressure on the police not to be seen to be resting on their laurels.'

I nod. She is making a fair point about the police. They aren't going to want to be seen to have abandoned all hope of finding Daisy, even if that is what has happened. My stomach twists though. Do I want to open myself up again, so publicly to scrutiny? Is it different now – now I have Brendan to think of too. And Luca. Because it's not just me anymore, is it?

Then again, I'm under scrutiny anyway. I can't imagine a time when that will ever go away. My card is marked. I haven't failed to notice the glances in our direction. I've seen how people lean in towards each other to whisper. I could draw the expression each and every one of them will pull without even looking. Wide-eyed. Slack-jawed. I'm the worst kind of celebrity. Infamous rather than famous – because who the hell would want to be known as the woman who can't remember what happened to her child? And when he is older Luca will hear those same rumours, the lies and the theories.

'You can change the narrative around this,' I hear Izzy say as I tune back in to her hard sell. I realise what I have to do.

'Okay,' I say, even if there is a part of me that screams this is not going to end well. Izzy grins back, as if she's a child who I've just agreed to take to Disneyland and not a professional documentary maker to whom I have just given access to my life.

Chapter Two

Izzy

Tom will be delighted to know he was right. I'm just so fucking relieved the gamble paid off. I'd wanted to lock Nora Logue into this documentary from the very start. Tom had told me to bide my time – to make sure whatever proposal I was bringing to Nora was as fully formed as it could be. And most importantly of all, he'd told me it was best to make sure it was all as time-sensitive as it could be.

'Don't give her the chance to say yes then go away, think about it and change her mind. Let her know the documentary is happening. Do it politely. Professionally. Make her feel as if you are doing her a favour by giving her a voice in it and not the other way round,' he'd said.

That approach didn't sit easily with someone like me. I like to plan and schedule and to know exactly what to expect from a project. I like to know exactly how the story will play out in its entirety before I start recording. Of course production can always throw a curveball in your direction and that does, and has, happened to me before. But for the most part if the research is done right, the pre-interviews are in the bag and the ultimate goal for the project is set in stone then things normally work themselves out without too many hitches.

I like that – in fact, I need it. Control freak is a phrase that has been used about me on more than one occasion. I don't apologise for that.

So to allow for a huge degree of uncertainty on the Daisy Logue project (we will come up with a better name, obviously) makes my teeth itch. That said, it's the only way we could really approach this one, and I've never felt as excited about a project before. I just feel, in my gut, that this is going to be something different. Something big – and I am so ready for that. It's why I've allowed Tom to encourage me to move outside of my comfort zone.

And now I owe him a drink.

We'll have to go easy though – we have a lot of work to do. Work I'm now extra buzzed about. Nora has agreed to meet with me again tomorrow morning, along with Tom, to talk over what exactly she can expect. If she feels comfortable we might try and get some material on film. We don't want whatever she has to say to feel too rehearsed or parroted. If we can get it the first time round, it will feel fresh to the viewer too.

So I'm grinning when I open the door to the Airbnb Tom and I have rented for the duration of our planned two-week stay in Derry, bursting to fill him in. His non-melodic tones are echoing through the house as he sings along – badly – to a Manic Street Preachers' song with not an ounce of self-awareness.

'Good thing I hired you for your film-making skills and not your singing voice,' I say as I walk into the kitchen-diner. But the music must be too loud and Tom doesn't look away from his computer screen, nor does he stop singing. It takes me tapping him on the shoulder for him to realise I'm home – making him jump.

'Jesus Christ, Izzy,' he says in his North London accent. 'You want to give a fellah a heart attack?' He mutes the song and clicks out of whatever document he has been working on.

'You'd have heard me if you hadn't been listening to that music so loudly! Tom, you'll annoy the neighbours!' I say.

'Okay, Grandma! Us young people just like blasting some tunes nice and loud,' he teases.

I raise an eyebrow. 'Grandma? You're older than me, Tom, and don't forget it.'

It's playful banter. The back and forth that makes working with Tom so *easy*. Leave your ego at the door. We are both ambitious, determined and we both enjoy cutting loose at the end of the day. I put my shopping bags on the worktop, take out a punnet of fresh green grapes and start eating them, savouring each refreshing bite. My stomach is rumbling. I'd been too hyped up when I was with Nora to eat the scone I'd ordered.

'Look, I can't help it if you're jealous of my incredible singing talent. Not everyone is gifted with a voice like mine,' he says, raising his shoulders in a shrug.

'Thankfully, you're right.' I laugh, aiming one particularly large and juicy-looking grape directly at his head. 'But seriously, we don't want to get on the bad side of the neighbours. This seems like a quiet street.'

Of course Tom catches the grape before it hits his head and pops it into his mouth. His reflexes are quite impressive. 'Izzy, have you always been such a worrier? This is a detached bungalow, in case you hadn't noticed. Plus I happen to know the resident of the house next door is eighty-five and deaf as a post.' Tom smiles. 'I had quite an awkward conversation with her earlier. She couldn't understand my accent, or hear me properly, or perhaps both, but she said she hoped that me and my "lady friend" had a lovely holiday.'

I laugh. 'I hope you corrected her and told her I'm your boss and not your lady friend?'

'I did not,' he says. 'She had a cheeky glint in her eye. I was worried if I told her we were *work colleagues*, she might've come on to me herself.' He stresses the words 'work colleagues' brushing over my assertion that I am his boss.

He digs into the shopping bag himself. 'Beer and wine?' he says, his smile growing wider. 'Am I to assume that the meeting this morning went as we hoped?' Tom is doing his very best to keep his tone jokey and light, but I know this project means a lot to him too. I'm not the only person looking to make a name for myself in this business. He may have been at this game a few years longer than me, but he's still chasing that elusive big break.

'It did,' I say. 'She's in. We are both to meet her at Shipquay Street tomorrow to talk it through more with her.'

He punches the air, a breathy 'Yesss!' sounding out around the room. 'I didn't want to call or text in case it was bad news and you were trying to work out how to break it to me.'

His enthusiasm is infectious and my smile is now a grin. 'I know, I should've called. But I figured I'd break the news with beer, wine and the announcement that you are cooking us dinner tonight while I pull together a plan for our pre-interview with Nora tomorrow.'

'You're a hard taskmaster,' Tom says. 'And I'm still waiting for you to say, "You were right, Tom. Thanks so much for suggesting that strategy. I never doubted it for a minute."'

'I've got you beer, and I've bought the finest steaks M&S could sell for you to cook later. I'd say that's thank you enough,' I retort, my mood buoyant.

He pauses for a moment, his face somewhere just outside of happy, and I can't quite read him. It looks as if he is about to say something, but then his face changes again and he breaks into another smile. 'Pass me some more of those grapes,' he says. 'And then let's get back to work. I promise I'll wear my earphones while I listen to my music.'

'And you also promise not to sing?' I ask.

'Don't push it, Izzy,' he says with warmth, and I decide not to, or to use more time bantering with him, because I have so much work to do.

And that includes logging into amateursleuths.com and updating my friends on the Daisy Logue documentary subforum about securing the interview. My phone has been hopping with notifications from people wondering how the meeting went. Both from regular forum users who just like to read updates and from some of those experts who are actively studying the case and who have agreed to be filmed as part of the documentary. I suppose they deserve to know how it went, but a little part of me wonders if I should keep that news to myself for now?

No, fuck it, I decide. It's too big. These people have been cheering me on.

They have inspired this documentary from the outset. There is no way I can leave them hanging.

Chapter Three

Nora

Brendan's phone rings three times before he answers and the wariness is obvious in his tone straight away. I've been putting off calling him, unsure of how he is going to take the news that I will be proceeding with the interview, but a second text message from him asking if I'm okay has just landed on my phone and it's better I get this over and done with.

'Hey,' he says, gently, clearly feeling the air around him for some sense of my mood. 'How did it go?'

'As well as could be expected,' I say. 'She seems on the ball. Passionate about our story, even.' I sit down at my desk in our small study and switch on my laptop.

'So, you've agreed to give her the interview?' he asks, his voice a little less gentle. I know this tone. This is Brendan going into super-overprotective mode. Not that I blame him. He's spent the five years we've known each other trying to piece me back together. He knows, more than anyone, just how broken I can be.

'She's making a documentary anyway. Whether I'm involved or not,' I tell him. 'After talking to her, I felt it was better to be able to at least control some small part of it.'

There's a pause while he tries to think of what to say next. I know he is concerned. He doesn't need to spell that out for me.

'Izzy, the producer, says she has a team of people from the true crime community looking at Daisy's case from all angles. These are experts, you know. She said they were ex-cops, a forensics expert, a journalist . . .'

'Ah, Nora. The true crime community?' he asks, his tone exasperated. 'You know what those people are like! And experts or not, they are not here and not able to access all the files from the case, or turn back the clock to examine the scene.' I can hear a mix of tension and weariness in his voice.

'I know that,' I say. 'I know it's not perfect. But they have requested access to the files . . .' I hear a sigh. He doesn't speak. 'If there is even the smallest chance – don't I owe it to Daisy, and myself, to look for answers?'

'Of course,' he says. 'You know I'll support you in whatever you have to do to feel better about this. But I thought we were finally in a place where, I don't know, we're living again. I'm not saying you've forgotten her or stopped wanting to know what happened, but things have been so much . . . calmer.'

It's my turn to pause because if Brendan thinks things have been anywhere near calm and normal then he hasn't been paying attention. The constant war in my head hasn't dulled anyway. Maybe I've just stopped talking to him so much about my grief, my fear because it's been making him increasingly uncomfortable.

It's more tangible for him now, as Luca grows. He can properly understand the strength of a parent's love for their child. That bond. That fierce protectiveness. He can now start to truly understand why what has happened to Daisy is incomprehensible. So, I think, a part of him just doesn't even try to comprehend it anymore because it's unbearable. It's easier to live in the moment.

'Would you be able to keep going if it were Luca?' I ask him.

There's a deep intake of breath. 'That's not fair, Nora,' he says. 'I'm not saying it isn't awful. Of course it is. And of course I would fall apart if it were Luca, but it isn't and we have him here now and he needs you.'

There's another sigh. A beat. 'Can we keep him out of it? I mean, don't put him on camera? Please? I don't want him to be defined by something that happened before he was born. Before we'd even met.'

My stomach tightens. I'd been expecting this and, to be fair, I've normally been only too happy to keep Luca out of the media but, today, for some reason, it stings.

Maybe it's the way Brendan has worded it. Whether or not anyone chooses to define Luca by Daisy's disappearance, the fact will always remain he has a half-sister. I will not protect him from knowing how amazing she was. Our lives are all intrinsically linked.

But I want to make this as palatable as possible for Brendan. It's bad enough I have my own concerns.

'Of course,' I tell him. 'He's too young to be a part of this.'

My laptop screen prompts me to enter my password and I do. I'm vaguely aware of Brendan talking in the background. Something about work and the weather. I'm only half listening, waiting for my home screen to boot up so I can use the internet.

'Nora?' I hear him say. 'I asked what you thought?'

'Sorry,' I tell him. 'I was lost there for a moment. What do I think about what?'

'Well, it's a sunny day,' he says. 'So I thought maybe we could go to the beach. Feel the sand between our toes. Build sand-castles and splash in the water. Maybe get an ice cream after.'

I smile. I would like that very much. The chance for some time with Brendan outside of this house. Somewhere warm and sunny where we can pretend, even for ten minutes, that we are a normal couple.

'That sounds like a great idea,' I say. 'I'd really like that.'

'Great,' he says, and the sombre tone is gone from his voice completely. 'How about you get some bits and bobs together. I'll pick Luca up from creche and be with you in about forty-five minutes.'

Momentary disappointment flickers inside me before I realise that of course he would want to bring Luca. He was unlikely to have been inviting me to build sandcastles and splash in the water with him when we have a perfectly good almost three-year-old who'd be in his element on the beach.

'Okay,' I say, glancing at the clock on my computer screen. I can probably still be online for the next twenty minutes or so. It won't take me long to throw some towels and a couple of water bottles into a bag.

'There's a new UV swimsuit in Luca's top drawer,' Brendan says. 'And a sunhat. Can you make sure to grab those? I have factor 50 in the car already.'

'Will do,' I say. 'And thanks, Brendan. For supporting me.'

There's a sigh. 'Let's just have a great afternoon with Luca and worry about everything else later.'

I envy his ability to do that.

When he ends the call, I open a private window on my laptop. I don't really think Brendan checks my online activity, but I do know he doesn't like it when I visit forums that discuss Daisy's disappearance, or if I read the comments under news articles about us. He hasn't forbidden me from doing so, but he gets tetchy about it all the same. I don't particularly like looking online myself, but the conversation with Izzy has intrigued me. I feel so stupid for not asking her the name of the site she uses – the one populated by specialists and experts who seemingly have nothing better to do with their time than try and solve cold cases.

I tap 'Daisy Logue missing' into Google. Immediately an image of my daughter's face appears on the screen. The photo that has become synonymous with her name. Long, wavy dark hair, a bright smile, a dimple on her left cheek. Beautiful, piercing and soulful blue eyes. Eyes that showed she was a deep thinker underneath her youthful joy and exuberance. The soulful eyes that some have taken as proof, categorical and emphatic, that she had a terrible childhood. The soulfulness mistaken for sorrow.

Even though there are pictures of Daisy everywhere in this house, seeing her face on a computer screen still takes the breath from me and that's before I even start to read the captions and the headlines. I blink the cruelness of their words away, realising I probably need to be a bit more specific in my search if I'm to stand a chance of finding anything useful.

So I type 'Daisy Logue Nora documentary new true crime forum Izzy'. It's a jumble of words that make no sense when put together in that order but it flags up a few recent hits. I look for the ones that aren't marked as 'missing word: Izzy' even though I know she will likely have a username that is not her own. I scroll through countless links, keeping one eye on the clock and mentally shaving off time needed to get our beach things ready. If I just lift bottled water from the fridge, I don't have to worry about finding our flasks and rinsing them out. That will save a good two minutes . . .

Within a few minutes I land on amateursleuths.com, which contains a Daisy Logue subforum and, I see, a number of posts by a user called IzzyTV, including a pinned post about an upcoming documentary she is making. I think it's fair enough to assume this must be the forum filled with experts and great people who will not only help Izzy make a great documentary but who might also be able to solve a case the entire Police Service of Northern Ireland (PSNI) with help from the Missing Persons'

Bureau have been unable to crack. Maybe they'll also be able to tell me how to access my broken brain.

It takes mere moments for me to be lost in the forum. It's bizarre to read about these people who I've never met and have no idea about, wishing Izzy the very best of luck with her meeting with me.

'I'll be surprised if she agrees,' one poster – a man with an avatar of Inspector Morse – has written. **'I don't think you should be going anywhere near her. She's guilty and that's an end to it. Any decent profiler would tell you the same just as I'm sure they'd tell you that dissociative amnesia doesn't last seven years. Something's not right with that one.'**

'Dissociative amnesia has no time limit,' a user calling themselves DrWatson has written. **'There have been cases lasting years, even decades. It's rare of course, but we're only starting to understand the real effect trauma can have on the human brain. If what happened in those woods was so horrific . . .'**

I blink, look away. I don't want to read more of that particular post, even though that user is sort of on my side.

For every post offering good wishes to Izzy there is another telling her that she's wasting her time with me, or that they have no doubt Daisy is dead, or mentioning the blood droplets in the hall. Nausea wells up in me again. I shouldn't have looked. Even those people who are offering to help seem to have their minds made up.

'I'll see what we turn up,' a ColonelMustard has written. **'But if I was a betting man I'd say Nora's up to her eyes in this and there's no way she's acting on her own. People don't just disappear without a whole lot of organisation. Not enough attention has been paid to the bigger picture. That child was most likely trafficked.'**

I read the first reply to that post, from 'IzzyTV' herself and I feel my heart sink, even though Izzy herself told me she doesn't know whether or not to believe I wasn't involved. **'You might be right, but she doesn't strike me as someone who is some sort of criminal mastermind or who has colluded with anyone. She seems genuine, but I suppose she might just be a good actress. And yes, that means I have met her and yes that means she has agreed to be a part of the documentary!!! Will post a new thread shortly!'**

I'm not sure how I'm supposed to react to that – the wishy-washy nature of it. Maybe I'm a good actress. I don't strike her as a criminal mastermind. I know obviously that's a good thing – but is she implying I'm stupid? It stings a little, perhaps because while I admire her honesty, I wish the reality was that she believed me, without question.

I'm about to close my laptop, conscious that really I should be just about ready to leave now, when a new reply pops on the screen.

'Izzy! Read your DMs! Been trying to call you too. This just got very interesting. Seriously!'

That one was posted by a user called DonegalDetective and the avatar is of a woman wearing sunglasses and a baseball cap. I click into her profile to try and find out more about her. Is she is a real detective? What does she know? How did it just get interesting?

Her location is listed as Letterkenny – a smallish town about half an hour's drive from Derry, across the Irish border in Donegal. She appears to be a prolific forum user, with in excess of five thousand posts to her name.

Her bio reads: **'True Crime obsessive. Loves a good puzzle. Particular interest: Daisy Logue case.'**

And that's it. No mention of a background in law enforcement, detective work or the like. Just 'loves a good puzzle'. I click through to her previous posts and see just how prolific she is on the Daisy Logue subforum in particular – and how she seems to be particularly friendly with 'IzzyTV'.

Just this morning she wrote: **'Best of luck for today. You've got this. Let me know how it has gone as soon as you're done!'**

IzzyTV had responded with a heart emoji before thanking DonegalDetective for her invaluable research help.

I feel as if I am outside of a bubble looking in, but if I try and push my way through, I might burst everything. I'm considering setting up an account to post a reply – which yes, of course I know is ultimately a bad idea – when the crunch of tyres on the gravel outside startles me. 'Shit!' I swear. I can't believe time has flown by and I'm here with not a thing ready and needless to say if Brendan finds me sitting on a true crime forum . . .

I slam the lid of my laptop closed and head for the stairs, closing the study door behind me. I just manage to reach the top of the stairs and the door to Luca's room when the front door opens and a small, incredibly overexcited child tumbles in ahead of Brendan.

Chapter Four

Izzy

As Tom has commandeered the kitchen-diner for his work, and his singing, I disappear into my bedroom where I have set up a makeshift workspace on top of the dressing table. It isn't an ideal set-up, but it's good enough and once we start with the interviews we'll be alternating between here and the room we have hired in the Shipquay Street townhouse anyway.

A beautifully situated and presented drawing room on the second floor of the Victorian townhouse, the space on Shipquay Street is much more suitable for filming than this Airbnb, which owes more to function than style.

Had the budget permitted, we'd have rented more space at the townhouse and stayed there ourselves but for now, we have to make do with the dual location.

So the dressing table has become my control centre. Colour-coded Blu-Tacked notes and Post-its on the mirror remind me of key details I have to keep in mind, and of ideas I want to follow up. Yes, I've also stuck up some affirmations, which I know shows me up as a millennial snowflake or whatever, but they work.

Already the mirror is filling up but I don't dare start sticking my notes to the pale-coloured walls in case the Blu-Tack leaves any greasy marks or pulls away the paintwork. I don't need to pay an extra charge to the Airbnb host on top of all our other expenses.

Setting my phone to 'Do Not Disturb', I scribble 'I can, I am' onto a fresh Post-it and tack it right at the top of the mirror – a very low-key way to celebrate securing the interview. I'd not wasted any time in logging into AmateurSleuths and updating the Daisy Logue subforum about securing the interview with Nora. I'd tried not to be too obvious, realising I'll need to play my cards a little closer to my chest. After all, I have no idea who might be reading this forum, and it wouldn't do to be scooped by myself this close to the finish line. There's little point in me pitching this to the big streaming services if they can click into a forum and read all the inside info. Similarly, I don't want the execs of those big streaming services seeing me post about the inevitable hiccups along the way, so I keep the details vague. Just that we met, it went well and she's on board.

People of course have a hundred and one questions and that's how, an hour later, I'm reading through replies and being selective in who I respond to. I know there are users who will happily piss all over every theory, piece of evidence or rumour that does not tie in with their preconceptions.

There are users who are just there to be nosy – to try and pick up some hint of scandal from what we are posting. I avoid those too – I know it sounds super nerdy but to some of us this is a lot more than that. I think I'm going to have shift some of this discussion to a WhatsApp group, or maybe a private Facebook group – one where I can control who joins and monitor what they are up to.

It might also help quieten some of the noise because it is much, much too easy to lose hours to this place, reading and reacting to what other people say. I'm already struggling to see all the replies I'm receiving.

I'm not surprised to see the icon indicating that I have private messages. It's not unusual for there to be several waiting for me even on an ordinary day, never mind today when I've met with the key figure in our most talked-about case.

Vowing that I will just give them a quick glance before logging out of the forum and continuing with my actual work, I click into my private inbox. I smile when I see a message from 'DonegalDetective' at the top of the folder. DonegalDetective is Jacqueline McLaughin, or Jacqs as she is more frequently known, and she is almost as obsessed with crime podcasts and documentaries as I am.

She knows her stuff. It's impressive really how she knows, in almost forensic detail, just about all there is to know about some of the most talked-about unsolved mysteries of the last thirty years, especially as she has no relevant background. She's not a former police officer, or lawyer or psychiatrist. She's a stay-at-home mum, but I swear she has the best analytical mind of any of my online friends.

We've never actually met, but I'm hoping we will one day soon, especially now that we are so geographically close to each other. In fact, that's why I assume she is sliding into my DMs today.

But when I start reading her message, it's clear Jacqueline isn't getting in touch to make plans with me. She has sent me a link to a photo gallery from a newspaper in Galway. One of those hyper-local sites that devote a lot of space to photo collages of fun days and birthday parties.

'I was sent this overnight. Fairly new user – IrishEyes? Do you know them? They said: "Show this to your friend" – but why they didn't just send it to you, I don't know. Anyway, I had a nosy first and maybe I'm seeing things. But here, have a look and let me know what you think!' Trusting that Jacqs is as clued in as she normally is I find myself not logging out of AmateurSleuths as I'd promised but instead scrolling through a slideshow of 'Fun in the Sun' pictures. I watch as the pictures shuffle their way through their display, utterly baffled as to what I'm supposed to be looking at.

I type a series of question marks back to Jacqs.

Three telltale dots appear on my screen indicating that Jacqs is typing, and I watch the slideshow again as I wait for her message to appear, still with no idea as to what this is all about.

'**Do you see it?**' Jacqueline's message reads.

'**Not sure what I'm supposed to be seeing, TBH,**' I type back.

'**This!**' She replies but there is no this, not for a moment or two anyway. Then a picture, screen-shotted from the slide-show, appears. A crowd scene. Smiling faces on the promenade at Salthill. Ice cream. Blue skies. I wonder if I'm looking at some sort of magic eye picture. Nothing in what I see seems in any way relevant or out of the ordinary to me.

'**???? What is it???**' I type back, beginning to feel impatient. It's unlike Jacqs to be so oblique.

A second picture appears. A close-up of the first, this time. A cropped section of a group at the very edge of the image. A woman grinning at the camera, her arms around two girls. At a glance I'd say they were maybe eleven or twelve. Maybe a little older. I find it impossible to age young girls these days – they grow up so fast. One of the girls is looking up at the woman I assume is her mother and grinning. The second is grimacing in the direction of the camera, and I smile in recognition of that look – it's a puberty special. I remember those years well. I'd rather have done anything than spend 'quality family time'.

'**IZZY!**' a message blinks – Jacqs obviously wondering why I haven't replied. '**You must see it. Really. Don't you think she looks familiar?**' I look at it again. It's not the clearest picture. And it's not until Jacqs posts another image, one that is all too familiar to me, that the penny drops.

The grimacing girl looks uncannily like the face before me now – the police impression of what Daisy Logue would look like now, if she is still alive.

'Holy shit,' I type back, before shouting out to Tom that I need him. Of course I realise straight away that he said he would be listening to his music through his headphones so shouting is no good at all.

'How did you find that picture? When was it taken? Do we know anything about the people in it?' I type furiously, before running back to the kitchen, MacBook in hand and thrusting it under Tom's nose. Clearly he hasn't heard me approach again and jumps, swearing loudly. 'For fuck's sake, Izzy!' His tone is less jovial than before but I ignore it.

'Look at this! Jacqs, DonegalDetective, has just sent me this picture.'

He pulls off his headphones, clicks off his own screen, and gives my MacBook his full attention. I watch his face to see the moment he gets it, his eyes widening, and he looks directly at me. Before either of us speak I snatch my computer back and sit down at the table beside him, waiting for Jacqs' response.

'It's probably not her,' he says. 'I mean, you can't even see her that closely. Where was that taken? When?'

"But it *does* look like her, doesn't it? We're not just seeing things,' I say, my stomach tight with anticipation. Securing an interview with Nora Logue today and now, possibly, just maybe, a sighting of Daisy Logue still alive. This could be the best day ever.

'Well, yes. But c'mon . . . it's not likely, is it? I mean we all think she's dead, don't we?' Tom says, looking at me as if I'm in danger of losing the run of myself.

I glare at him because as much as I do think it's most likely

Daisy Logue is dead, I don't really like to say it out loud. I might be a true crime fan. I might have learned that most of these mysteries don't have a happy ending and that many of them in fact have pretty horrific endings. But I still like to hang onto a bit of hope. And today feels like a good day to have a bit of hope. I've already pulled off something I thought would be basically impossible by getting Nora to speak to me in the first place. Maybe there's room for something a little more impossible too.

'We said we were going into this with open minds,' I remind him, and he pulls a face that lets me know exactly what he thinks of my open mind and my optimism. He starts to speak but I cut him off, my attention drawn to a new message on the screen from Jacqs.

'This IrishEyes person. They said they had more info. I've messaged back to ask what they know but I've not heard from them yet. I'll keep you posted.'

It's the strangest thing. It feels as if I might have seen something momentous but I don't actually have much more information other than a girl who fits the description of what police think Daisy could look like has been spotted in Ireland. Just outside Galway if my Google search of Salthill is right.

I have my private messages filtered on the site so that I only hear from people I follow, so I click into the folder where all the other message requests go. There is no message for me from IrishEyes. I scan through the forum, searching for that username but just as Jacqs says, they are a relatively new user, and a quiet one at that. They've been a member of amateursleuths.com for seven months, posting roughly once a month and offering nothing of any real value. A GIF response here, an 'I agree' there. They have primarily posted in the Daisy Logue subforum but that's not an awful lot to go on. There are no biographical details in her (I'm assuming IrishEyes is a 'her') profile, no location more specific than 'Ireland', and her avatar is the shadowy detective figure that is the site's default. Maybe I should send her a message myself? But what if she's flighty? Easily scared? Both Jacqs and I asking questions might spook her.

'So what does this mean?' Tom asks.

'It means we have a photo of someone who looks a helluva lot like Daisy Logue.'

'From an unknown source, with minimal details and no guarantee they will give you any more information?'

Tom seems to have switched into prime pissing-on-my-chips mode. I glare at him.

'Izzy, part of the reason you brought me on board with this project was to help keep you grounded. You know that. This isn't like anything else you've worked on. This case has been an obsession of yours. You are already incredibly emotionally invested, which could mean you don't look at things as objectively as possible. As interesting as this picture is, it isn't even a firm lead. And how many other times have pictures of "Daisy" shown up before now?'

Of course, he's right – every year or so another picture of another child who looks similar to Daisy shows up and the papers run with sensationalist 'Could this be Daisy?' headlines. It whips everyone up into hysteria for a day or two and then, when the lead inevitably goes nowhere, it all dies down again.

'There's still a chance though,' I say, while I continue to click through the forum and read more messages, hoping something more cast-iron reveals itself. It only has to be her once. No body was ever found. No trace of her, even – apart from those blood droplets in her house. As unlikely as Tom may think it is – it *could* be her.

'Izzy, do you need me for anything else?' Tom asks, cutting through my thoughts. 'I have stuff I could be working on.'

I shake my head. I don't want his negativity, even if he feels it's him just keeping me grounded. Today has been a good day and I want to enjoy it. 'No. No. That's it. I just wanted to show you that. I think it's big but, look, I get what you're saying. We'll not count our chickens just yet.'

I lift my laptop from the kitchen table and go back to work in my room, where I can at least do a bit of digging on my own. Maybe it is nothing, but maybe it is everything.

Chapter Five

Nora

'You seem a little distracted,' Brendan says. We're at the beach, the three of us sitting as far from other families as we can. I don't like to be close to people – not because I'm some antisocial freak but because I cannot tolerate the constant judgement. I have a sunhat on, glasses and a maxi dress, and yet I know people will still recognise me as Nora Logue, the woman who lost her own child. Or the woman who murdered her own child, depending on their perspective.

I give a small smile. 'I'm okay,' I tell him.

'I get this morning was strange and you probably have a lot on your mind mulling it all over,' he says. 'But try and focus on the here and now. Just for a bit. Look how much fun Luca is having.'

Hearing his name, Luca looks up from where he is driving one of his toy diggers through a mound of sand and he grins at me from under his sunhat. Pearly white teeth and chocolate brown eyes that you could lose yourself in. 'Mummy, I love the beach!' he chirps. 'You want my digger?' He thrusts the plastic yellow toy truck at me and I take it from him, switching into engaged mother mode and running it back and forth across the sand making a 'vroom, vroom' noise.

'Isn't Mummy a good digger driver?' Brendan asks, his voice light and carefree, and I envy that. Really, I do. I envy how he can fully embrace parenthood. He knows about Daisy, of course. He knows how it affects me, but only on an abstract level. He can't feel it. He can't feel the pain of missing her because he never knew her. He can't feel that every day with Luca reminds me of a day I'll never get again with Daisy.

My beautiful boy nods vigorously before reaching his chubby hand out once again to get the digger back. He doesn't want to be parted from his favourite toy for long. Brendan chats with him while I make appropriate noises and smile in all the right places.

'I think,' Brendan says after a few minutes, 'we should go and dip our toes in the water! Shall we see how cold it is?'

Luca whoops with excitement. 'Can I bring my bucket too?' he asks.

'Well, of course you can!' Brendan says as if no right-minded person would ever dream of walking into the sea without a small, colourful plastic bucket. Brendan gets to his feet, kicking off his Converse and letting warm sand seep between his toes. 'I think I'll bring my bucket too,' he adds.

'And Mummy come too?' Luca asks, blinking at me and then back at his daddy.

'Ah pet, I have to stay here and mind our things. But you wave to me from the water and I'll wave back. Okay?'

Luca pauses for a moment, his little brow furrowed as if he is considering his options. 'Okay, Mummy,' he says, before adding: 'Be good!' and taking Brendan's hand.

I smile. I always tell him to be good when I leave him at creche or with his daddy. It's strange, but sort of lovely to hear him say it back. I marvel as I watch the boy and the man in my life walk hand in hand, carrying their buckets, towards the shoreline. Luca is unspeakably cute in his one-piece UVA suit and aqua shoes, his bright yellow bucket swinging as he walks. The outline of Brendan against the sun has its own appeal. I know I should be happy in this moment. I know that Brendan is right and I should focus on the present, right here, with my family, but my mind just keeps wandering back to that post and the assertion that things 'just got very interesting'. I want to know what exactly this DonegalDetective meant by that. I want to sit down with Izzy again and ask her as many questions as I can think of about this forum and these users.

I try closing my eyes against the bright sun and settling myself in a mindful moment of just feeling the warmth of it on my face, but all I can see is Daisy's face. That day was warm too. Warm and bright, and we decided to go exploring in the woods before having a picnic. She'd been so excited, wanted to bring her favourite teddy and sing 'Teddy Bear's Picnic' on a loop. Dressed in lemon yellow leggings, and a white T-shirt with a daisy pattern. Her dark hair in bunches. Sparkly sandals that I'd bought her the week before in Dunnes on her feet. She'd begged me for those sandals. Said they were her best ever. I can still see her singing and dancing, the sequins catching the light of the sun.

It plays now in my head, never quite reaching the end, and I'm happy to lose myself into the fractured memory until I hear a scream and my head snaps up, back to the shoreline. The scream is Luca's; I know it is. I would know his voice anywhere. My heart thuds as I scan the length of the beach to try and find my son and my husband. Instinctively, before I'm even aware I'm moving, I'm on my feet and running towards the incoming tide, panic rising like the crest of the waves rushing towards the shore. Noise distorts around me, the rapid thump thump thump of my heart dulling the chatter, the breeze, the gulls, the laughing children and I want to find my voice and scream out. It cannot be happening again. The screaming has stopped now – everything is muffled, but I know I can no longer hear my boy.

My vision blurs, the sun too bright, the movement of people around me making it impossible for me to focus properly on what is in front of me, or beside me, or . . . my ankle twists as I tumble on a mound of sand, dimly aware that someone is shouting at me for ruining their sandcastle, but even though my ankle hurts like a bastard, I still stumble forward until I see him.

I see them. Ankle-deep in the water, grinning. Luca bending to fill that yellow plastic bucket and a wave, merely an inch or two taller than the one that came before it rushes forward and hits Luca on the legs, as high as his knees, and he screams again, but it's not fear or peril. It's pure, unbridled joy. I watch Brendan throw his head back and laugh while Luca splashes his feet up and down, enjoying the coldness of the water licking at his bare skin.

I stop, stand and watch. Wait for my heartbeat to slow. Wait for everything around me to come back into focus. Wonder if anyone close by noticed my dive for the shore, if anyone clocked who I am. If anyone is holding their own child a bit closer, either because they fear me or they fear what happened to me. Who wants to contemplate a lost child?

I'm about to turn and walk back to where I have just abandoned our belongings when I see Luca turn, his smile growing wider as he spots me. He shouts, 'Mummmeeee!' and waves as if he hasn't seen me in a month and it hasn't just been five minutes. I wave back, pushing the swell of emotion that is threatening to choke me down. I keep pushing it down and I smile broadly, blowing him a kiss before turning and walking back across the beach, leaving a rather bewildered-looking Brendan still standing ankle-deep in the foamy tide.

I am so glad, truly, that Brendan doesn't understand fully what it's like to have lived my life. So glad, but also so incredibly jealous.

I shiver in spite of the warmth and keep my head down, determined not to draw any more attention to myself than is strictly necessary. It's all I can do to not burst into tears. I sit for a few minutes before I hear Luca's voice again, this time approaching.

'Mummy, we bringed you some water and three shells,' he trills, uncurling his chubby fist and dropping a sand-covered mix of tiny pebbles and broken shell onto my palm.

'Well, look here,' I say, sure there's no wobble in my voice. 'This is some great treasure. Are you a pirate?'

His eyes widen and he looks at me as if I've just revealed the greatest secret in the world to him. 'I fink so,' he says, looking to his daddy, who has just put the two buckets, filled with water onto the sand. 'Is I a pirate?'

'Oh yes,' Brendan says, immediately dropping into faux pirate speak. 'You be the Dread Pirate Luca. The fiercest pirate on the seven seas. Avast, me hearties!' Luca repeats 'Avast, me hearties!' four times, laughing louder with each go. Who'd have thought something so minor could be so incredibly entertaining.

While Brendan talks about buried treasure and walking the plank, my mind flits to Daisy in a Tinker Bell costume asking me to make sure Captain Hook stayed away because he was a baddy. Daisy didn't like baddies.

My shiver turns to a shudder. 'Brendan,' I say. 'Do you think we could just go home? I'm not feeling great.'

Luca has planted himself firmly on the sand again and is trying to work out how to get sand into his bucket while still keeping the water he just brought up from the sea. I can see that despite his unbridled enthusiasm for the beach, he is starting to tire. This is so much excitement for him and he's already missed out on his afternoon nap. I'm hoping I can use this to bolster my case.

Brendan looks disappointed, but he wraps an arm around me and pulls me close to him, kissing the top of my head.

'I was hoping we could stay a bit longer,' he says. 'But I know it's a lot. I know today has been tough. Thanks for coming with us. How about we round the afternoon off nicely by grabbing some fish and chips on the way home?'

I daren't tell him my appetite has completely deserted me. I daren't tell him that after this morning, and after the fear I felt when I heard Luca scream, I'm doing all in my power not to throw up. I don't want to disappoint him further. 'Sounds great,' I say and nuzzle into him a little further.

'Today has been a good day,' he says, before pulling away and announcing to Luca that it's time to start packing up because there's a special pirate tea of chicken nuggets and chips waiting at home.

Ten minutes later, and after two very sad goodbyes to the seawater we could not bring home with us, we are trudging back up the beach to the car. Luca is on my hip, his head already starting to loll against my shoulder. A couple of hours on the beach has been too much for him. I know he'll fall asleep in the car and I only pray it won't be for long or else there is no chance of him sleeping through the night.

I spot it from a distance and my heart sinks. The closer we get, the further it sinks. Brendan stops dead for a moment when he sees it, before walking on again, telling me he'll deal with it and that I'm not to take any notice. It's probably nothing to do with me anyway, he says. 'This is just some lout acting out. Savages that were dragged up, not brought up.'

His voice is measured, but he's used to that now. Keeping his tone even so as not to frighten Luca.

'I'm sorry,' I mutter as we get closer still, and then the smell hits me. I gag.

'Get in the back seat with Luca,' Brendan says, before dropping our bags into the boot and retrieving a couple of plastic carrier bags. It doesn't take him long to remove the shitty nappy from our windscreen, but it does take a little longer to clean the excrement that is smeared across the glass. Luckily we keep paper towels and a spray cleaner in the boot of the car for this type of incident because this is far from our first rodeo.

Luca just watches on with confused interest.

'Is that poo, Mummy?' he asks.

'It is indeed! Stinky, smelly, yucky poo. A nappy must've fallen off a flying poopy baby!' I joke, because there is nothing funnier to almost three-year-old boys than poo, except perhaps the thought of flying babies with bare bottoms.

But it's not actually funny. I'm just trying to distract him from what has happened because I don't want him to be scared. This isn't random. It isn't just some lout acting out. It's just another very public assertion that I am not welcome in this world of happy families.

Brendan is silent when he gets back in the car. I stay in the back seat with Luca, who immediately launches into telling his daddy all about the flying baby whose nappy must've fallen off.

Brendan laughs, but it's forced, tense, and when I catch his eye in the rear-view his expression is grim. I already know what this will lead to. This will just feed his assertion that I shouldn't be doing anything to draw a lot of attention back to us.

'Let's go and get some chips!' I say, to a cheer of excitement from Luca and a nod that speaks a thousand words from Brendan. I can't help but look all around us as we drive out of the car park and away from the beach – aware that it could've been any of the happy families on the beach who decided to leave us a very clear message.

Chapter Six

Nora

'I might do some work before bed,' I tell Brendan as we pick at our fish and chips, still in the paper at the kitchen table. Luca's nuggets and chips are wrapped and sitting on the countertop while Luca is now fast asleep on the sofa, still in his swimsuit. The sea air and the car journey clearly exhausted him. I'm exhausted too but I want to get back to picking through the AmateurSleuths forum to see what else people are saying, especially now they know I'll be talking to Izzy for the documentary.

'I didn't think you had any projects in place just now,' Brendan says, and he's right of course. My work is piecemeal at best. On the infrequent occasions I feel able to take on a project, I work as a freelance copy editor. I haven't done any paid work in the last four months.

'I've decided I want to chase down a few leads,' I lie. 'You know, get in touch with some of my old contacts and tell them I'm open for business again.'

He dabs a chip into tomato ketchup before deciding against eating it and dropping it back on the paper.

'I'm all for you working, but I'm not sure now is the best time. This documentary will unsettle you. It might unsettle a whole lot of people – I don't want you setting yourself up to fail.' He doesn't meet my eye while he talks, and I wish I hadn't lied to him and had just told him the truth instead – that I need to see exactly what I'm up against out there. I need to see the kind of people Izzy is talking to. He won't understand though. He doesn't get how I feel defeated. Not quite trapped, but maybe stuck. Maybe mired in a moment that no matter how we try I can never get out of. Not while there are still questions to answer.

'I suppose you're right,' I say. 'I just wanted a bit of a positive focus, you know?'

I hope this will do the trick – will convince him that I'm feeling more upbeat, more inclined to move on just a bit.

'There's a beautiful wee child lying on that sofa in the living room who is the most positive focus you could ask for,' he says and I wince at his words. I do my best to be a good mum to Luca. God knows I do. He wants for nothing. Despite how hard it can be for me, he still gets my attention. But it's not enough for Brendan. My inability to always be carefree and silly with our child is a constant disappointment to him.

'Not today, Brendan,' I say, my voice small. I don't think I can handle having this conversation again, and certainly not now.

He sighs, scrunches up his remaining food in the paper and stands up, stalking to the bin where he throws it as if he's a basketball player dunking the winning hoop. I can feel tension radiate from him as he stands, his muscles taut, the strain in his back evident. He takes a few deep breaths while I feel what little was left of my appetite evaporate entirely.

'We had been having such a lovely day,' he says. 'Even with everything – the documentary and all – it had been lovely. And then there it is, waiting for us when we get back to the car.'

I don't say anything, unsure of what I can say to make it better and afraid of making it worse.

'It's there all the time,' he says. 'That threat. And, Nora, I'm not saying it's your fault. Of course I'm not. I know you'd never have done a thing to harm Daisy, but don't you think this might be actively harming Luca?'

I bristle. 'Luca thinks a flying baby's nappy fell off,' I say. 'I think you're overestimating his trauma.'

Brendan just shakes his head, leans back against the countertop, presses the heels of his hands into his eyes to rub them. I see his wedding ring glint in the sunlight, am suddenly aware of the plain gold band on my own finger and our promise of new beginnings.

'How will you explain away the next lot of graffiti on the front door, or the next brick through our window? How will you stop him being ostracised by the other children at creche? He'll be in preschool in just over a year – how will he make friends?'

The feeling of being trapped grows, claustrophobia pushing in on me. I don't, or can't speak.

'And when this documentary airs – when it goes viral as some stupid trend on TikTok or Snapchat or whatever – what will happen then? How can we live with this?' His voice is raised, and I am now pinching the skin on my wrist tight enough to distract me from raising my voice back.

'How can we live with this?' I say, eventually, a shake to my voice. 'You know what I'm living with every day, Brendan. Every day not knowing where she is. Not being able to remember what happened. Can you imagine for just one moment what that is like?'

He stares at me but I don't drop my gaze from his. I will not be guilted into pulling out of this project. In fact, his stance just makes me more determined to see it through.

Eventually he shakes his head. 'I know it must be horrific for you,' he says. 'I just want to protect Luca. That's all. Protect us and protect Luca.'

'I know,' I say, finding the will to stand up and wrap up my own dinner. It's pointless carrying this on and I'm tired now. There's an implication in his words that *I* don't want to protect us or Luca either, and I don't know whether I'm more sad or angry at that.

'I'll take Luca up to his room and try and get him changed into his PJs without waking him,' I say, walking past him and lifting our sleeping boy. I'll wait until later, until Brendan himself is asleep, before I go back to my laptop.

Chapter Seven

Izzy

The phone rings three times before a woman with a cheery voice and a beautiful West Coast accent answers.

'Good evening. GalwayLive, Maureen speaking. How can I help?'

I'm a bit thrown, because I certainly wasn't expecting anyone to answer at this time. It's almost seven in the evening and after all day talking back and forth with Jacqs, I decided the best thing to do was to try and find out as much info as possible about the photo. Okay, so Tom is right. These kinds of photos do show up relatively frequently and they've never amounted to much, but I can't ignore it.

Jacqs still hasn't received a reply from 'IrishEyes' so I decided a two-pronged approach was best. I'd expected to leave a message on an answerphone and hopefully have someone call me back in the morning. If I did it now, before dinner, then Tom wouldn't have any further chance to talk me out of it.

I had prepared myself for the message I would leave. I was not prepared to talk to an actual person, but there's something about Maureen's voice that puts me at ease. She sounds like the kind of woman who always has paracetamol and tissues in her handbag. The kind of woman who gives good hugs.

I introduce myself, and tell her I want to speak to somebody, maybe their photographer, about photos that appeared online.

'Now what photos would those be?' she asks, in a manner that leads me to believe there is no task too big or too small for Maureen. She gets stuff done. I've met her kind before. My Irish granny was one of those women.

'A fun day at Salthill,' I tell her. 'They were posted online a few days ago – Sunday maybe. I don't live near Galway, so I'm not sure if they appeared in print or not.'

There's a little laugh. 'Well, now I could tell by that accent that you're not a Galway girl, but what I can tell you is that if they were online on Sunday, they'll have been in print. Or some of them will, at least. We have to keep people buying the paper and not just getting all their news for free. I'd have nothing online if it were up to me. We're cutting our own throats,' she says. I sense it's not the first time she's made this argument.

There is a rustling of what I assume is newspaper and then she is back on the line. 'Yes, I have them here. They appeared in yesterday's print edition, as it happens. We only publish once a week, you see.'

'Ah, okay. That's great. Look, I was wondering would it be possible to get the name of the photographer who took them. Maybe even speak to him or her? I realise it's outside normal hours but maybe if I could get a message to them? Would your photographers be due into work tomorrow?'

There's a snort on the other end of the line. 'Ah pet, there's only two of us here on a good day and none of us are photographers. This is what I'm telling you. We're cutting our own throats. We used have four staff photographers here, and now? Not a one. We use freelancers now. Pay them a pittance. Hardly covers the cost of their diesel when we've got them driving round half the county.'

As much as I thought Maureen sounded lovely at the beginning of this call, I am starting to lose my patience with her. I don't need to hear chapter and verse on the past of GalwayLive, or the disastrous impact of the internet on print media. I just want to talk to whoever took the photos.

'And do you know which freelancer was paid a pittance for these photos?' I ask, trying to keep my growing impatience out of my voice. I remind myself I wasn't expecting to get anywhere with these pictures tonight anyway. I take a deep breath.

'I do,' she says. 'It was Paddy McGilloway. Great fellah. Brilliant eye for photos, you know.'

'And could you possibly give me his number so I can call him? Or maybe even his email address?'

There's a slow sucking in of breath through teeth. 'Ooh, I don't think so. No offence or anything, pet, but we don't give out personal details over the phone. But I can take your details and forward them on to Paddy and I'm sure he'll get back to you soon. Although I think he's been out working at a country fair or festival or something today, and he'll be in rubbish form this evening. He was in here swearing earlier because the skies were about to open and he'd get mucked to his eyeballs standing in a field all day. I said to him he should've packed his wellies.'

I pinch the bridge of my nose, fighting back the headache that is threatening to send me over the edge into the realms of rudeness.

'If you could give him my details that would be great. And could you tell him I'm a documentary maker and his help could be invaluable to our project?' I say before reciting my name, phone number and email address.

I cut her off just as she says, 'A documentary maker, indeed. This all sounds very glamorous . . .' telling her I have another call coming through but thanking her profusely for her help.

By the time I've ended the call, I feel like I've gone ten rounds with Mike Tyson. If Mike Tyson were a talkative woman from Galway. It's a good thing my granny prepared me well for such situations.

The smell of steaks cooking reminds me I'm actually starving and really should've eaten an hour ago. It also reminds me about the bottle of wine I stashed in the fridge earlier – even if I've vowed to only have one glass with dinner.

I close my MacBook, stretch and pad through to the open-plan living area, where Tom has cleared and set the table. My wine is already poured.

'Well?' Tom says. 'Did you uncover any more hidden gems today? Maybe find the Ark of the Covenant, or the—'

The look on my face cuts him off mid-sentence.

'Okay,' he says. 'I can read the room.'

'I did get through to GalwayLive just now, about the picture.'

Tom starts to plate up the steaks, serving them with seared asparagus and a peppercorn sauce. My mouth is practically watering. 'And did they have more info?' he asks, his back to me.

'Well, I did learn that the newspaper industry is struggling and Maureen, who might be the receptionist, the editor or the cleaner for all I know, isn't very happy about it.'

When Tom turns around he is holding the two plates of food and gives me a sympathetic smile. 'So, no new info then?'

'She's passing my details on to the photographer,' I say. 'And when he isn't so grumpy because he's been standing in a rainy, muddy field all day, he might get back to me. Maybe my excitement earlier was a bit premature,' I say. He has the good grace not to agree with me, opting to sit down and lift his bottle of beer instead.

'But you did get Nora Logue on board,' he says. 'And we should definitely drink to that.'

I lift my glass and clink it against his bottle.

'I wonder what her reaction to the picture will be,' I say.

'You're going to show it to her?' he asks.

'Well, yes. Of course. It might be something. I can't exactly keep it from her.'

Tom sits back in his chair, head tilted ever so slightly to one side as if he is thinking. 'I think we should film her reaction to seeing it. Let the psychologists and experts read what they can from that.'

It's a good idea. Actually in terms of material it would be gold, but she seems a little fragile. No, I tell myself. I knew this was going to be challenging going in. I knew I was going to have to ask awkward questions and not pander to Nora's emotions. Filming her is the exact right thing to do.

'Okay,' I say, a fizz of excitement bubbling in the pit of my stomach. I'll choose my moment to make sure it lands right, but yes, we should film this. We *will* film this.

Chapter Eight

Nora

Brendan lies snoring gently beside me, his face a picture of perfect relaxation – jaw slack and a slight smile playing on his lips. Dreaming happy dreams, no doubt. I nudge him probably a little too harshly with my elbow, causing him to roll off his back and onto his side. The snore becomes gentle and rhythmic, breath in and out. But it's no good. Even without his snoring, my body refuses to sink into sleep.

In the early days, after Daisy went missing, I'm told I was given sedatives to help me block the world out.

But getting sleeping pills or sedatives now would require a battle of wills with my GP that I'm not up for, or capable of just now. According to her, I took them back then for too long. Became addicted. It was a wonder I could function at all, she said. Maybe that's why it's all so hazy. Maybe that's why there are huge chunks of time that I don't remember.

The pills came with their own set of problems. There were times when I found myself in a half-sleep state, unable to move and unsure of what was real and what wasn't.

That's the place where my nightmares really came to life – where reality and the dreamworld mix. That's where I'd see

Daisy again, walking into my room, and I'd try to fight to get to her but I couldn't wake up enough.

As the light streams through the gap in our bedroom curtains, the warmth of the early morning sun lets me know it's going to be another hot day. Brendan may well suggest another family adventure – there are perks to being your own boss, and July isn't a traditionally busy time for accountants. He could take the day off if he wants to with no one to answer to.

But I have to go and meet with Izzy again today, and meet with this Tom person she's working with. Brendan might not be happy about it, but he'll have to learn to live with it.

After slipping out of bed, I pull on my soft pink cardigan over my pyjamas and pull my unruly dark hair back in a scrunchie. Very quickly I realise the pink cardigan is a mistake. The wool brushes like sandpaper against a patch of sunburn on my shoulder. 'Fuck!' I swear under my breath, stripping it off and dropping it on the floor before going to the family bathroom where I slather on a liberal dose of after-sun. Some natural aloe-type concoction that Brendan swears by. The relief is almost instant.

I pad my way downstairs to grab a coffee that will pull me from my fugue. If I'm not able to sleep I might as well wake up properly.

Five minutes later, with a full mug in my hand, I go to the study where I fire up my laptop. It's early enough that Brendan should be sound asleep for another hour or two. This gives me ample opportunity to have another look around AmateurSleuths, although there's a big part of me that is nervous to see what they have written about me now. But now I know it's there, and I know 'IzzyTV' is posting, it's not something I feel I can stay away from.

The documentary thread has been busy since I last looked – there's a flurry of activity. Congratulations to Izzy on bagging such a great interview. Lots of questions – lots of people asking how Izzy will approach the interviews, asking if she could ask questions on their behalf, snippets of rumours and theories half discussed. Some of them I've heard before – that Daisy and I never went into the woods together the day she disappeared, that I'd killed her days before. Or that I'd taken a massive cash payment from Daisy's father, Conal, so he could bring Daisy to live with him – that one makes no sense. Why would I hide that? Why wouldn't Conal just show everyone she is okay? But sense doesn't always come into it when it comes to these theories.

I scan through the thread, half-reading but really only looking for that name again – 'DonegalDetective' – to see if there is any indication on how things have just got more interesting. What lies are doing the rounds now? What has she heard that has sparked her desperation to get in touch with Izzy? Is it something new? Is it something I should know?

I feel jumpy, nervous, extra aware of the sights and sounds around me. Listening out for a telltale creak on the stairs or perhaps the sound of movement from my bedroom overhead. I don't want to be caught off-guard by Brendan.

I'd asked him if he wanted to come and meet Izzy and Tom with me. Told him it might help assuage his anxiety if he could talk his concerns through with them personally. He refused – telling me his concerns are not something that could be eased by any conversation with a TV producer. He suggested I speak to the police, to Heather – my family liaison officer – to ask for her take on whether or not I should be involved. I didn't tell him how the police were being cagey with getting involved themselves. I'd just nodded. Said I'd think about it.

But I won't. Because I want to see what these people come up with. I'm curious if they can solve the puzzle that I've been unable to.

There are no new posts from DonegalDetective, and none

from IzzyTV either. It's unusual for both of them from what I can see of their posting history. Frustration nips at me. This is not what I need. It's not as if I can arrive at my meeting with Izzy and Tom later and ask outright what this 'DonegalDetective' person meant. Izzy didn't tell me the name of the forum she uses so she'll know I've been snooping. And while that might be a perfectly natural, human response, I don't want to appear overly needy or unhinged. Especially not when so many people seem to think I'm unhinged anyway.

Maybe I should set up my own account – anonymous of course. I'm not a glutton for punishment. It might allow me to lurk a bit more freely? Maybe ask a question or two? Eke out what information I can without feeling as if I'm interrogating Izzy.

My hands hover over the keyboard, my brain racing. This might just be a spectacularly bad idea. I tell myself I'll wait until I've finished my coffee and then I'll decide, but I notice my coffee cup is already pretty empty. Jittery enough, it's probably a bad idea to make a second cup. Nonetheless I wander into the kitchen and stare at the coffee pods anyway, before deciding I'll be okay with a second cup as long as I eat something too. Yet my appetite is still almost non-existent. I pop a single slice of bread into the toaster, already knowing I won't eat it, but I go through the motions anyway until I can take both the coffee and the toast back to the study.

As soon as I sit back at the desk I start to set up an account for myself, kidding myself that I'd not made the decision as soon as I'd opened the browser this morning.

I don't want to use my real name – obviously. Which means I also don't want to use my real email address. Nora.Logue@ gmail might be a giveaway. So I set up a new email account using 'JustLurking' as my username, and then I complete my forum registration. I don't fill in any significant bio information.

Anyone clicking on my profile will see the generic avatar that comes with the site, and they'll see I'm from Ireland. I don't specify north or south. I decide against enhancing my forum signature with any quotes, or stats or indication of what my special interests might be, noting that other users have links to conspiracy theories, podcasts, subforums or declarations as to their own take on high-profile cases.

'Mummy, I waked up. Can I have a go on your 'puter?' I jump at the voice and turn to find Luca, bleary-eyed, one leg of his pyjama bottoms pulled up on his leg in his sleep. His morning bed head sits at all angles, but his eyes are wide and there's a tremble to his lower lip.

I realise I didn't just jump, I shouted. Swore. Shit. What if Brendan has heard and wants to come and find out what all the commotion is about?

Reaching my arms out to Luca, I gesture for him to come and sit on my lap. 'I'm sorry, baby,' I tell him, burying my face in his curls and closing my eyes to breathe him in. His hair smells of a mix of apple shampoo and salty sea air. I'm struck by a memory – fleeting – of how Daisy's hair smelled after her bath. How soft it was. How she'd cuddle on my lap just like this as we talked about her day.

'You've gave me a bit of a scare,' I tell him. 'I didn't hear you coming down the stairs.' He cuddles closer to me for a moment, before reaching his hand out towards my computer.

'What's that?' he asks, pointing to the screen.

'Just some work Mummy has been doing,' I lie.

He nods, never doubting me for one moment. 'Can I watch *Paw Patrol*?'

'Yes, pet,' I say, relieved that he hasn't asked any more questions about what exactly my work involved. 'How about you watch *Paw Patrol* in the living room on the TV and I'll make some breakfast.'

'I watch it here,' he says, his hand already reaching for the mousepad. Not quite three years old, and he is already able to find his way around a computer screen. Gently, I place my hand over his. 'Luca, this is my computer for work. Let's go and watch *Paw Patrol* in the living room or we can bring your tablet to the kitchen table.'

I feel his body tense, the beginning of an epic-scale tantrum sure to be on the way. If that happens, then Brendan will definitely wake up and things will get more complicated. 'Okay,' I say, already annoyed at myself for capitulating so easily. 'Just let me set it up.'

Quickly I click closed the AmateurSleuths screen and open YouTube, where I find enough *Paw Patrol* content to keep Luca busy for as long as it takes for me to make his breakfast. Damn it, I hate that I have to sneak around in my own house and may God forgive me but right at this moment I feel more than a flash of irritation towards Luca for interrupting me.

Of course he has no understanding of what is going on. Daisy is an abstract figure to him. A picture on the wall he says hello to. He's told he has a sister but he doesn't get it. How could he?

I set to work making him a breakfast of pancakes and Nutella – a treat usually reserved for weekends but which I'm making today to make up for my frustration with him. A mother's guilt is a powerful force.

They're almost ready when I hear Brendan on the stairs. 'Nora, is Luca with you? He's not in his room,' he calls and I hear our son call out to him.

They chatter, discussing the merits of Chase over Marshall in *Paw Patrol* before Brendan, already dressed for work, walks into the kitchen. 'Bit early for Luca to be on the computer, isn't it?' he asks, as he slots a pod into the coffee machine.

'He's only watching *Paw Patrol*. I've been keeping an eye on him,' I say.

'So you were . . . online already this morning? Sending out those work emails?' he asks. Brendan is not a controlling man, but there is suspicion and something more – something darker – in his voice.

'Yeah,' I say, cutting up Luca's pancakes onto his plate before calling him.

'Because I don't think you should be taking too much on,' he says.

'Yes, I know. You said,' I say, trying to keep the terseness from my voice. He makes to speak again but I am in no form for it, and I call Luca to come and get his breakfast instead. 'I'm going to get a shower,' I announce. 'I've to go and meet with the TV producers this morning and I don't want to be late. You know how crazy parking can be in the city centre.'

When I leave the room I nip into the study and shut my laptop down, just in case Brendan has any notion to snoop.

Chapter Nine

Nora

There's a strange energy in this room. I can't quite put my finger on it, but I'm not long in noticing that Izzy seems a little jittery. She was all smiles and warm welcomes when I arrived, leading me through to a beautiful drawing room, complete with period fixtures and a heady, musky smell of beeswax polish and lavender.

'We're all set up in here,' she said, gesturing to a sofa and armchairs positioned in front of bookcases filled with leather-bound tomes. A camera is positioned facing the seats, lighting set up around them. My head buzzes and fizzes as I try to take it all in.

I hear a cough from behind me, and turn to see a very tall, slim man giving me a small, gentle smile. Unlike Izzy, who is once again dressed in a sharp suit and white shirt replete with an on-trend oversized collar, the man, who I assume is Tom, is dressed casually. A T-shirt. Jeans. Rough-shaven, but in a fashionable way. When he reaches out his hand to shake mine, I notice some leather bracelets wrapped around his wrist and some sort of minimalist tattoo. I try not to stare. There's just so much to take in.

'Nora, I presume?' he says, his London accent throwing me

for a moment and I don't know why it does, given that Izzy has an English accent too.

'And you're Tom,' I say, noticing my voice sounds shaky, nerves twanging again.

'I am indeed,' he says. 'We're really grateful that you've agreed to come on board for this project,' he says. 'Shall we sit down? Can I get you a tea or coffee? Or a cold drink? We have water here, but there's a café next door and I don't mind running out.'

'I'm fine,' I tell him, taking a bottle of water from my bag. 'I came prepared.'

'Is anyone joining you?' Izzy asks. 'Brendan maybe? A friend.'

I shake my head, feel the urge to scratch at my wrist again. If the truth be told, I'm embarrassed that it's just me and that I don't have friends who come and hold my hand at these things. Not anymore anyway. People peel away bit by bit after a while.

'Brendan has mixed feelings about my involvement in this project,' I say. 'He's concerned it might just stir things up again. Hate towards me, you know.'

Tom looks at me, sympathy drawn across his face. 'That must be tough all the same,' he says. 'Not getting the support you need from him.'

I bristle. I don't want to paint a picture of Brendan as unsupportive. Not at all. 'It's not like that,' I say. 'He has been a rock to me these last five years. But we have Luca to consider now, and he's getting old enough to notice when things aren't quite right.'

I think of the excrement-filled nappy wiped across our windscreen. How Brendan was so quiet as he cleaned it the best he could – the smell stomach-churning in the heat – but how unsettled he seemed later.

'Of course,' Tom says. 'I suppose having Luca does complicate things.' He disappears behind the camera. Are they filming this?

I wasn't expecting this today. I was only expecting to chat things through some more. I shift in my seat, pull the sleeve of my dress down over my arm to hide the scratch marks, the red lines now livid. I can't talk about Brendan or Luca. I have to keep them out of this as much as possible.

Probably sensing my discomfort, Tom speaks. 'Don't worry about me. This isn't for the documentary. I'm just practising some shots for when we do this properly. Getting the light levels right and the like. But if you'd prefer I didn't . . .' He leaves it hanging, gives me that same soft reassuring smile from behind the lens. I shake my head. I don't want to come across as more neurotic than I am.

'No. It's okay. I'm fine,' I lie, before sipping from my water bottle, my mouth now dry.

Izzy sits down opposite me, but she looks about as comfortable as I feel. I wouldn't have taken her for someone nervous. If anything she seemed a bit overconfident when we met yesterday.

'Look,' she says. 'Before we start, we think there is something we should bring to your attention. I've tried to have this verified and find out as much about it as possible.'

I stiffen. Is this what 'DonegalDetective' was talking about yesterday?

'We received this picture yesterday. It was sent to my friend, Jacqs, on Amateur . . .' she stops, no doubt realising she's about to reveal the name of the forum she hasn't mentioned before, '. . . on the forum we frequent. We can't track the user who sent it, but we're trying to get in touch with the photographer who we think took it – he's supposed to call me at some stage today. But long story short, this picture has appeared online and possibly in print. It was taken in Salthill, near Galway, a couple of days ago.'

She turns the iPad she has had resting on her knee towards

me, before pinching and stretching her thumb and forefinger to enlarge the image.

It takes a moment for my eyes to focus on the image in front of me. I see people, standing, smiling at the camera. A summer scene. Happy families enjoying a day out. At first glance there's nothing particularly remarkable about it. I blink at Izzy, my confusion written all over my face.

'Here,' Izzy says, reaching over and zooming even closer. 'This girl here. Does she look familiar to you?' She points a short scarlet gel nail at a figure on the screen. My stomach lurches. She does look familiar. It's almost as if I'm staring at myself, but myself if there was a piece of Conal Arbuckle, Daisy's father, mixed in.

This figure in front of my eyes looks like a perfect mix of us both. And very much like an older version of the little girl I loved with all my heart. Yes, her hair is longer and slightly lighter than the police image, a grimace on her face rather than the neutral expression in the computer-generated picture the police have shared.

An ache unlike any other I have ever felt squeezes my heart, and I feel the colour drain from my face. And it keeps on draining, lower and lower – while the spaces left behind become cold and clammy and my lungs fight to suck in air.

'Breathe,' I hear a voice in the distance, but it's as if I don't remember how. Things aren't working as they should be. Panic sets in. The back of my neck prickles, and I can feel a pressure, a blackness, start to form at the base of my skull.

I'm going to faint. I don't know how to stop it. I don't . . . know . . .

The warmth of the sun beats down on my bare skin, so pale against the bright blue of the sky. Almost translucent. As if I'm here and, at the same time, not here. As if I'm watching myself striding through the long grass, the cool blades tickling the bare skin of my legs. My maxi skirt is bunched up at the sides into my knickers. Daisy laughed so much when I did that, so amused by my folding and tucking and flashing of the sides of my pants. But the sun is so warm and I want it to touch my body in as many places as possible. I want to savour the feeling of it bouncing off my shoulders, exposed by my coral cotton vest top. I want to feel the freckles blossom on my face and arms.

I want to savour her hand in mine. Always. Our arms swing back and forth as we walk – no, as we march – in time to the song we are singing. Our smiles are as wide as our notes are out of tune, and I am so unashamedly, blissfully happy that I feel my heart swell and I squeeze her hand as we walk out of the clearing and into the shade of the woods.

All my life I have been waiting for love like this. This person who would love me unconditionally. Who would see me as their hero. Who would make me laugh until my sides ache and tears run down my face. And here she is. Everything I've ever wanted. I did not expect to love her so fiercely. I had not expected her, my darling girl, to be the love of my life but there's no other way to describe her. No other love could come as close.

She is as perfect as this day.

I feel her hand slip from mine as her voice falls silent. My hand is more than empty without hers in it. I am untethered. Weightless and useless. Looking around, my eyes search for her but she has vanished. How? It must be a game. Hide-and-seek. In this place, with its trees and leaves and long grass housing a million great hiding spots.

'Daisy!' I call, my voice shaky. Not able to hide my fear at not having my eyes on her. I can't believe I've been so stupid. I should've stayed where I would have her in plain sight at all times. I shouldn't have let go of her hand. I have one job. Keep her safe. That's the only job that matters. I can't fail at it.

'Daisy! Okay, you win. I give up. You are the hide-and-seek champion!' I call, hysteria distorting my voice. I hear a noise. I can't pinpoint *from where. I don't know if it's a scream of fear or of laughter. There's a strange buzzing in my head and dizziness washes over me – the sky changing from the dappled light of the woods to black, to grey. My throat is sore, hoarse from screaming.*

The temperature has dropped now and a fat drop of rain has just landed on my face, its coldness feeling as though it's carving icy rivulets in my skin. How can it be so cold? How can it be raining? There wasn't a cloud in the sky a minute ago.

Blinking to see through the downpour, I hear someone say my name. They say it again and again, distracting me, but I want them to stop. I have to concentrate. I have to use every part of myself to find Daisy, but the voice only gets louder until I am suddenly back in a room in a nice building and someone is putting a glass to my lips and encouraging me to take a sip of water.

There's a cool compress on my forehead – a muttered back and forth between two voices. 'I think she's coming round,' says a male voice, an English accent.

'Let's just give her a little space. Nora? Nora, sip this water. It's okay. You've had a shock.'

A memory of the sullen-faced girl in the picture comes back to me. It's her. I feel it in my bones. That girl is my daughter.

Chapter Ten

Izzy

Tom is helping Nora back up onto her chair, telling me he'll run out to the café next door and grab a cup of hot sweet tea. Nora meanwhile has grabbed onto my hand and is squeezing it incredibly tightly, the iPad having crashed to the floor already. She stares at me, her eyes wide. 'Oh my God,' she mutters. 'Oh my God.' Her eyes flutter again and I'm not sure if she's going to pass out a second time.

'Just try and focus on your breathing,' I tell her. 'Should I call Brendan for you?'

She shakes her head, releasing a single tear, which slides its way down her cheek. 'I need to call DI Bradley,' she says, her voice thick.

'Of course,' I say as she stares into space, in a daze. Her right hand fumbles at her side, reaching down to try and find her bag. She's still an awful colour, but her breathing seems to be regulating itself now. It has slowed but is still shuddering on each exhalation.

'Let me help you,' I say and make to reach for her bag. At my movement, she blinks and looks at me, her eyes wide.

'That's my girl. I'm sure that's my girl. How . . . ?'

Her eyes flutter again, and I grab her to make sure she stays upright. 'She was just here,' she says. 'When . . . I saw that picture . . . and then it was dark and she was there and she was just like she was that day and I shouldn't have let go of her hand . . .'

I gulp. I definitely shouldn't have let Tom go. I should've got him to film this. She's so far out of it I doubt she would even notice.

'Did you remember something?' I ask, gingerly, wondering if the picture might have unlocked something from her lost memories. 'Something new about that day?'

She shakes her head. 'No,' she says, and it's as if saying the word has taken every last ounce of energy from her body. 'It's the same. Always the same,' she says and her tears start to flow freely now. She makes a half-hearted attempt to wipe them away with the sleeve of her dress, while I reach for the box of tissues on the coffee table and hand one to her.

If this woman is an actress, she is a damned good one because I feel the power of her loss. It's in this room, weighing us down, and suddenly I wonder how she ever finds the strength to pull herself out from under it.

'You can use my phone if you like?' I say, fishing it out of my pocket.

'Who did you say sent the picture? Did they send a message? Do they know these people, the other people, in the picture?' Nora is throwing questions I can't answer at me.

I take her hand in mine. It's cool, clammy, and I can feel her tremble. 'I'm trying to get you as much information as possible,' I say. 'At the moment I don't know anything more than I've told you. It was taken in Salthill, a few days ago, and it appeared online on a website called GalwayLive. I can show you the link – there's just a generic caption, no names unfortunately.'

Nora nods, taking it in before turning her attention to her

phone and scrolling down the screen until she finds the right number. I listen in as the call connects and a female voice answers.

'It's Nora Logue here. I need to speak to DI Bradley. It's urgent,' she says.

I can't hear what the woman on the other end of the line says, but by the expression on Nora's face it isn't the answer she was hoping for.

'It's in relation to my daughter. Daisy Logue. You know the Daisy Logue case?' Nora says, exasperation seeping from every pore. She is gripping her phone so tightly, her knuckles are sheet-white.

Just as I hear a male voice sound on the other end of the line, Tom walks back into the room balancing three cups of tea along with a bag of pastries. Spotting that Nora is on the phone, he mouths 'who's that?' to me and I mouth back 'police'.

With a nod, he gestures to me to follow him into the hall, but I want to stay where I am. I want to hear what DI Bradley has to say. But when I shake my head, Tom raises his eyes to indicate that he wants to talk to me. Now.

'What is it?' I ask, having pulled the door gently behind me.

'I was just talking to a woman in the café next door,' he says and I'm sure by talking he means flirting.

'And?'

'She says she worked with Nora when they were teenagers. A Saturday job,' he says, in a half whisper, his eyes darting to the door behind me. Okay, he has my attention now.

'She said we should be careful around her,' he says. 'That she's not quite right in the head.'

My attention wanes as quickly as it arrived. This is not a new take. Hasn't Nora herself just told us of the high number of people who are resolutely not on her side?

'That's hardly ground-breaking news,' I snap. 'And you'd be

"not quite right in the head" if your child had gone missing, taking your memory of the event with her.'

'No,' Tom says, and I can see I have rattled him with my tone, but I just want to get back into the room to listen in on the chat between Nora and the police.

He continues, 'The woman said she was always a bit odd. Bit of a loner, you know. Even as a teenager. Didn't have many friends.'

'Again,' I say, 'this isn't new information.' There have been a hundred and one profiles done on Nora Logue and many of them have touched on what was a pretty strict childhood. Her parents – both in their late thirties when Nora was born – had been religious, her father a teacher. They'd lived in a small village on the North Coast, and Nora had been packed off to attend a grammar school in Derry when she was sixteen, after her father's health deteriorated and her mother felt unable to cope.

Arrangements were made for Nora to stay in accommodation normally reserved for students at Ulster University at Magee, and by all accounts Nora was a serious, studious young woman. She took her studies, and life in general, very seriously. Her mother died when she was twenty and her father is in the advanced stages of dementia – and has never even been aware he has a granddaughter.

Young Nora Logue did not have the time, nor the social skills, to make a large circle of friends.

'Yes,' Tom replies, his face taut and his eyes boring into mine. 'If you'd let me finish.'

Chastened, I nod at him to continue. 'Well, the café was pretty busy and there was a queue building up behind me so she said she couldn't talk just then, but we needed to know Daisy wasn't the first.'

A flicker of something – fear, or maybe excitement – pulses through me.

'Wasn't the first what?' I ask.

'She didn't get to say,' Tom says with a shrug of his shoulders. 'But she asked for my phone number and said she would be in touch.'

Here it is, I think, the same old story. Someone falling for Tom's charm and good looks and taking extraordinary measures to make sure she got a hold of his phone number and Tom, being Tom, would fall for the flattery every time.

'I think you've just been taken advantage of,' I say, my voice clipped. 'This is an exceptionally high-profile case. So, Daisy wasn't the first what? The first child Nora had? Pretty sure someone would've known about another child – all these doctors and professionals who have been supporting her. I imagine it would be on her records. Or the first child who went missing? Things like this don't just get forgotten and brushed under the carpet.'

'Say what you want, Iz,' he says. 'But I'm old enough to know when someone is coming on to me. This girl, she was serious. It was almost as if she was scared.' It dawns on me that Tom isn't smiling. This isn't playful banter. He's a little shaken.

'She said it again as I was leaving,' he says. 'To be careful.'

A cold shiver runs up and down my spine.

Chapter Eleven

Nora

DI David Bradley sounds distracted and I feel my temper start to rise, but I must not lose my cool. Even if I think this man has let me down, I need him onside. I need him to take this lead seriously and to find the girl in the picture as soon as possible. If it was taken 'a few days ago' like Izzy said then this girl could be anywhere now. Thousands of people holiday in Galway each year – there's nothing in that picture to indicate they are local to the area. If DI Bradley doesn't get his colleagues in the Garda Síochána involved immediately, we could miss them. We might already have missed them.

'There's been a sighting,' I tell him. 'I have a picture here in front of me of a little girl who looks just like Daisy. How Daisy would look now. The picture was taken in Galway at the weekend. The girl is with a family. This is the strongest lead we've had yet,' I blurt. 'She's practically identical to the girl in your e-fit.' My voice cracks, just as I hear the door to the room open and Izzy and Tom walk in together.

'Okay,' DI Bradley says. 'And this picture? Where did you find it? What information do you have?'

'I was sent it,' I tell him, then immediately correct myself.

'Actually, I've been shown it by the producer working on the new documentary about Daisy's disappearance. She received it from a friend last night.'

'That's convenient,' DI Bradley mutters not quite enough under his breath. I tense. 'And where did this friend receive it?'

'She was sent it by a user on a true crime forum. You know, where people talk about old cases and try to solve them?'

He sighs. 'Yes, of course. So the person who sent it in the first place – do you know who they are?'

My heart sinks. He's not buying this and I shouldn't be surprised. When looked at properly, we have very little to go on at all.

'It's an anonymous user,' I tell him. 'But the picture appeared on GalwayLive – that's a website about Galway.'

'And did they give a name or any details of this girl? In the caption perhaps?'

'It's my daughter,' I say, slowly.

'I'm not telling you you're wrong,' he says. 'I'm just trying to find out as much information from you as possible. And, Nora, I'm urging you to be cautious. For your own good as much as anything. It doesn't seem as if we actually have a lot of information to go on, outside of this picture.'

'These forum users,' I say, 'they seem to know their stuff. They're ex-police, specialists, you know.' I'm parroting what Izzy told me just yesterday, which I'm not even convinced about myself.

There's silence on the other end of the line. DI Bradley is not a bad man. Despite his failure to find my daughter, I wouldn't even say he was a bad police officer. But in this moment, it feels like he isn't interested in what I'm telling him. Maybe it's compassion fatigue. Maybe he's just had enough of seeing all the things police officers have to see. Or maybe he has just had enough of this case, of the brick walls and the leads that go nowhere. Maybe he has moved on.

'Okay, Nora,' he says after a moment. 'Send it over and I'll have the team look at it. Please give us any more information as soon as you get it. We'll need to speak to these producers you're working with, and some of these true crime people as well – so get their real names and contact details if you can.'

'Can't you access them some way?' I ask, hoping if nothing else the police would be able to track down the new user who sent the link in the first place. Surely the police have access to all sorts of technology that can track down the location and identity of internet users?

'We can,' he says. 'But if they are really trying to help you, it's quicker all round if they volunteer the information to you. I'm sure they'd be happy to,' he says but he doesn't sound sure.

I nod, before I remember he can't actually see me. 'Yes, of course,' I say.

'Nora,' he says and the tone of his voice has changed now. It's softer. More caring. This is the ultimate 'lay it on thick' voice that he normally keeps for press conferences and the like. A consummate professional when it comes to tugging at the old heartstrings – or telling grieving mothers what they want to hear. 'Just before I go, I need to say that I don't want you to get yourself too excited by this. We've been in this position before. More than once. You know the chances are not great—'

'Not great is better than non-existent,' I interject.

'Indeed,' he replies. 'But measure your expectations, please. You know that we believe if Daisy is still alive, she is unlikely to be in Ireland. Every police force north and south of the border have been on the lookout for her all this time.'

I'm not sure, but I think I might detect a defensive tone to his voice.

He says his goodbyes and ends the call, leaving me to think about just how hard we have all looked. I'm trying to grasp on the fragments of my memories from back then because I had to have looked. Right? Even that day? I had to have combed that woodland. I wouldn't have just walked away.

I know what I've been told about that afternoon. About how I was seen wandering onto the Limavady Road close to the Foyle Bridge in the heavy rush hour traffic, commuters heading in and out of the city to their homes. It's one of the busiest roadways in the city and often gridlocked at peak times.

It didn't help that the woods we had walked in also happen to be in extensive grounds surrounding the old mental health hospital. 'Gransha' is long gone and with it the many horror stories that probably owed more to urban myth than reality. In its place now is the much more palatable Grangewood – a much smaller but state-of-the-art 'intervention centre' for those who are actively suicidal. But the association with the old 'madhouse' still stands and the ghost stories are still whispered to terrified children on dark nights.

I'm sure I looked every inch the madwoman stumbling into the road. I *was* every inch the madwoman by all accounts. I don't remember it. Every now and again I get a glimpse of something that I try to hold onto but as soon as it arrives in my head it is gone again. I do, however, know that I stumbled into that road just before five. My last memories of Daisy, of our lunch and the buttercups and her marching ahead of me, were at half past two. Three at the latest. The time in between? I have no idea. But it's a popular spot. People would've been there. Dog walkers. Families. It was such a nice day and the woods are so beautiful . . .

I'm pulled from my reverie when Izzy comes back into the room, her face a mask of concern. 'I need to send that picture to Bradley,' I tell her. 'And I need details of the forum users – especially the person who posted the picture to your friend.'

'I'm on it,' she says, as she taps at her phone. Less than ten seconds later, the image appears as a WhatsApp message on my own phone screen. I waste no time in emailing it to DI Bradley. We need to act now.

I can sense Izzy watching me intently, and Tom approaching me with cups from the café.

'Here,' he says, handing one of them to me. 'Hot, sweet tea. For the shock.'

I thank him and take the cup because it's the appropriate thing to do. In a minute I'll pretend to take a sip from it and then set it down on the table. Hot, sweet tea does nothing for me except make me feel sick to my stomach.

'You really think it might be her?' he asks as I watch Izzy drink from her own cup. She takes a long drink and I wonder if it has been sweetened as well. She has a pallor about her that she didn't have when she left the room.

'I do,' I say, looking at the image on my phone again. The face of the girl in the picture is more defined than the little face I kissed that day. Her hair straighter. Her body taller and leaner. But I know that face. I know those eyes. God, I spent so long just staring into those eyes when she was little. The draw I feel towards her is magnetic and it's only all the warnings to be cautious, to get more information, to not hope too much, that are stopping me from jumping in my car and driving towards Salthill right now. I'd knock on every door and stand in every hotel lobby to try and find her.

'There must be so many emotions running through you right now,' Tom says, as if he is the person supposed to be interviewing me and not Izzy, who is still uncharacteristically quiet.

'You've no idea,' I tell him, my voice cracking. I think of the times I have imagined a reunion. Imagined being able to hold her hand again. Imagined being able to tell her I'm sorry. Imagined what it would feel like to have her forgive me. In the darkest days, the days when I have wanted to escape the horror of not knowing, of not remembering, it's that thought that has kept me going. 'Fear. Hope. Grief. I don't know which is strongest. What if it isn't her? How will that feel? But I have to hope, you know. If I don't have that, I don't have anything. That's what Brendan struggles to understand.'

I should probably stop talking, and certainly not talk about Brendan, but adrenaline is flooding through me and Tom and Izzy seem just so easy to talk with.

'Why do you think it's such a struggle for him?' Tom asks, as he pulls across a seat and sits down opposite me. I take another fake sip from my tea. Even though I don't let it touch my lips, the sweetness still invades my senses.

'He says hope can be cruel more than kind,' I say. 'It strings you along and you invest everything in it. It's addictive. You can't give it up because the alternative is unthinkable. But it keeps you in a moment that has passed, and for me it's the moment she disappeared. Or at least my next memory of that day. I can't exist outside of it. So it's killing me,' I shrug my shoulders. 'I'm not living anymore. I'm existing. It's not a life.'

'I don't know how you keep doing it,' he says. 'I mean I get there's no real alternative but you must feel like you're living under a cement block of pressure.'

I shrug again. 'You answered that with the first part of your sentence. There is no alternative. And there are occasional moments when it feels like my hope will be rewarded. If I'd given up and accepted that I'd never know, then we'd never have been looking for this picture and we wouldn't have this lead.'

'I suppose,' he says and I see him glance towards Izzy, who is still drinking from her tea – totally silent. As I look in her direction her gaze catches mine. Something has changed in the way she looks at me. There's something there that wasn't there before.

Suspicion, I think. I've seen it enough times to recognise it when it is staring me straight in the face. It comes to everyone eventually. They start off on my side but then doubt creeps in. Or the voices of the people convinced I'm responsible for Daisy's disappearance get too loud for them to ignore. The knot in my stomach tightens further. Already that wee sliver of hope I had is already starting to shrink.

Chapter Twelve

Nora

The urge to ask Izzy if everything is okay is strong, but I push it down. I do that because I'm afraid of what she might say. So I play over what I've said and done in the last five minutes to try and find a clue as to what has changed.

It dawns on me that she left the room briefly while I was on the phone and maybe it was when she came back in that the mood seemed to shift. Of course, I might be paranoid. The incident at the beach yesterday with the shitty nappy has perhaps unsettled me more than I realised. It's one thing to come at me, to think of me as somehow to blame. To think of me as a liar, but it's another thing to direct your hate where an innocent child can be hurt by it. God, maybe Brendan is right.

'So, you'll never guess what?' Tom says, cutting through my thoughts. 'When I went to get the coffees there was a woman there who said she used to work with you when you were teenagers.'

I stiffen. Run over the people I worked with in the Saturday job I had when I was still a student. I'd felt like an outsider even then, and had never really made any friends. My experience now is that anyone who comes out of the woodwork to say they knew me is either looking to hear gossip or to spread it.

My mouth dries and I look down to the teacup. Instead I lift my water bottle and take a sip.

'Really?' I say, realising that a prolonged silence might not come across well.

'Yeah, she realised I'm not a local once she heard my accent and asked what had me in Derry. I mentioned the documentary and that's when she said she knew you. Worked with you when you were sixteen or seventeen.'

'Did she give you her name?' I ask. If I can at least narrow it down, I can try and figure out if this is a friend or a foe. I suppose I could call into the café and see for myself, but even the thought of doing that makes me nervous. That was a difficult time in my life – suddenly on my own away from home for the first time.

'I didn't catch it,' he says. 'And she wasn't wearing a badge. Big queue too, but she took my number and she's going to call me when she gets a chance.'

The feeling of dread washes over me again. It comes in waves, threatening to knock me over. I take a deep breath.

'Why does she want to call you?' I ask. 'I don't keep in touch with any of the people I worked with when I first came to Derry. I wouldn't describe any of them as friends even. I was just trying to get on with my studies – to do the best I could. I didn't go in for after-work drinks or the like. So I'm not sure what she could tell you that you don't already know.'

Tom shrugs, casts a quick glance at Izzy, and I can't help but feel they have their own unspoken language. The comfort I felt with both of them is evaporating. Nervousness forces me to keep speaking. 'People like to claim their part in big stories don't they? Even if the link is tenuous to say the least.'

'What do you mean?' Tom asks.

'You must have experience of this,' I say, trying to keep the tremble out of my voice. 'Everyone likes to think they have something to add to the story. They want to be part of it. Enjoy their fifteen minutes of fame by association or whatever. Some people don't care if what they tell others is the truth, or helpful or both. All the crazies come out of the woodwork. As do the bullies. People will say anything if they think it will get them on TV.'

'It must be very hard,' Izzy says, reaching across to take my hand. It's only when she pulls it away that I realise I have been scratching at the daisy tattoo again, faint pricks of red starting to break through my skin.

'Of course it's hard,' I snap. 'That's what you need to realise. Because I don't know who to trust. I don't know who to believe. I don't even know whether I can believe myself, or trust my own memories. People can and will say what they want and as much as I might feel in my bones that they are wrong, I can't say they are for sure. That's what it feels like to properly lose your mind.' I sound borderline hysterical.

Izzy is silent for a moment. 'Look, I can't make you any promises that we will be able to get to the bottom of everything, but I can promise you that we have good people working on this and researching it for us. You're welcome to come and meet them when we have them in for interview, although we will be recording some of the interviews remotely.'

I blow out a long breath, suddenly tired. We've not even officially started filming yet and already I'm starting to feel overwhelmed.

'I think I want to go home,' I say. 'I think I need to think about things a bit more. This is all a lot. The picture. Whoever it is in the café. What happened at the beach yesterday.'

'What happened at the beach?' Izzy asks.

I tell her about losing sight of Luca and Brendan for the

briefest of moments. About hearing the scream and fearing the worst. 'It wasn't just because I know that the very worst things can happen to a child in a heartbeat,' I admit, 'or because the thought of losing Luca would be unbearable, but also because the reaction of everyone around us would've been so utterly horrific as soon as they realised who I was.' Even before I lost sight of them, I had to make sure we kept to ourselves. I did my best to hide my identity, covering up as much as possible. Because even on a nice family day at the beach, I'm always aware I could so easily become as much a spectacle as the waves themselves.

'Everyone watches me, everywhere. Everyone judges. Everyone tries to see something in how I interact with Luca, or with Brendan. Everyone watches to see just how broken I look – to see if it suits their idea of how grief-stricken I should still be. If I'm in pieces, I'm letting Luca down. If I appear happy with him, then I've clearly forgotten all about "that wee girl". What I really want to do, most of all, most of the time, is to stand up and scream at the top of my lungs for them all to just fuck off.'

Izzy blinks but doesn't speak, giving me space to keep going. 'And when we left, when we walked back to our car to go home, someone had left a present of a dirty nappy wiped across the windscreen. Another message. This is what my life is like now. Don't you see? I can't trust anyone. I can't even trust myself.'

Chapter Thirteen

Izzy

'Izzy. Tell me I'm amazing.' I can't help but feel he is reading the room all wrong. I'm not in the mood for telling anyone they're amazing. Nora has gone home, too shaken to stay any longer. It had been heart-breaking listening to her talk of how she is always watched, how not remembering what happened makes life impossible for her.

Of course I knew this in theory. I'd seen it written down in think pieces and interviews from the earlier days before she withdrew from giving interviews or giving live statements. But it's very, very different to see it up and close and personal. It's raw. I don't think I fully appreciated what raw would look like.'

'Not now, Tom,' I say, stretching to try and ease the tension in my neck and shoulders. I hate that every time I feel remotely stressed every muscle in my body decides to seize up in protest.

'You really need to learn to trust me more,' he says. 'This is gold. What we recorded today is absolute streaming gold. The faint! The freak-out over the old friend.'

I tense, a feeling of deep discomfort washing over me. It was one thing to talk about filming, but this feels really intrusive.

'I'm not sure it's right to use that,' I say. 'I mean that was pretty intense and you didn't tell her that you were filming . . .'

'I did tell her I was filming. I said it wasn't for the documentary just yet. And I asked her if she wanted me to stop, so . . .'

I'm still not convinced his actions were entirely ethical, but if he caught the footage . . . It would be a shame to waste it. Yes, it feels voyeuristic and a bit creepy but this was never meant to be comfortable.

'Why did you think I kept asking questions?' he says. 'I figured she'd be more candid if she didn't realise there were cameras on her. And I was right.'

She certainly had been candid. And that faint . . .

'Did you catch the audio?' I ask, aware that if we were to use the footage we might have quality issues. 'We weren't mic'd up,' I say.

'It's not the best quality, but we do have it. Or most of it anyway. I figure we could still work with it − and edit the video to look like grainy CCTV,' he says excitedly. 'It'll make her reaction look more authentic anyway as we'll be able to say she didn't know she was being filmed. We could say we didn't realise the camera was running, maybe.'

The issue of recording someone without their express knowledge is still nipping at my conscience though. 'Do you really think we can use it and not compromise our integrity?' I say.

'Look, Nora has never said anything is off the record − just that she wants to do whatever she can to find Daisy, and I think this all falls into that category. The thing is, when we pull all this together, when we edit it as part of the series and show it to her, I'll bet she won't even remember that she didn't know it was being filmed. Worst case she does, and we convince her it makes her more likeable, more believable. I doubt she'll be able to resist that.'

He is speaking with such authority that I ignore my own misgivings and choose to believe him.

'Play it back for me,' I say, and he taps the keyboard on his laptop and an image of Nora appears. She looks nervous – her body language screaming that she is out of her comfort zone. A thought crosses my mind to get a body language expert to examine the footage because there is something that makes me feel uneasy about her behaviour, but I can't put my finger on it.

Maybe I'm allowing the woman in the café – who I've not even met – to cloud my thoughts. What the hell did she mean about it not being the first time? Or maybe, I think as the footage plays, it's because every now and again I'm sure I see something flicker across her face that I can't quite name.

It's just a moment or two every now and then where perhaps her guard slips or perhaps it's a shutter coming down – but when I see that expression, a coldness in her eyes, a total lack of expression, it makes my blood run a little cold.

'Tell me you see it too?' I say, reaching across and hitting the pause button. And there it is, that flicker. The tautness of her jaw. The whitening of her knuckles. The expressionless moment.

'Can I be real? Tom says.

'Ideally,' I say. 'It's why I brought you on board after all.'

'Something about her gives me the creeps. Maybe that's wrong to say, but there's something not right with her, and I don't think it's just grief or trauma or whatever. I can't help but feel we're being played. And that girl in the café? She seemed to know exactly what she was talking about. I don't want to say she looked scared, but she definitely looked wary and she wasn't acting. She seemed pretty genuine.

'If only we could get Brendan to be interviewed,' Tom says. 'To tell a little more of their story.'

'I get the sense that's not going to happen, but that doesn't stop us talking about it or doing some digging ourselves. Same with following up with your woman in the café. I want to know what she meant,' I say.

'You and me both,' Tom says, before looking back at the screen. I watch as Nora fidgets in her seat. She scratches at her arm; I noticed that earlier. How she seems to compulsively tear at a small tattoo of a daisy on her wrist. Her eyes dart around the room. She is clearly not comfortable, hovering on the edge of fight or flight.

I can see why people can't take to her. She can say all the right things, can pull you right into her grief, but there is always something standoffish in her manner. Or maybe it's because we expect to see that. Tell enough people someone is shifty and they will automatically see them in that light.

'It's complicated, isn't it?' I say, more as an observation than anything else.

'C'mon. You didn't expect this to be easy, did you? I mean, this is one of the most controversial missing child cases in the world. You want easy? Go and do some two-bit documentary on a fading rock star, or a reality TV show. You need to remember you're not here to make Nora Logue your best friend. You're here to tell this story, no matter where it takes you.'

I can't decide if this is a pep talk or has crossed the line into some epic mansplaining, but either way I don't like how Tom is talking to me. This is my project and I never said it was too hard. Simply that it was complicated. His words make me bristle, and I feel the need to be away from him for a while. Perhaps living and working together wasn't the best idea in the world.

'I do know that,' I tell him, trying my very best to keep my tone even. 'And I don't care if it's hard. I'm ready for it to be hard. Yes, maybe I was a bit naive but I didn't think I'd feel so conflicted about her. I did my research, Tom. You know that. We've been over this a thousand times and watched almost every moment of footage that exists of her, but that's all very different to being face to face with her and don't dare tell me you don't feel it too.'

He shrugs. 'It's all part of the job. It will be worth it in the end when you're picking up your BAFTA.'

'It had better be,' I tell him, 'but if you don't watch how you speak to me I won't thank you in my acceptance speech.'

'Yeah you will,' he says with a wink. There are times when I truly hate him.

Chapter Fourteen

Nora

My hands are still shaking when I get to my car. I don't feel particularly safe to drive, but it's not like I can sit here all day. Or maybe I can. Maybe no one will notice me. Then again, what if someone does? What if someone sees Nora Logue just sitting having a never-ending panic attack in her car in the city centre? How long would it be until that was all over social media?

I take several deep breaths in a row. I know I need to be home. I need to be within my own four walls. Curtains drawn. Door locked. Away from the world. Sat in a quiet corner. While Brendan is still at work and Luca is still at creche. On another day I might pick him up early. I might hold him to me and breathe him in and remind myself of the good in the world. I might try not to think about how he smells different to his sister, how his body moulds against mine in a different way. The different timbre of his voice.

The fact he is almost three, and then he'll be four and then older than I have ever known her to be. That he will have existed in my life longer than she has.

The ache for her never goes away. It's a constant hunger. A

need. I consider driving to Galway anyway. To the streets of Salthill. Handing out fliers with the police image and asking if anyone has seen a child resembling this picture. At least I would feel as if I was doing something positive. Something active.

So much of the last seven years has been spent waiting. For news. For my memory to come back. But being terrified of both of these things happening at the same time. Being paralysed with fear. Wanting to remember but being terrified of what remembering might bring. The brain shuts down in the event of a trauma. What trauma have I blocked out?

I know, of course, no body has been found. And the area was searched, extensively. It's possible, however, that someone disposed of her body in the nearby River Foyle, the fastest-flowing river in Europe. Dump a body at the right time and there's a chance it will be swept out to sea never to be found again. The river usually gives up her grim treasures eventually, but a child's body — small, light — could be carried further and faster than an adult's.

That's one of my nightmares. Of her floating endlessly in dark waters, unable to see. Unable to reach me. Unable to breathe. Even now, awake in the daylight, in a public place, the thought of that is enough to have me bent double with fear.

I push down the urge to scream. With shaking hands, I turn the ignition and even though the tremble in my legs makes it difficult for me to hold down the clutch, I know I need to get home before the full weight of a panic attack kicks in. I just need to breathe, I tell myself, swearing and jumping when my phone rings. Instinctively I hit the dashboard display to answer the call, unable to find the words or breath to speak at first.

'Nora?' It's Brendan. I nod as if he can see me.

'Nora? Can you hear me? Are you driving?'

I manage to make a small noise, enough to let him know that I can hear him.

'Are you okay?' he asks.

'Go . . . ing . . . home,' I stutter between breaths.

'Nora, you're scaring me.'

I shake my head but I can't speak. I pull the car over. I have to use every ounce of energy I have simply to control my breathing.

'Is it another panic attack?' he asks, and again I make a noise – somewhere near a yes but not quite fully there.

'Okay, Nora. If you haven't pulled over, then do that for me now,' he says, his voice calm and in control. 'Then we'll remember your breathing, okay? You're safe right now. I have you. Do you understand? I've got you. I'm looking up your location on find my phone right now. I can come to you. You don't have to worry about anything but breathing in and out. This will pass. This always passes. Just breathe in for me . . .'

His voice is so calm, so gentle that it reaches inside my panic and stills me. I let him guide my breath in and out. Let him take control until the struggle for breath eases, and is replaced by a steady stream of tears.

'I'm going to come and get you now,' he says. 'Just stay where you are. It's okay, Nora. I promise you that it's okay. I love you.'

He ends the call and I play his words over and over again in my head. *I promise you that it's okay. I love you.* I breathe in and out just as he told me, concentrating entirely on the feeling of my lungs inflating and deflating while imagining the oxygen travelling through my bloodstream. I do that until Brendan's car pulls up behind mine and he does just what he said he would. He walks up to my door, opens it, and helps me out, pulling me into a giant hug.

'I'm going to take you home,' he says, his voice soothing what is left of my panic. 'I'm taking the rest of the day off. I'm going to look after you. I promise.' Sagging with relief I allow the warmth of his hug to ground me, and then I feel tiredness wash over me. It's the kind of tiredness that only comes when a spike of adrenaline has started to ebb away, and so I let him lead me to his car. I even let him help put my seatbelt on.

We drive home in silence, my thoughts too jumbled for me to speak – and Brendan gets that. He gets that sometimes I need space. What he doesn't quite get is why, when we get home, I close the blinds in the living room and curl up on the sofa, pulling a soft green velvet throw over me while I shiver.

Sitting down on the other end of the sofa – far enough away to give me space but close enough to help me feel secure, he sighs. 'Do you want to talk about it?' he asks.

I nod, but I don't speak. I still can't find the right words.

'I assume this is about the documentary?' he probes.

'Yes and no,' I say, my voice small. 'There's a picture,' I tell him and his eyes widen just a little. 'Of Daisy. Or at least we think it's Daisy or it might be Daisy.'

'Okay,' he says and again falls silent, allowing me the time to fill in the gaps.

'A photo taken a few days ago. In Ireland. In Galway,' I say. I reach for my phone and scroll through to the picture and show it to him.

'And you've spoken to the police?' he asks.

I nod. 'DI Bradley is looking into it. Izzy and Tom are looking into it too. The person who sent it isn't answering their questions.'

'Well, I'm sure the police can compel them to talk,' Brendan says.

'If they can track them down. It's an anonymous account on a forum Izzy uses. Where she has been discussing the case.'

Of course he stiffens when I mention a forum because he has no time for this nonsense. 'So it could be any crazy with any agenda?' he asks, and his tone is a little harsher.

'Or it could be legitimate. It could be my child.' I try not to sound defensive but it is so hard. 'This user could be someone who has seen that a documentary is being made and may have decided they want to help. People can be good like that. People can want to help.'

'People can also be cruel,' he says. 'Look at you, Nora. Look at the state you are in. The state you were in when I phoned you. That's what digging into this again does to you.'

'I'm not digging into it *again*,' I tell him. 'I never stopped digging. I'm looking for her and I'll keep looking for her.'

'Regardless of the toll it's taking on you,' he says.

'Brendan, what choice do I have? I can't give up on her any more than I'd give up on Luca.'

He drops his head to his hands. 'And if Luca had been with you today? When that panic attack hit? What would that have done to him? Can you tell me he would've been safe?'

'He wasn't with me,' I say.

'But he could've been. And yes, this might be Daisy and please God it is, but if it isn't and we go through this again and again and again? How will he feel being the target of cranks and vigilantes? How will he feel seeing people abuse his mummy?'

'That's why it's important!' I shout, frightening myself with the volume of my voice. 'Because the only way to stop this is to find out what happened. The only way to shut people up is to find Daisy. The only way for me to stop going through this torment again and again and again is to know.'

I can see Brendan's jaw tighten, his body tense, and he gets up, stalks across the room. 'There has to come a time when you put us first. If not us, then him. Can you ever put him first?'

I don't answer because the only answer I am able to give him wouldn't make him happy. No. I can't put Luca first.

My silence hangs in the air until Brendan gives me a defeated look and leaves the room.

Chapter Fifteen

Izzy

I've reviewed the footage we took of Nora three times, taken notes on her body language. I'll send the footage to Jim Porter, a profiler who has shown an interest in the case — another AmateurSleuths user, of course, even if he's not so amateur. I've verified his credentials though and he's not some fly-by-nighter. He actually knows what he is talking about, and more than that is willing to go on camera to talk about his views on Nora — albeit via Zoom. Our budget doesn't quite stretch to a cross-Atlantic flight to speak face to face with him.

I make a note to collate headlines of think pieces demonising Nora, which I'll get Tom to edit into a montage. Perhaps I'll use the audio of her talking about being targeted over that rather than use all the freshly recorded footage of her. It might be more palatable to her if we do that. It might even have more of an impact.

'Do you think we should go and scout the woods?' I call to Tom, who is once again sitting at the kitchen table, his head bowed over his computer, fingers moving like lightning across his keyboard.

'What?' he asks. 'Did you say something?'

'I said do you think we should go and scout the woods? I

think I'm getting cabin fever sitting here. I feel a bit restless. Feel the need to get up and do stuff.'

'I'm kinda in the middle of some stuff here,' Tom says. 'I'm not sure we've looked enough into Nora's past.'

'Plenty of others have and it's not been relevant,' I say.

'Well our mystery woman in the café would say differently,' Tom says.

'If she isn't just an attention seeker like Nora says she is? After all, we don't actually know anything much about her, do we?'

Tom pulls a face. 'That's why I'm trying to find out more. Look, I get that this morning was a bit intense. We weren't expecting a sighting to land on our first day of filming but don't look a gift horse in the mouth. Has that photographer phoned you back yet?'

I shake my head, wondering if I should ring the very talkative Maureen at GalwayLive again to make sure the message was passed on. Maybe I'll post openly on the AmateurSleuths page as well. See if we can't rattle this IrishEyes into replying to our message.

'Let's power through for another hour or so and then maybe relax with a cold one later?' Tom says. 'I'll even cook again, or if the cabin fever really is getting too much let's go out for a bite?'

'I'm trying to watch my budget,' I tell him. Until we get snapped up by a streamer we are doing everything – from research, to travel, to accommodation – as economically as possible. I have invested more than I'm comfortable with already without splurging on fancy meals.

'My treat,' he says. 'We'll get that smile back on your face.'

'Okay,' I say. 'I suppose there's plenty to be doing here anyway.'

'That's the spirit,' he says. 'Now get to work and I'll make you a cuppa.'

It's an offer I can't refuse. I lift my MacBook and bring it through to the bedroom where I prop myself up against cushions and get comfortable. I suppose I shouldn't be surprised to see that there has been a flurry of activity on the Daisy Logue subforum – much of it driven by news of us securing the interview with Nora.

Much of it is congratulations from long-term users. There are a significant number of suggested questions. And perhaps least surprising of all, is the amount of hate directed not only at Nora but also at me for giving her a chance to speak. I should follow my usual block and delete advice – knowing full well that answering back to angry people on the internet rarely ends well. But I also want to professionally defend my work and some of these accusations are deeply unfair.

'Media bias will mean the truth of what happened to that child will never come out. Children are being bought and sold around the world and the MSM covers it up time and time again. We know who is in power here – and it's those who would have us believe that Nora Logue is a victim. She sold her child and you can't tell me otherwise. There's big money in feeding the perversions of paedophiles and satanists. People think it doesn't happen here – but when things get too hot to handle stateside, they find their pickings elsewhere. Epstein's cult has a wide reach,' Truthseeker101 has posted.

'And all this bull about not being able to remember what happened? I bet if you looked hard enough you'd find a nice, healthy payment into an offshore bank account somewhere. Everything is for sale as we head towards the new world order. Mark my words.

'That woman should not be walking free. She should have been sterilised and never allowed to carry another child. Lock her up!' Truthseeker101 concludes.

'In my expert opinion, we are all overlooking the one obvious thing in this case. There was no forensic evidence linking Daisy Logue to the woods at Gransha on the day of her disappearance. That means none at all – not just no evidence that she was injured, or worse. No traces of her at all. Why are we so willing to believe she was there in the first place? This is not that quiet and secluded a spot. I've looked at the maps – the woods run alongside a school for God's sake! Surely someone would've seen them if they were ever really there?' JessicaFletcherFangirl has posted.

I don't have to reply with the derision I'm feeling to that one. But thankfully there are posts already pointing out all the flaws with that particular theory.

'Are you forgetting that CCTV footage captured Nora leaving the woods later that afternoon? Or that Daisy disappeared outside of term time? There may be a school close by but it was summer recess. Those are the facts. I'm sorry they don't align with your theory!' Spook76 has posted.

Several posters – new, of course – have already linked to blog pages that claim to have 'explosive evidence' that Nora Logue murdered her daughter and the PSNI helped cover it up. They provide lists of allegedly buried information, cite off-the-record sources 'close to the investigation' and have provided their own unique analysis of every single movement Nora has made on screen since the day Daisy went missing. I'm familiar with these dossiers. I've read through them, examined them, discussed them and discounted many of them. Others I have passed on to experts to examine. None have been verified as having any real standing in the truth.

I read through these as the unread message count on my DMs grows. I'm almost afraid to look, but I can't hide from the fact these people are also the ones who are helping me, who I am relying on to put meat on the bones of this documentary. Even the controversial opinions are valid. Okay, well maybe not the satanist trafficking opinions, but I try to keep an open mind. The reality is though that I can't follow up every allegation – I have to go where I'm guided by other people who have examined this way more closely than I have.

I stretch, rub my neck to ease the growing muscle tension while realising that perhaps sitting on top of a bed is not the best research position. My DMs are mostly more of the same style as the posts on the main forum page, but when I click into my unfiltered inbox, things quickly get more sinister.

Anon895013 writes, **'Fuck you and fuck that child-murdering bitch. I hope you both get raped an slaughtered.'**

So that earns Anon895013 an immediate block and report.

Justice4Daisy writes, **'Why would you give that woman a platform? How can you call yourself a serious documentary maker when you come down on the side of a she-devil like Logue? Some people don't deserve a chance to spin their lies even further. I don't believe in the death penalty but I'd make an exception for that one.'**

Message after message is filled with similar ranting. All from new users. It's clear someone, somewhere, has started to spread the word and I wouldn't be surprised if this is some sort of orchestrated campaign to try and silence not only Nora, but me as well.

I expected some hate, of course. But I did not expect this level of anger and vitriol. Maybe I was naive. I'm tempted to just switch off my computer and go out for a drive, or maybe a run. Derry's close enough to the Donegal coastline, I could even drive across the border and walk along the beach and clear my head of all this hate.

But I have to remind myself that this is what I signed up for. The bad and the good. The anger and the hate. It's all part of the story. It's all part of Nora's life. Still, it's okay for me to look at it in smaller doses if I need to. I'll just give it ten more minutes.

The next message I click into is a strange one. Another new user – this one with the name 'TheFour'. I'm intrigued from the start.

'We are The Four. We do not believe Nora Logue should be given a platform. If you knew what we do, you would agree. Nothing good will come from encouraging so much attention on this case. There is no happy ending here. But things can get worse. We promise you that. More people can, and will, get hurt. We are watching very closely.'

I click into their profile but of course there is no information given. The moderators of the page wouldn't even be able to help me out on this one. Data security comes first at all times. And it's easy to set up a fake account. All you need is an email address and, if you want to be relatively untraceable, a VPN (virtual private network). I'm a total luddite and even I could figure that one out.

Chances are this is just a crackpot, just like the other crackpots. Those who have extravagant conspiracy theories or want to threaten violence against Nora, and against me for daring to make a documentary, but I don't know. There's something about this one that makes the soft downy hairs on the back of my neck stand up. Maybe it's gut instinct. Maybe it's having spent the last hour reading increasingly batshit messages. I don't know, but it definitely feels just that bit different.

Does The Four have any significance? Is that in itself some kind of a clue? Daisy was four when she disappeared but beyond that I'm stumped. I type a quick message to Jacqs, asking if it rings any bells with her, or if she has heard from this mysterious poster as well. It doesn't take long for her to reply that she has no idea, but she'll do some digging, of course.

'**Oh, another thing,**' she types. '**The IrishEyes account appears to have been deleted altogether. This place is going batshit today. Hope all is going okay your end?**'

I type back a quick response, filling her in on how the morning went and telling her she really ought to come up to Derry so we can have a proper chat face to face. I've no doubt I could use this woman on my team.

By the time Tom pokes his head around the door to see if I want to go and grab a bite to eat, I've a headache, and am famished.

'You still paying?' I ask him, closing my laptop and getting off the bed with a much-needed stretch.

'Yup,' he says. 'I think cabin fever is setting in here too. This is heavy stuff.'

'And that's before I tell you about the death threats and the abuse online,' I say.

'Internet crazies,' Tom says with a shrug. 'Brilliant TV but not the most pleasant people to try and work with.'

'Some of them are deranged. Let me show you . . .' I'm reaching back for my computer when he cuts me off.

'No. No, Izzy. Don't show me anything. I'm starving with hunger. My head hurts. I want a pint. So unless it is Daisy Logue standing in this room right now ready to tell us exactly what happened, I'm voting we take a night off.'

Despite my growing sense of unease about some of the messages, not to mention the disappearance of IrishEyes, I decide to err on the side of keeping on Tom's good side; after all, he's paying.

Chapter Sixteen

Nora

I struggled to make sense when they found me. A passer-by had pulled his car over to the side of the road and had come to guide me away from the traffic. This is what I'm told. It's a blur to me. It's noise and shapes and an overwhelming sense of dread.

I'm told I said my little girl was gone, but I couldn't elaborate further. The driver, a nurse on her way to work at the nearby Altnagelvin Hospital, called the police and an ambulance. I'm told I was taken to A&E with signs of extreme emotional distress. I remember none of this. I don't remember talking to the police. I don't remember that I was sedated for my own safety. These are things I learned later when people started to drip-feed me information about what happened that day.

It's four in the morning, almost daylight, but everyone is asleep apart from me. I've barely closed my eyes. Brendan decided he was going to sleep in with Luca and not in our bed with me. His anger from earlier has not abated. I don't suppose I blame him. Luca is his everything. Luca is here and real and tangible. To him, Daisy is an idea of a person, not a real living, breathing, beautiful, bewildering little girl.

I've been scouring the internet on my laptop for hours now, watching footage of myself from news reports on Daisy's disappearance. I wonder what Izzy's profilers and experts will make of it. What they will make of me.

I know it's me in the footage, of course. I recognise myself in the film of a police press conference. Wide-eyed, pale. Gaunt. Wrapping my arms around myself as I sit behind a table and cameras flash, people shout questions. I barely blink. Barely register what is happening around me. I'm told I was out of it on tranquillisers at that stage, but you'd think I'd remember something. I stare at the person I know is me and I don't know whether I want to shake her, to shout at her to wake up, or to hug her. She looks so alone. She was so alone.

That much I can remember, feeling there was no one to turn to.

Yes, of course we had some neighbours who were lovely and brought food, patted my hand, said they'd offer prayers, but there was no friend I could cling to while I sobbed into the night. Conal had already upped sticks and moved to Australia – not that I think that would've made much of a difference anyway. He and I were never more than a fling. An unusual act of rebellion on my part. He's not a bad man, even if he turned out to be a pretty shit father who paid little attention to his child. Then he realised he could make some money by playing the part of the grieving daddy to the media when she disappeared.

So instead I'd relied heavily on Constable Heather Williams, my family liaison officer, but I'd never have said we were friends as such. She was professional enough to maintain the distance she was supposed to. In fact, it was only when I got chatting with Brendan two years later online that I finally felt as if I had a true friend. We'd met through a befriending site – one aimed at helping adults find friends in this increasingly digital world. For me, it was a safe place to reach out to someone without immediately having to put all my history out there on the line for them to know from the very start. It seems my history makes people uncomfortable. But it was different with Brendan. With no expectation of romance – it was the furthest thing from my mind – we started to chat, laugh and check in on each other. Before too long I wanted to open up to him and he gave me the space to do that. He didn't judge. He looked after me and I had so needed someone who was willing to just look after me at that stage. It wasn't long before I considered him a true friend, and even less time from that moment on until we shared our first kiss. From then on, it was love. He became my friend and my protector.

So the tension between us now unsettles me, more than I can admit to myself. Shivering, I pull the throw from the sofa up around myself as I click through more links to old footage, stumbling across a clip from an old documentary in which the presenter talks to camera while walking through the woods. I shudder, panic clawing me as I watch the presenter walk in through the old gate and down the path that leads to the darkest corners of the woods, where it is overgrown, and pathways lead off in all directions.

The presenter on my laptop screen walks, stony-faced through the woods, filmed to make them look as dark and threatening as possible. Even though I know there is no chance of it, I can't help but scan the footage anyway in case there is a trace of Daisy. A scrap of material on a branch. A shoe. A fallen hair ribbon. Anything. Even though this documentary was made more than a year after she went missing, I still cling onto hope.

At some stage I fall asleep, drifting into a dream where I am in the woods myself, wandering up and down the overgrown pathways, which never seem to go anywhere. I hear a voice calling. Shouting 'Mammy' and it's her. My God, it's her and I run towards her voice. Sweet and happy. 'You can't catch me!' she sing-songs and I call out to her to wait where she is, that I'm coming to get her. I hear laughter, footsteps crunching the leaves. Repeated calls of 'You can't catch me,' and I'm running still but always ending up back at the entrance of the woods, alone.

I turn and run back in, calling to her. My voice cracking now. It's not a game. I've realised this is a dream and that it isn't real, but even in my sleep I am wishing that I'm wrong. I keep calling until I see shadows cross behind the branches, hear more footsteps. But there is more than one person. There are two, maybe three children running and laughing. I try to distinguish their voices. I call at them to be quiet until I find Daisy but they don't stop their laughing or their running.

The air around us suddenly feels thick with malice, and threat hangs heavy around me. The refrain of 'You can't catch me' plays over and over again but in a distorted voice. Desperation claws at me. Please don't be a dream. Please be real. Please stop running! Please just be here. Just stop and come back to me. I stop running, my breathing now laboured, but there is someone or something now behind me. Tall, dark, ominous. A muffled low voice booms and I run, stumbling, willing myself to wake up. A child's voice, clear, loud, icy. 'Why didn't you catch me?' sounds out as I stumble on a broken branch and fall into darkness.

A loud crash pulls me from my sleep, my eyes flying open just after my laptop hits the floor. My breathing is hard, laboured, as if I have actually been running in the woods and not simply sleeping on my own sofa. Echoes of the childlike voices seem to hang in the air. The laughter and the screams and the accusation. I try to tease apart the details of my dream, wondering if there is something there that I have missed – that could be of use to DI Bradley, or even to Izzy and Tom and their band of amateur sleuths.

As consciousness further returns I realise how stupid that is. No one can be expected to rely on a dream as evidence and what did it show me anyway? That I'm scared of being chased? That I'm scared at how this hunt for Daisy will impact on Luca and my family. I'm pretty sure his was one of the voices I could hear mingled with Daisy's. I imagine them, my two babies side by side. They are so unalike in so many ways but they are both a part of me. Of course, the Daisy I imagine by his side is not the Daisy who exists now – if indeed she does still exist. Maybe the worst of my fears are correct and she was cast out in the river to sea.

My mouth dry, I go to the kitchen and pour myself a glass of cold water, my hand still shaking as I bring the glass to my mouth. There's something about the dream that is nipping at me, something I can't put my finger on. Just like my memory of that horrific day, it exists just out of reach.

A fat tear of frustration rolls down my cheek. This is all such a mess. Every part of it. Glancing at the clock I see it's already six. Even though tiredness is pulling at me, or maybe it's just the need to escape into some form of unconsciousness again, I know there is no point in trying to sleep anymore. I don't want to risk drifting back into that nightmare. And anyway, Luca will no doubt be awake again soon and he won't understand if I slip past him and into bed. I contemplate a shower, but I don't want to make any unnecessary noise that might wake either Luca or Brendan before they have to get up.

Clearly a masochist, I carry my laptop back into the study and opt to have another look through amateursleuths.com. Sometimes the only way to push away pain is to find a new, sharper pain to replace it with.

I go straight to the Daisy Logue subforum. Top of the list is a fresh post from today, titled 'Nora Logue: Mother of the Year?' My heart sinks.

Chapter Seventeen

Nora

There's a photograph on my computer screen, but it's not of the wee girl in Galway. Nor is it of me. Or Daisy for that matter.

No, this is an up close and personal shot of Luca. My head spins and I grab the desk as if that will ground me. The sound of my own blood rushing through my veins drowns everything else out but the thudding of my heart. Luca. Yesterday. In his *Paw Patrol* swimsuit on the beach. His dark curls escaping out from under his sunhat. He is hunkered down in that gravity-defying way only toddlers seem to be able to manage, his expression serious, his yellow bucket by his side, toy digger in his hand.

From the angle of the picture it looks as if he is entirely alone. I know, absolutely and utterly without doubt, that Brendan or I would have been at most three or four feet from him when that picture was taken. Most of the time we were closer. Most of the time he was sat on the edge of the picnic blanket we'd brought with us.

In this picture he looks lost. There's a sadness in his eyes that I don't recognise and maybe it's just that the picture is lying, or maybe I've been too blind to see it. Or maybe I'm reading too much into a snapshot because my own sadness is so huge it can't help but frame everything else I see. But it feels like more than the soulfulness that existed in the eyes of his sister.

Scanning the words below the picture my head swims more.

'Is it not enough this woman "lost" one child? Here is she letting another wander! This is Luca Pryce, aka Luca Logue. This week. On the beach at Ludden, in County Donegal. See how he's on his own? Where is his mother? Is she too busy off cashing in on the disappearance of her beloved Daisy, making this new documentary? What age is this child? Two or three and yet here he is, on his own. Anything could have happened to him. Or maybe that's what she's hoping for.'

There is only one reply but it's not any comfort to me.

'What age is that child? Four maybe? The same age Daisy was when she went missing. And him on his own? That woman doesn't deserve to be a mother. That child should be taken away from her before she "forgets" what happens to him too.'

Each word is like a punch in the stomach. These posters don't know me. They don't know what I've been through – what I'm still going through. They don't know that Luca is never left alone. Ever. Okay, so it might not be me who is with him at all times, but what mother is with her child twenty-four hours out of every day?

But I wouldn't and don't endanger him.

I don't know who took this picture or why. Is it the same person who left us that message on the windscreen of the car? Or multiple people watching and judging and actively trying to attack me? Anger surges within me. The kind of anger that comes from not having had enough sleep – not just last night but every night for the last seven years.

I remember the account I registered yesterday, still untouched, and I'm tempted to use it. To explain to these people, and to the entire internet if they want to read it, that he was with me. And his daddy.

And it must just be the angle of the photo that makes it look as though he is alone because we would never, ever leave him on his own or let him wander out of our sightline. And that he has every chance a mother could give her child. I yearn to say all this but I know it's better that I ignore it. Just take it on the chin. Do not engage with trolls – that's what Brendan would say.

But I can't help but wonder if I'm the troll in all this. Am I the evil lurking in the shadows and I just don't remember it? Glancing at the image of Luca again, I blink back tears. Brendan's question – asking why I don't put him first – comes back to my mind. It's not his fault he's not Daisy. I wish I could love him as deeply and unconditionally as I love her. But I can't.

The tears flow freely as I read the hateful words again, getting some perverse pay-off from them. The sting of them is a special kind of self-flagellation – the least that I deserve. I must remind myself that whether or not I remember what happened, she *was* in my care. That's inescapable.

'Mummy, why are you crying?' A small hand rests on my knee, making me jump. I turn in the direction of the voice and there he is, Luca, eyes wide, startled not only by my jump but by my tears, his face too close to mine in that way small children with no sense of personal space seem to be able to master. Perhaps he thinks that if he looks close enough into my eyes, he might be able to see what's wrong.

I swallow the sobs that I've become so good at hiding over the past seven years and plaster on a bright, false smile. 'Oh my goodness, Luca! You've managed to startle me again! I'm okay. I'm not crying. I was a little sad,' I tell him as he clambers onto my knee and pats my hand like someone much older and wiser than his years. 'But I'm okay, now you're here. Where's Daddy?

Is he still sleeping?' I say, kissing the top of his head, guilt at not loving him just as much biting at me.

Luca shakes his head. 'My whole body is awake,' he says. 'And Daddy is getting up and he's going to make pancakes and 'tella for me.'

'Nutella, again?' I reply, testing my voice to hear if it sounds normal. 'That's a big breakfast treat.'

He nods solemnly, his curls bouncing as he does so. Something, a moment of sunlight and curls and warmth, comes to mind but it leaves as quickly as it arrived. ''Cos I'm a good boy,' he says proudly. 'Can I watch YouTube?' he asks, turning towards the computer where his image is displayed.

I don't want him to see it. I don't want it to be any part of his day. That picture. Those words – God knows I don't want Brendan to see those words. Today is not the day where I will give in to his request to have a go on my computer. I slam the laptop shut, just as he reaches out to tap at the keyboard, and after a moment of stunned silence he emits a siren-like wail and I feel a dart of dismay. I didn't mean to hurt him. It was an accident. I didn't know he would reach out or that the laptop would slam closed onto his fingers. I didn't realise how much force I'd used, not until now as Luca withdraws a red hand, a darkening purple line already indented into his skin.

'Oh, Luca!' I say, as I stare at him and catch the look of horror on his face – one that is no doubt mirrored on my own face. I just hurt him. His mother just hurt him. He looks at me as if he doesn't know me, while the pitch of his crying gets louder, and I try to look at his hand, to examine it and make sure nothing is broken, but he is doing his best to pull it away from me. 'No, Mummy! No!' he yells.

'Sweetheart, please let Mummy kiss it better.'

'No, Mummy! Want Daddy!'

And of course Daddy appears, his still-sleepy face a perfect picture of confusion. 'What on earth . . .' he begins.

'It was an accident,' I stutter. 'I reached out to close the laptop and didn't realise he'd reached out to try and find bloody YouTube at the same time and I didn't know—'

'Mummy hurted my fingers,' Luca wails, wasting no time in jumping from my knee and running into Brendan's arms. Of course he lets his daddy examine his injured hand. Of course he lets him soothe him. And of course the pair of them look at me, with matching accusatory expressions. Luca is so like his father and nothing like me. Nothing like Daisy. In that moment, I feel more detached from them both than ever.

'I was checking our online banking. Getting a head start on the budget for this month—'

'Nuh-uh,' Luca hiccups, his sobs starting to subside now. 'You were being sad and crying and I seed my picture on the TV.'

'The TV?' Brendan asks and Luca points to my laptop.

'The 'puter TV. I seed a picture of me at the beach.'

'What?' Brendan asks, but his question is clearly directed at me now and not at Luca, who is still nursing his hand as if he's afraid I might launch a second attack. 'I didn't think you took any pictures yesterday? You left your phone in the car?' he says.

'Look, he's mistaken. It was another child. On a friend's Facebook. Luca *saw* that picture,' I say, placing the emphasis on *saw* to try and correct our son's grammar. 'Seed isn't a word,' I say softly at Luca, who stares at me in defiance.

'Yes it is. I knowed it is. A baby flower is a seed.'

Brendan is at least momentarily distracted from questioning me to beam with pride at our almost three-year-old and his lovely take on the world.

'Are those pancakes ready yet?' I ask, and am delighted that the further distraction works. His tears now dry, Luca's eyes light up at the thought of pancakes and 'tella.

Brendan looks at me for a moment and I know what he's thinking. No matter how many times he tells me he loves me and he knows my heart as well as his own, there will always, always be a part of him that subconsciously doesn't trust me. I can't judge him for it. I feel the same way about myself, if the truth is told. But then he blinks and smiles at Luca. 'You can even help me chop the strawberries!' he says.

'And bananas?' Luca asks.

'Well of course,' Brendan replies. 'You can't have your favourite pancakes without bananas.' He swoops our son up into the air, holding him by tummy and legs as if he's flying, and the pair leave the room with Luca pointing his non-injured hand forwards and pretending to be Superman.

I know that when they have eaten, and when Luca has been dressed, Brendan will make his way back to this room and he will ask to see what I had been looking at. He'll be jokey about it. Playful even. 'Here, show me this picture of Luca's evil twin at the beach.' He'll laugh. But we both know it's not a laughing matter. Brendan will want to know what exactly made me slam my laptop lid with such force that our child's hand has been left bruised.

I don't want him to see this page. I don't want him to see what these people have written. Those vile things. That I do not deserve our son and I do not look after him.

I decide I'll simply click out of the page and delete the browser history from this morning. Simple. It won't be hard to find a picture of a child at the beach on a friend's Facebook page.

But I can't resist reading the comments one last time, and I see that a new one has been posted.

Chapter Eighteen

Izzy

'Sorry for calling so early,' Jacqueline says as soon as I answer the phone. My brain is still thick with sleep and it takes me a moment to work out who I'm talking to.

'Jacqs?' I say, briefly pulling my phone from my ear to check the time. It's not long gone seven in the morning.

'Well, who else would it be calling you from my number?' she says, her voice light.

'Is everything okay?' I ask, pulling myself up to sitting and sipping from the now tepid glass of water on my nightstand. I'd been so sensible and brought a pint of water to bed with me after drinking a little too much at dinner last night – it's just a shame I didn't get round to actually drinking it. My head throbs. I look to the floor to see if that's where I left my bag, in which I know there are paracetamol.

'I'll assume by the fact you sound like one of the undead, that you've not been awake and online already this morning?'

'Erm, no. I might have overindulged last night,' I croak, grimacing and taking another drink of the water to tackle the arid conditions in my mouth. Did I smoke last night? It feels like I might've smoked. I could kill Tom.

'Well, I've been on the forum and there's a new user in town. And a new post you'll definitely want to check out – like, now.' I've already reached for my laptop and switched it on, and I tell Jacqs to give me a minute for my ageing MacBook to power up.

'When you're logged in, go straight to "new posts". What I'm talking about will jump out at you from the first page, I promise.'

I do exactly as she says, and there is one post that does jump out at me. There it is, a thread entitled 'Nora Logue: Mother of the Year?' Is this what Jacqs is talking about? I can see from the thread title there is an icon indicating a photo has been attached.

Clicking the link, an image of a young child, seemingly alone on a beach, appears before my eyes. Blinking, I reach for my glasses on the bedside table to be able to see it more clearly. It's only when I read the accompanying post that I'm able to make full sense of what I'm seeing.

Some absolute ghoul has posted a picture of what they claim is Luca Pryce, alone on a beach. I assume this would've been taken on their family day out – the one Nora told me about that ended with the dirty nappy on their windscreen.

'Jesus,' I mutter under my breath, taking in the image of the curly-haired tot crouched down, his face set in concentration, but indeed looking as if he is very much alone. I scan the caption, wincing at the anger in the words.

'That *is* Luca, isn't it?' Jacqs asks. 'The poster doesn't have it wrong?'

She does well to ask. There are very few pictures of Luca in the public domain. There was an article shortly after he was born, where they were all pictured together – under a headline about their new baby joy helping to ease the heartache of not knowing what became of Daisy.

There isn't much joy on Nora's face in that picture, but

Brendan is luminous with new-father pride. I found it oddly unsettling. Very few of the quotes in the piece were accredited to Nora, most coming from Brendan who said the birth of Luca would hopefully help his wife heal. 'It's only now,' he is quoted as saying, 'that I truly understand the depth of Nora's loss. I can't imagine what it would be like to lose a child. I don't think I'd be able to go on if anything were to happen to Luca. Already he has my heart.'

There have been no further family interviews since then, and any pictures of Luca that have emerged seemed to have originated from Brendan Pryce's social media. They never stay up long. I wonder how hard he finds it – this need to mute his paternal pride to save Nora's feelings or protect Luca from prying eyes.

'I'm pretty sure it's him,' I reply, reading the caption again and feeling the sense of unease that is becoming more and more familiar to me rise up again.

'Pretty sure? Have you not met him?' Jacqs asks in her lilting Donegal accent.

'Erm, no. I haven't. But I only met Nora herself two days ago. It's early days, you know.' I look at the picture again and wonder if the camera really does lie. I can't imagine the Nora I've come to know to be someone who would allow that boy outside of an arm's reach at the very most.

'That's another new user too, isn't it?' Jacqs asks, and I hear clicking in the background. 'Yep, registered their account yesterday. No biography. No avatar. Do you think that username means anything or is it one of those random ones the system throws up?'

I look at it, and something about it seems a little familiar. I read it again, out loud this time. DL180715. Is it a car registration? No, I think there would be more letters. And it doesn't actually read like an auto-generated name.

I read it out loud again. 'There's something about this . . .' I say to Jacqs.

'Shit,' she gasps. 'I think I've got it. If DL is Daisy Logue, then . . . yes . . . 180715. The eighteenth of the seventh . . . July . . . and then 15 is 2015, the year she disappeared.'

God, but people are bastards, I think. I know they think that they aren't. They think they are fighting the good fight, but they have no understanding or compassion for all the grey areas that lie between their opinions and the truth. They invest so heavily in what they believe that they can't even contemplate that they might be wrong. All that self-righteous anger transforms into hate. Does anyone keep an open mind anymore?

'Jesus,' I sigh. 'This is clearly someone on a mission. The number of posts we've seen in the last twenty-four hours alone, Jacqs. I'm struggling to keep up with them. And that's not even mentioning my DMs, which are a shitshow.'

'And you think the picture is legit?' she asks.

'If you're asking do I think it's a picture of Luca and the beach, then yes. If you're asking if I think Nora and Brendan let him out of their reach for even a moment then, honestly, I don't. Unless the woman is a complete sociopath, that is not the vibe I get from her at all.'

'I'm going to bring this to the attention of the mods,' Jacqs says. 'I think maybe we should get it taken down. Or locked at least. If that really is Luca, I don't like having his picture doing the rounds. Or the thought that anyone might be actively following them and taking surreptitious pictures.'

My initial reaction is to agree with Jacqs, but almost as soon as I think that another idea arrives in my head.

'I think I might send this DL person a private message,' I say. 'See if they want to talk? Clearly they know about the documentary and they want to get my attention – so maybe I should give it to them?'

116

There's a pause before Jacqs speaks again. 'Do you think that would really be a good idea?' she asks.

'I think it would make a good angle for the documentary,' I tell her. Now that the thought is in my head, I think it's going to be a hard one to shake off. I like the idea of talking to these people – asking them what drives them to behave the way they do. Why do they feel so passionately about this case over others? What level of obsession pushes them forward? That's what people want to know – the inner workings of people's minds.

'Maybe get in touch with the police?' Jacqs says, cutting through my thoughts. 'There are a lot of crazies out there, Izzy. We know that more than most. If they're following her, that's not to say they won't follow you. You don't know who you're dealing with here and you don't want to put yourself in harm's way, do you?'

As she talks I read down the replies, limited as they still are. The third is from that account that slid into my DMs yesterday: 'The Four'.

'Hang on a minute,' I say, cutting Jacqs off. 'Just . . . let . . . me . . .'

I read the message.

'We fully intend to make sure no harm comes to Luca Pryce at the hands of the woman who refers to herself as his mother. No child deserves a "mother" like Daisy Logue. She is reckless and cruel. We have seen it first hand and leopards are not known to change their spots. Some people cannot be fixed. We are watching and we are going to make sure that child is safe, and away from that monster.'

My blood runs cold. The same threatening tone from yesterday, but this is more blatant somehow. This is stating that 'they', whoever the fuck they are, are going to take action.

'Jacqs,' I say, 'have you read that last post on the thread?'

'The one from The Four? Just reading it now.'

'Yes,' I say.

'Fuck,' she exclaims. 'Look, Izzy. I can't tell you what to do, but this needs to go to the police and now. Those are the people you were asking me about yesterday, aren't they? The Four? That sounds like a threat to me. Look, I'm going to get this particular thread shut down. You should contact that Bradley guy. Or I will. Either way I don't think I'd forgive myself if I'd sat on my laurels and said nothing or did nothing. I know we've experience digging into crimes and all, but this is hardcore. This is on our doorstep. You're working with this woman right now. And this wee boy might be in real danger. You know people don't think twice about taking justice into their own hands, especially when there's a child involved.'

I know she's right, of course, but informing the police, who will inform Nora, could throw up some problems. If Brendan is already spooked, I can't see this helping matters and this might just be enough to spook Nora too. Now that we have her on board, I don't want to lose her. Yes, we have some footage but it's nowhere near what I was hoping for.

No. I shake myself. I must think positively. I must try and find a way to make this work. I realise, of course, that there is nothing stopping me from sending 'The Four' a private message as well. If they want to warn me off, if they want to protect Luca, then they might just want to tell their side of the story.

'I'll talk to the police,' I tell Jacqs. 'The senior officer was on a day shift yesterday, so chances are he will be today as well. I promise I'll get in touch with him as soon as I can. And Nora too, of course.'

'I think that's wise,' Jacqs says. 'You don't want any of this to come back and bite you on the arse. Protect yourself, Izzy. As well as Nora and that wee boy.'

'I will,' I say, and we end the call with the promise that I will call and speak to DI Bradley as soon as he's on shift. I don't tell her that while I'll keep that promise, I will also be contacting both DL180715 and The Four and asking to speak to them. My heart may well be thumping harder than usual in my chest, and the fear that I'm feeling may well be more than just the after-effects of a heavy night on the drink – but if I'm to look at this story from every angle I need to push past my feelings and ask the difficult questions. The best approach, I decide, is to just do it. So I start typing. This is my documentary, and I will tell this story.

Chapter Nineteen

Nora

A long, slow breath leaves my body as I hear the front door close behind Brendan and Luca, and I listen to the hum of the car engine as they drive away. It's only then I allow myself to read the post again, to see 'The Four' say those things – those horrific things – about me. Are they right? Am I a monster? Do they know something I don't? I don't know anymore. I don't know who or what to trust.

But my God, if Brendan sees this post, this picture – if he reads these threats, he will lose it. He will insist that I pull out of the documentary. Or maybe he will lose what little patience he has with me. He'll be furious that my stepping back into the spotlight is putting Luca's safety in danger. He'll try and be understanding of course. He's not a bad man. In fact, he's a good man, and a great husband and father. Fiercely protective of both Luca and me. But I have no doubt that if it came to choosing between supporting my need to find my daughter, and his need to protect his son, I would ultimately lose. Part of me admires him for that, and another part of me hates him for it.

Shortly after Luca was born, and with as much compassion as he could muster, Brendan told me that I need to stop chasing a ghost. I'd looked at him, my eyes wide, my temper fraying. I didn't care how much concern was on his face as he spoke, or how much love he felt for me and our baby son. I didn't understand how he could say such a thing and not realise how deeply it would wound me. Immediately, I saw the regret in his eyes and he apologised. He told me he didn't mean to use the word 'ghost'. That he wasn't trying to dismiss my grief or imply that Daisy was definitely dead. He just wanted me to be able to live again. He'd been patient – so tender with me. So understanding. But now, with a new baby, he hoped I could find new joy and comfort in the child in front of me instead of focusing all my attention and all my love on the child who was gone. He'd gently told me, as if I needed telling, that Daisy was gone and wasn't likely to ever come back, but Luca was right here in front of me and he was perfect.

I understand what he meant of course, and his desire for us to be a normal family, whatever that means. But there is nothing on this earth that could stop me looking for answers about Daisy. And I realise now, reading this post again, that is still true, despite the cost to my sanity, to my marriage, and now to my son.

I have to speak to DI Bradley again, and soon. I need to find out who these people are flooding the forum, who took the picture and who 'The Four' are or is. I need Bradley and his team to track them down and let them know in no uncertain terms it is not okay to threaten to take my child or to assert that I'm a bad mother.

My entire body is tense with the strain of it. And anger floods me, right there in my bedroom. A furious, fierce and deep anger that someone or something, man or beast or some god-like entity not only took my child from me but also my memory, my contentment, my sanity. And now someone is coming for whatever I have left, or have managed to claw together of my life without her. I have always known the world is not a fair place but today it feels like all it has left is cruelty.

I know the advice is not to engage with trolls. I know, deep down, that the best thing to do would be to let DI Bradley handle it. And I will, but I have to say something. With fury flowing through my veins, I storm back downstairs to the study and fire up the computer again, logging into AmateurSleuths. I find the account I set up just two days ago and change my username. I will not hide my anger from these people. They want Nora Logue? Well, that's who I'm going to give them.

Maybe it's time they realised I'm not going to sit back and listen to shitty conspiracy theories anymore. If you want to claim I'm a monster, then you better be ready to prove it.

Taking a deep breath, I start to type.

'I'm the terrible mother you're talking about. I'm Nora Logue. The woman you think of as unfit. The woman you think would wilfully hurt her own child or children. This picture is bullshit. Yes, that is my son. And I was just feet away, just out of shot. If it was you who took the picture, you'll know that. You'll know I was watching him like a hawk. I always do, because God forbid I didn't. People like you would never let me get away with it.

'I was there. My husband was there. We were trying to create a normal, happy memory for him. But that's not enough for you, is it? You have to lie and threaten and try to scare me. Take a long, hard look at yourself before you cast aspersions on my character. I'm not the stranger with a camera taking pictures of other people's children on a beach and sharing them to the internet. How close were you to my boy to get that shot?

'You know nothing about me. You've not lived my

122

life or experienced my pain. I wouldn't wish it on my worst enemy.

'But I promise you this much: if you come near my child again, if you threaten my family again I will wish it and more on you. I won't rest until I know who you are, and I will show everyone what kind of sick-minded bastard you are to stalk innocent children and grieving parents.

'I've stayed quiet for so long but I'm not doing that anymore. My life – my daughter's life – is not a game. We're not players on a Cluedo board. We're not puzzles to be solved. We're real people and the pain is real. So stop it, now, unless you want a taste of that pain yourself.'

Chapter Twenty

Izzy

I have reached out to both DL180715 and The Four with identical messages. I spent twenty minutes drafting what I would say, asking too many questions, making too many assertions before I opted instead for a simple 'I would be keen to discuss your latest posts with you. You can call me on . . .' inserting only my mobile number before hitting send. Maybe it was a stupid move to send my mobile number to people I know nothing about except that they like to post vitriol online.

Maybe I should've nipped out and bought a quick Pay-As-You-Go phone that could be used as a burner, but it's too early for the shops to be open and I have a feeling this forum is about to attract a lot of attention. And, of course, if Jacqs gets the relevant thread shut down or deleted, I risk losing contact with them altogether.

They could disappear as quickly as IrishEyes did. (Jesus was it really not even forty-eight hours since the picture of the supposed Daisy landed on the forum? And still, I've heard nothing from Paddy McGilloway in his muddy field in Galway.)

But now I have sent the messages and my need for caffeine

to tackle the hangover I more than deserve has grown to critical levels, I get out of bed, pull on a hoodie over my vest top and shorts and walk through to the kitchen, stopping on the way to knock on Tom's door. He will want to see what has been going down this morning, and my money is on him being impressed at my reaching out to the suspect accounts.

If I'm expecting to see my hangover reflected in his eyes, I'm disappointed. He looks vaguely human. Actually, he looks remarkably good for a man last seen ordering a third bottle of wine. Then again, he did most of the pouring and I suspect I might've done most of the drinking.

'You need to see this now,' I say. 'The forum. It has all kicked off.'

'I've just looked,' he said. 'Do you think that's really Nora posting? It's all a bit Liam Neeson in *Taken* isn't it?' He gives me a crooked smile and while at another time I might have laughed or agreed, despite the poor taste of joking about an actual missing child, I feel a spark of irritation.

'If it really is Nora, then we need to get to her. It means she's been reading the forum, Tom, and she has seen all the hate and all the threats about Luca. She'll be spinning out. Brendan will be spinning out.'

Tom nods and lifts his phone. 'I'm sending her a text now to tell her to be ready in thirty. You'll pick her up, and Brendan and Luca if necessary.'

'Thirty minutes? I'm still in my pyjamas,' I say, the thought of coming face to face with Brendan making me nervous.

'Then you better get yourself dressed, or head out in whatever combination of bag-lady clothes those are.' He nods towards my uncoordinated loungewear look. I can tell he is fizzing with excitement. 'If word of this post gets out – and it will get out, considering the picture – I imagine every journalist worth their salt will be on to it. Not to mention that it will attract the attention of the police and God knows who else. Every gossip-monger in the vicinity,' Tom says.

'Gossipmonger?' I raise an eyebrow. In amongst all the drama, his choice of words amuses me. It feels very old-worldy for him. I feel something bubble up inside of me. And I think I'm almost ashamed to realise that it's excitement. My worry about whether or not to tell Nora about the post is gone and replaced again with a sense that this has all just got really, really juicy.

We've got Nora Logue on our side, at a time when she has vowed she won't be listening to any more lies or threats. The meek, shaking woman who was locked in her own pain has just come out fighting – and we have ringside seats.

Tom shoos me to get ready and I don't need telling a third time. As I dress I can hear him on the phone to her, telling her he understands why she has posted it and telling her not to talk to anyone else if they phone her about it.

'Izzy will be with you shortly,' I hear him say. 'She'll bring you here and we can come up with a plan. Look, we're here to help you. If you need to bring Luca, or if Brendan wants to come too, that's fine. We understand that neither are to be filmed.'

He sounds sincere. I think he is sincere, although with Tom there's always the chance he'll stretch the boundaries a little. It's also clear he is as excited as I am. I switch out my pyjama bottoms for jeans and slip my feet into my Converse mules. I don't stop to put on any make-up. I don't even brush my hair, simply running my fingers through my short crop, not even worried if it is still sticking out in one hundred different directions. I haven't had my morning coffee and I don't care. There's a natural energy battling this hangover now, a buzz that is fizzing through my veins. I'm struggling to hold in the sense that this has just gone next-level. I have to keep my cool, I remind myself. I must be professional. I must make sure that Nora still trusts me. I can't arrive hyped up.

Tom is still talking to Nora as I leave, giving him a thumbs up. I should be with Nora in about twenty minutes according to the sat nav on my hire car. Surely no one will have been able to get to her before then?

Chapter Twenty-One

Nora

My heart is racing, blood pumping through my veins. My lips are tingling, my face flushed. My hands, when I look down at them, are trembling.

I can't quite believe that I posted that message. I know I've started something that I can't stop. It's already too late to stop it being seen by countless people. It will have been screen-shotted into the record books by now. Izzy and Tom have already seen it. I wonder how many other people have. Is it already whizzing its way around countless WhatsApp groups or Twitter feeds? I'm too scared to log into Twitter and search my name. I slam my laptop closed – tempted to throw it in the bin even though that's hardly going to undo the damage I have just done to myself.

I need a coffee. Or a drink. Or something. I don't know what I need.

Tom has phoned me. He has done his best to soothe me and told me Izzy will bring me to their Airbnb where I can at least have peace to think about things. He said I can bring Luca and Brendan if I want. Christ, I can't even think about Brendan right now. This will be the final straw for him.

I want to go back to bed and hide under the covers but Tom

is right – I can't stay here. It's only a matter of time before the phone starts ringing, or journalists show up at the door. From what little I remember of the aftermath of Daisy's disappearance, they can be incredibly persistent. I have, in a box in the study, scores of business cards and scrawled-on jotter pages that were pushed through my letterbox in the weeks and months after Daisy disappeared. The hall carpet was blanketed with them at one stage. Fresh cards arrived every day until slowly they petered out, then stopped altogether.

Each hand-scrawled note was asking me to call the journalist in question. Each offered assurances that they weren't like the journalists portrayed on TV or in films. That they could be trusted. Journalists from a hundred different organisations. Different countries. All falling over themselves for an exclusive.

They must've thought I was stupid. That I really believed they cared. I know it's not their place to care. Their role is to get the woman losing her mind to do so publicly. To grab headlines that feasted on my pain, and my possible guilt. To get people asking questions about me. I became a villain the day my daughter was taken.

I kept their cards and their notes though, stuffed them in a box along with newspaper clippings covering Daisy's disappearance. I have more boxes. Letters and cards that came by the sackload. All were opened by the police just in case they contained something that could help, or something they thought I should be protected from. There are some sick bastards in this world. Most of them were passed on to me. Words of sympathy and solace. Offers of prayers and blessings. Some people sent money, as if I could buy my memory, and my daughter, back.

I was so lost at the time that I decided to keep them all. If I'm honest I've always hoped that one day looking through them might just unlock the broken part of my brain that can't unlock itself. Nothing has.

Maybe the users of that forum are right. Maybe I don't deserve to be a mother. Whatever secrets are locked inside me, maybe they are proof that I am not a good person. Maybe I could've done more. For the last seven years I have sat and waited. I've made measured statements through the police. I've behaved myself in the hope that people would believe the truth – that I don't remember what happened. I have behaved in the hope that the attention would stay where it needed to – on Daisy and not on me. But it hasn't, has it? And it never will.

People are more interested in finding guilt in me than they are in finding Daisy herself.

A fresh wave of anger and grief rises in me and my heart feels as though it might explode with the force of it. I feel as if I am on the precipice of exploding.

My stomach tightens and I know I can't hold in this ball of fury any longer. With a roar that feels as if it has been seven years in the making, which comes from the tips of my toes and fills my entire body, I start to pull apart the study. Pulling out the boxes that are filled with these mementos of loss and grief. If Izzy wants to see what pain looks like, I'll show her. If people in these online communities want to see grief up close and personal, I'll show them. I'll show them these papers that I have searched through hundreds of times while Brendan has slept upstairs. I'll show them the clothes that belonged to my beau-tiful daughter, which I have packed in boxes and refused to get rid of even if people have told me it would be a kindness to myself to let them go. They didn't understand how I could no more get rid of them than I could cut my own arm off. I'm so angry. So angry with them for even asking me.

Everything. Every little thing from that day has been taken out of my control. Even my own damn mind has betrayed me. I pull box after box from the cupboards at the back of the room, swearing and crying as I do. I run up the stairs and pull down the loft ladder before climbing up into the dark. By the light of a single, naked bulb, I go to the corner of the attic where I know I will find Daisy's belongings. Things that should be in a room. Her room. Still laid out, waiting for her to come back. They shouldn't have been touched. I shouldn't have let them be touched. I shouldn't have let Brendan persuade me it was time to move house – to move on and start again for the sake of the baby that was then growing inside of me.

There is so much that I should not have done but I failed myself, and other people. I failed her. A resolve washes over me that I'm not going to continue to do so.

I lift the boxes from the darkest recesses of the attic; boxes that are filled with vacuum-packed bags of her clothes and soft toys, and I tear them open, before breaking the airlock seal on the bags. Please, I pray, can these clothes still smell of my child? Just a little? Just a trace? Can I feel as if I am lost in hugging her once again? Holding a small pink pyjama top to my face, I breathe in, chasing memories of a long-forgotten fabric softener mixed with the scent of lavender shampoo. I'd stopped using both after she disappeared. I couldn't bear to catch a trace of her in the air, only for her not to be there.

But there's nothing there anymore. No smell. No warmth of her body. No trace at all of the wee girl who was there. Who existed and lived. Who laughed with her head thrown back and her eyes wide. Who liked to sing. Who would tenderly stroke the downy hairs on my arms as she soothed herself to sleep. The girl who made me a mammy. My girl. The pain of her loss is now screaming through me with the force of the blood pumping through my veins and the pain growing in my heart.

I want to break something. I want to run through the streets and scream like the madwoman they think I am. I pull through every box, spilling the contents on the floor. Grabbing everything to me. Trying to feel something. To remember something. To conjure her back.

The doorbell rings but I ignore it. Could it be a reporter already? If it is, they can go to hell. It rings again, more persistent this time. The loud ring continuing. All I can do is cover my ears to block it out, but still I'm deafened by the sound of my own blood pulsing through me.

I push against my head harder, trying to make it stop. The pressure grows as my hands squeeze tighter still. Closing my eyes, I swear I hear a voice. Small and sweet. I swear I feel breath on my cheek and a brush of something soft against my arm. It takes everything else away. For a moment I know she is with me. As I rock back and forth, the words and that wee voice come into focus. It's an echo. I know it is. Of another time.

'No! Don't. I'm frightened.'

My eyes flash open and I expect to see her. I expect her to be right there in front of me. I expect to be in the woods on the day she went, and I expect to see whatever it was that took her from me. I feel as close to it as I ever have. As close to remembering.

When I realise that all there is around me are the boxes with their contents now scattered on the ground, and when I realise I'm in a house she never set foot in, pain slams into me again, and that damn fucking doorbell is still ringing. My hand starts to throb and I look down to see blood dripping from a gash on my palm. A gash I've no memory of happening, but I can guess it's from tearing at the boxes. The blood is real and it's warm and wet, and I see it drip, drip, drip onto a pale blue dress that is on the floor in front of me. I watch as it leaches through the material, reaching through the cotton fibres, and I hear that voice somewhere in an echo or a nightmare or a memory.

I try to grasp onto it, to pull it back into focus, but the real world is crashing in. My phone is ringing now too. And the trill of the doorbell is accompanied by banging and a loud voice.

'Nora!' a woman with an English accent is calling. 'Nora!'

And it's gone. Whatever trace of her was with me for that moment, it's gone. Her words aren't though. 'No! Don't. I'm frightened.' I can hear her voice. I can hear the tone of it. The fear in it. I feel the blood trickle down my hand, and the two sensations feel like they are entwined.

Dear Jesus, what did I do?

Chapter Twenty-Two

Izzy

Okay, so I'm worried. Very worried. I've been ringing this blasted doorbell, banging on her door, and shouting through the letterbox and she hasn't appeared.

I know she's in. Her car is still in the drive for one and for two I can hear someone shouting, or crying or something from the bowels of the house. It sounds like it might just be Nora.

Scrabbling around, I lift plant pots and look under the doormat hoping a spare key will reveal itself to me, but there's nothing. So I try dialling her phone and while I can hear it ring inside the house, she doesn't answer. I shout some more. A neighbour walks past, two children in tow, and when I start to speak, start to ask if she knows Nora well and if she might know where there's a spare key, she bows her head, wraps her arms around the children's shoulders and ushers them away as if I'm some crazy woman.

So all I can do is call out again and bang harder on the door.

'You're scaring me now, Nora,' I shout through the letter box. 'I'm going to phone Bradley. Do you hear me? Are you okay? Are you hurt?'

But for the keening coming from inside the house, I'd fear

she was hanging from the rafters or opening her veins in a warm bath. For all her talk of fighting back, her mental health is at best fragile. A momentary thought to call Tom and tell him to get here with his camera is overridden by my panic that she may actually be in danger.

'Is anyone in there with you?' I shout. 'Luca! Brendan!' I can't quite keep the growing hysteria from my voice. 'It's just me. I'm here to help!' I shout again. 'Nora! Luca! Brendan!'

'Brendan left with Luca already,' a voice from behind me says and I turn to see a man, in his late thirties maybe, standing at the bottom of the short drive. 'I saw them leave. Probably taking Luca to the childminders.'

'And you are?' I ask, as if I'm likely to recognise a name or a face.

'A neighbour,' he says, nodding in the direction of the end of the road. 'I live up that way.'

'Do you know if they have a spare key anywhere?' I ask.

The man looks at me as if I'm not all there. 'Erm, I haven't a baldies who you are. Do you really think I'd tell a stranger where a key to someone else's house might be?'

'I'm . . . I'm a friend of Nora's,' I lie. It's easier than explaining that I'm a documentary maker.

'Not a good enough friend that she'd tell you where she hides the spare key though, so if you don't mind . . . maybe you should leave.'

'But I know she's in there—'

'Clearly she just doesn't want to talk to you. So again, maybe you should just leave.'

My temper is starting to fray now. With every minute that passes I'm more and more convinced that Nora has hurt herself, or is in the process of doing so.

'If you, sir, have nothing of use to say, then I suggest you fuck right off,' I snarl as I press my finger on the doorbell once again. I've only glanced away momentarily but when I look back the annoying neighbour has indeed fucked right off. It's something at least.

Tears prick at my eyes and I lift my phone, to call the police and beg them to get someone here on a safeguarding call if nothing else.

It's then that the front door opens, and Nora, looking diminished from yesterday, her pale skin almost translucent, is staring back at me. Her eyes are wide as if she is truly terrified.

'Nora! Jesus, are you okay? I know it must've been a shock. That picture. And you've every right to be angry.'

She pulls the door open wider to allow me to follow her in and it's only then I notice her left hand is wrapped in blue fabric. 'I cut my hand,' she says, but her voice is flat, monotone. 'I was going through some old things and I cut my hand.'

'Is it bad?' I ask. 'Can I see it? Do you need to go to A&E?' I reach out to her but she pulls her hand back.

She shakes her head. 'No. I'll just sort it here.'

I can see the red stain of blood seeping through the pale blue material. 'I think maybe we should get a doctor to—'

'It's fine,' she says, cutting me off, before turning and walking to the kitchen. Gingerly I follow her, casting my eyes around her house. This is my first time in Nora Logue's home and maybe my imagination is running away with me but I am not getting a good vibe from this place. It's all very ordered. Tidy. None of Luca's toys strewn around the place, none of his drawings on the fridge. There are pictures on the walls, a couple of Daisy but many more of Luca. A giant collage of him from the moment he was born until now takes pride of place on the kitchen wall. He's a beautiful child, different to his sister, but still beautiful. I wonder how hard it is to have all these pictures of him here and only a few of Daisy.

'He's a happy-looking boy,' I say and it feels like the absolutely most stupid thing I could say. Nora looks as if she's on the edge of a complete mental breakdown, with blood now trickling down her arm, and I'm admiring photos of her son.

I watch as Nora, appearing to not have heard me, reaches into a cupboard and pulls out a first aid kit before running her injured hand under the cold tap. The water flows red and Nora winces. Before I can suggest once again going to the doctor, she says: 'So you've seen it then. Tom said so.'

'I have. I can't say that I blame you. It must have been awful to see Luca's picture like that, never mind what they wrote. Those threats. And accusations . . .'

She has started to wind a bandage around her hand, grimacing as she does so. 'Look,' I say, 'do you really not think you should—'

'It's fine,' she says, matter-of-factly.

'It looks like you're in pain.'

'It's no more than I deserve,' she says and there's no self-pitying tone to her voice. She is stating this as if it is merely fact. I wish I was the kind of person who knew what to say in circumstances such as these, but I'm not and I don't. So I stay quiet and watch until she asks me to help her cut some surgical tape to secure the bandage. It's impossible not to notice how her hands are trembling.

'Maybe a cup of hot—' I begin.

'Izzy,' she says. 'Please don't suggest hot sweet tea. I'll turn into a bloody cup of hot sweet tea at this rate and I don't even like tea.' She doesn't make eye contact when she talks, and it's clear she's still lost in her own thoughts. Closing the first aid box, she slips it back into the cupboard. 'Right, Tom said I should go with you. Before the phone starts ringing.'

I wonder if she hasn't noticed that her phone has been ringing almost incessantly since I arrived. 'Yes,' I tell her. 'Or before people – you know, journalists – show up.' A little prickle of shame creeps up inside me that I also want to make sure we don't get scooped, but very quickly, I push it back down. I'm here to do a job; it's as simple as that.

She nods, but doesn't speak.

'I spoke to your neighbour outside. He told me Brendan left for work. Do you need to speak to him? Maybe he wants to be here with you?'

She laughs – a sharp, brittle laugh. 'No. No, he won't. But thanks for asking.' There's a beat. 'You spoke to my neighbour? Which one?'

'He didn't give me his name,' I say. 'And he was a bit, you know, grumpy so I didn't ask. Tall man, mid-thirties. Dark hair, beard. Local accent. Looks like most of the men of his age seem to look these days.'

I watch as her brow furrows. 'A beard?'

'Yep. One of those full hipster efforts.'

'I can't think of who that might be. But he said he was a neighbour?'

Replaying the conversation in my mind, I'm pretty sure that is exactly what he said. I remember the head tilt towards the top of the street and I relay this information to Nora. She still can't think who I might be talking about, but she shakes her head, and the question from her mind. She lifts her phone, keys, and then the bloodstained piece of blue fabric and slips them all into her handbag. I say nothing.

'Let's go,' she says, as her phone trills to life again.

She doesn't answer it.

Chapter Twenty-Three

Izzy

Nora doesn't say hello to Tom when she arrives. She just allows me to guide her past him to the sofa in the living room. I put the kettle on, now desperate for that hit of coffee myself, and I pour two glasses of water – one that I quickly drain and a second that I bring to Nora. I'd noticed the way she has been smacking her lips, a sign her mouth is dry, most likely brought on by the adrenaline pulsing through her body. Her hands still shaking, she lifts the glass and takes a small sip. Still she doesn't speak.

With a nod of my head towards my bedroom door, I let Tom know I want him to follow me. For a moment I can see the confusion on his face. He is torn between wanting to follow me and wanting to stay here to keep an eye on Nora. I give him a second look – wide-eyed and urgent – before nodding my head towards my bedroom again. He catches on and follows me.

I reach over and push the door closed behind me, wondering if this will make it all too obvious to Nora that we're talking about her. Then again, she is likely more than aware that we're talking about her anyway. Everyone will be talking about her.

'What's with the bandage on her hand?' Tom asks as I fill the kettle.

'She cut her hand. It was bleeding quite a bit. It looked deep to me, but she insisted she didn't need to go to A&E and bandaged it up herself. Tom, when I got to her house I had to ring the doorbell a dozen times or more. Shout through her letterbox too. I was really starting to worry she'd done something stupid.'

'Like what?' he asks even though the answer is obvious.

I can't help but roll my eyes. 'You know what "something stupid" means,' I say. 'That message is really out of character for her. You know that. She's kept her distance from the media. Everything has been managed for her or by her and then this online tirade . . . It doesn't speak of a stable mind, does it?'

He shrugs. 'I think it's understandable that she would lose her shit when she thinks someone is threatening her child,' he says. 'I don't think it screams insanity.'

'Have you seen her?' I ask, my voice thick with sarcasm. 'She's not exactly herself, is she?'

'Again,' he tells me, 'this is all understandable under the circumstances.'

'The cut on her hand,' I start. 'When she came downstairs she had it wrapped in this blue piece of fabric. Looked like a top, or a something. It was very small though.'

'She has a small child,' he says.

'Yes, but small boys don't often have frills on their clothes. I'm pretty sure I saw a frill. And here's the thing. When she bandaged up her hand, what would you expect her to do with the makeshift dressing she had been using?'

He shrugs. 'Throw it in the washing machine, or the bin, or rinse it out?' he says.

'So not slide it into her handbag and bring it with her?'

He has the grace to look a little flummoxed at this.

'And she didn't speak in the car. Not a single word. But her phone – her bloody phone kept ringing and I didn't have the heart to tell her to put it on silent. She didn't even reject the calls – just let them ring out.'

At that precise moment the sound of Nora's phone ringing – and ringing – chimes from the other room. I give Tom a 'told you so' look.

'I set the camera up while you were away. It's on in there now. Capturing this. I thought it would be better to have it running rather than for her to notice us switch it on and maybe start to doubt whether or not this is a good thing,' he whispers.

'That was smart thinking,' I say, picturing the footage we'll have of this woman on the verge of God knows what and how this story is playing out with more drama than we could've dreamt of. If there's a little knot of doubt over just how exploitative we're being, I push it down. We're not driving the story, we're simply telling it. 'Just let it roll and we'll see what we have at the end of the day.'

Tom furrows his brow, pinches the bridge of his nose. 'You know, I think we should try and get what material we can sooner rather than later,' he says. 'And definitely before the police arrive and put any media strategy in place.'

'They wouldn't?' I say, my stomach now so tight I think I might actually puke.

'They more than likely will,' he says, reaching for the door handle to go back out. 'They'll want to control this, and get on top of any threats being made by anyone – including our friend out there.'

He nods to the door and before I can say anything else he opens it and we walk back to the living room. Nora is sitting in exactly the same position that she was in when we left her five minutes ago. And not just in the same position but the same pose. Precisely. It's as if she hasn't moved a muscle except those required to keep her alive. Breathing in and out. Heart beating.

'I've called the police,' Tom says. 'But maybe you've spoken to them yourself?'

She looks in his direction and then at me, but her gaze is unfocused, as if she is looking past me. 'No,' she says, in a small voice. 'I . . . I meant to but . . .'

'Well, don't worry,' Tom says sitting down opposite her, but leaning forward, adopting his best 'I'm listening' pose. 'DI Bradley wasn't at his desk yet, but the officer I spoke with said she would pass a message on for him to call back as soon as he could. Do you think he might be trying to call you?'

I glance towards her phone, which is ringing again, and she blinks at Tom as if trying to process what he's saying. 'Erm, I don't know,' she says as she slowly turns her gaze to the table, lifting her phone and looking at the screen.

'Someone has been very persistent in trying to get through,' I say.

She looks at the screen, taps at it to unlock her call history. 'Brendan,' she says, that one word – her husband's name – a sentence in its own right.

'You don't mind if we film?' Tom says, in a small voice. Nora blinks and looks at me, shakes her head a little, but it's almost indiscernible. I look at Tom who nods back at me before getting up and walking behind the camera. This is easier than we'd thought it would be.

'Does Brendan know about the forum – the messages?' I ask, as I sit down beside her.

She gives a strange, half-smile before her face darkens again. 'You know, I think given all these calls he probably does now.'

'So he hadn't seen it with you?' I ask and she shakes her head.

'No. You know how he feels about forums. He doesn't know

142

I was looking. I saw the picture of Luca this morning but I didn't show him. I . . . he'd be angry, you know.'

'How did you know which forum to look at?' I ask.

'Well, it didn't take a lot of work to find a forum that mentioned a new documentary being made. Once I saw your username, IzzyTV, I figured I'd landed in the right place. Sorry but I had to look for myself.'

I blush, run through all the things I've said publicly, hoping I've not said anything she might find offensive. But then again, I think she might have bigger things to worry about just now.

'I didn't expect to see the picture of Luca,' she says. 'I mean . . . you believe me, Izzy? Luca was not on his own. He was nowhere near on his own. I was within arm's reach. Brendan was too. And the thought that someone was up close like that, and would write things like that . . .' Nora makes for a pitiful sight as tears slide down her face. She doesn't even make an effort to wipe them away. Her phone rings again, and she winces at the sharp tone.

'Are you going to answer it?' I ask her, glancing at the screen and seeing Brendan's name emblazoned across it again.

She shakes her head. 'No. I don't know what to say to him. He's going to be so angry. And God he must be so scared too. Luca is everything to him. Every last part of him.'

'Surely he'll know this isn't your fault,' I say.

She gives a small, brittle laugh. 'If it's not my fault, whose fault is it? He warned me that doing this documentary would bring the wrong kind of attention and we're barely two days into it and . . . this . . . And he won't be happy I responded to them. God, I know it was foolish but I can't just sit and do nothing, can I? He's going to be so angry. Christ.' She looks at her phone again before switching it off and I can't help but feel that will just infuriate Brendan to a whole new level.

I've not met the man but I can't help but feel uneasy about

Nora's entire dynamic with her husband. There's a hint of control about him that feels as if it goes a little beyond just being concerned for her welfare. I get that he must be worried about Luca's safety. Of course I get that. But surely he should be supporting Nora to do whatever she wants to help her find peace. It's not like Brendan didn't know exactly what he was getting into. They met two years after Daisy disappeared, and it wasn't as if her history was a secret. It never could've been.

'Of course you can't just do nothing,' I soothe.

'I just don't know what's happening. All these things . . . Why now?' Nora says.

'What do you mean?' I ask, more for the benefit of the camera than anything else.

She shakes her head. 'The picture from Galway. The picture of Luca. The way I . . .' and she is interrupted by the ringing of a phone – Tom's this time. I glare at him for not having it on silent but he glares back. 'It's the police,' he says and I see Nora stiffen. She can't hide the grimace as she lifts her water glass with her bandaged hand.

I don't speak. I don't think I even take a breath as Tom answers and says that yes, Nora is here and yes it's okay for an officer to call over. He rhymes off our temporary address and hangs up.

'Was that Bradley?' I ask him, but he shakes his head.

'A woman. Eve King? Something like that.'

'She's his second in command,' Nora says. 'Is she the one going to come round?'

'She didn't say,' Tom says. 'Just that someone would be here shortly.'

Nora gets to her feet – almost jumps to her feet in fact. 'Okay. Okay.'

Tom gives me a look that says, 'If she's standing, she's not on camera,' and I reach out, placing my hand on Nora's arm. She's clearly agitated but I'm sure if I can just reach her, I can keep her from spiralling further.

Turns out I'm very, very wrong about that. As my hand brushes against her arm she flinches with such force, her eyes wide with terror, as if my touch has burned her, that she bangs her injured hand against the sideboard and lets out a shrill yelp. I glance at Tom, see his eyes widen, but he swings the camera around, making sure to keep her in frame.

'Are you okay, Nora?' he asks as she cradles her injured hand, tears pooling in her eyes.

As she blinks one rolls down her cheek, tracing a perfect line on her skin. She doesn't answer him. I suppose it's a stupid question all the same. But that pause is enough for her to soothe herself and sit back down on the sofa.

'I don't know what's going on,' she says. 'I don't know what I did to my child but *something* inside me is screaming that it was *something* bad . . .'

Chapter Twenty-Four

Nora

Almost immediately, I regret my words. I see the subtle changes on the faces of Izzy and Tom. They're doing their best not to react, but I know the look well. It's the look people get when they *really* question my innocence in all this for the first time.

'What do you mean?' Izzy mutters as she sits down opposite me. I can see the blinking red light on Tom's camera.

'No! Don't. I'm frightened,' plays in my head again, and again. That voice. Small. Light. A memory, I'm sure, and not a hallucination. A pale face flashes into my mind but it leaves again so quickly I can't grasp what I'm seeing, what I'm feeling.

I blink at Izzy but I don't know how to answer her. I don't know how to explain this feeling inside me. Fear and guilt and so much pain. I gasp, trying to pull air into my lungs.

'I don't know,' I murmur. 'I just don't know.'

Only the throbbing of my hand is stopping me from floating away into a different reality altogether.

'Was it you who posted the picture of Luca?' Tom asks me, his voice distant and muffled. Why does it sound like he's talking through cotton wool, from behind a filter? Something is humming in the back of head. No, not humming, it's incessant. A warning almost. Tom's face is earnest. He looks sincere in his concern but why on earth would I post a picture of my own child, and why on earth would he think that I would?

'No,' I tell him. 'No. Why would I do that?'

'No! Don't. I'm frightened,' echoes in my ears again, I blink and try to grasp what is real and here in this moment.

Tom colours and while I can see he wants to say something, he either can't find the words or can't find the courage to do so. I question the tone in my voice. Was I sharp? Angry? Confused?

'You said you think you did something bad. What do you mean by something bad?' Izzy cuts in, her voice gentle. 'I think that's what he means.'

I bristle, even though I have no right to, at her probing. It's too late to put the words back in my head until I can make proper sense of my feelings, and try to make sense of the memories tapping at my brain. They're there, but not there at the same time. Echoes of an echo.

Nausea swirls in the pit of my stomach. I've not eaten breakfast. Just had some coffee. I feel almost seasick as I imagine it swirling around deep inside me, fighting to stay down. I know I should eat something but . . .

I have to breathe. To get through this. I close my eyes as if the rest of the world is too much of a distraction – because the rest of the world *is* too much of a distraction right now. It's loud and filled with lies.

'Did you just mean the post on the forum?' I hear Tom cut in, breaking the silence. 'Because I'm sure everyone will be able to understand why you did that. You're a mother who wants to protect her child. Oldest instinct in the book.'

'I'm not sure it is,' I say and my voice sounds alien to me. I know it's me speaking. I can feel my tongue move in my mouth as I form the words. 'It's not always an instinct. We don't know how to do it. Any of it. Not really. Not when it gets hard. Or at least, I didn't know.' I'm speaking but I can't make sense of what I'm saying. It's as if someone else is talking for me. Maybe the real me? Maybe the me that disappeared the day Daisy did? As much as I try, I can't really remember that woman. I can't remember who she was or what she did, or how she spoke. She's hazy, like an old movie when the starlets were blurred. Vaseline on the lens. That's what my mum used to tell me anyway. I've assumed it's true. I don't really know. The room around me now is hazy too, as if it's not real. I don't know if I'm real. If I'm here in this moment, or lost in a place where my child is shouting – no, screaming – at me. In a place where blood is vivid red.

I know I feel it now. Fear. And it's familiar and stark. I close my eyes again and I don't know if it's because I want to escape it, or I want to be right there in the moment. I feel closer to it than I have done in seven years. As if the key is in the lock and all I have to do is turn it, if I can just catch it in my grip.

Words swim in and out of focus. *Mother of the year. Doesn't deserve her children.* 'No! Don't. I'm frightened.' Over and over again but the record keeps jumping back to the start and it won't move past it. My stupid head and my stupid memory. Anger rises in me. Strong and fierce and loud. They're right. They are all right. I am a shit mother. Luca would be better off without me. Daisy deserved better than me. I can feel a blow to my head and I don't know if it is now, or then, or both. I don't know, and if I'm being completely honest I don't care. I don't care about anything anymore except remembering.

It's a tight grip on my wrist and a voice repeatedly saying my name – not Mammy – that blinks me back into reality. Izzy is kneeling on the floor in front of me, pulling my arm from my face. My hand aches and when I glance at it, I see that blood is seeping through the bandage.

Wide-eyed, I stare back at Izzy, completely at a loss to understand what has just happened. All I know for sure is that she looks scared. Her eyes are wide, her face just a shade paler than it was before. 'Are you okay?' she asks. 'Should we call a doctor?'

'Why?' I ask, confused. Not for my hand, surely. I just need to wrap it again. Be more careful. Or go to A&E. I certainly don't need a doctor to come and see me.

'You . . . well, you kinda . . . spaced out a bit there,' Izzy says.

'Did I?' I ask, even though I know myself I was not in this room with these people moments ago.

'You were babbling,' Tom interjects. 'I couldn't make out what you were saying.'

I think of the fuzzy thoughts fighting for space in my head right now and I tense. What did I say? What could I have said?

'And then you started hitting yourself,' Izzy says, her hands still holding my wrists but more gently now. I come to realise she must've been restraining me in some manner. I feel the heat rise in my face as shame nips at me.

'That's how you hurt your hand again,' she says, her voice soft. 'I think we really need to get that looked at and dressed properly.'

I started hitting myself? I think of the pain in my head and an image, unbidden, comes into my mind – an image of me, like a lunatic in an asylum, rocking back and forth and pounding on my head as if to try and shake the memories out of it.

I have a feeling, a knowledge deep within my bones, that this is not a recent memory. This does not relate to what has just passed but to a long time ago. To the madness that went before.

Because I was quite mad. I know that. Back when Daisy went. When I was strung out with grief and pain and my body was trying to heal.

And I was mad the day they found me on the road coming out of the forest, completely unaware of how I'd got there, how long I'd been there and why my hands were blackened and bruised. My nails torn off, and my fingers splintered and bloody. Had I been digging? Did I know something then?

I blink, as if the act will change the scene – turn the page to the next one. I want to see more. Even if I'm scared.

'The police are coming,' I say. 'About the picture of Luca. And my post on the site. I need to talk to them. That's the most important thing.' Luca's name feels wrong in my mouth, heavy on my tongue. I am acting, I realise. Masking my real feelings because they are too horrific to put a voice to.

My mouth is dry. I sip from the glass of water Izzy brought me, but I find it hard to swallow. It would be a relief, I realise with a heart-stopping wrench, if someone else did take Luca. It would be a relief not to have to pretend anymore. Not to have to act as if this child – this beautiful boy – has caught my heart in the same way Daisy did. He has not.

He could not.

When Luca was born I both longed to and dreaded giving birth to a carbon copy of Daisy. I longed to see a replica of her, her wispy dark hair. I wanted to gaze into the stark blue of her eyes. I wanted to see that one dimple in her right cheek again. I'd know, of course, that it wasn't her, but it might help to see her. It might help me hold onto the fading memories of my child for a bit longer. I wondered, would he smell the same as she had? Would his smile curl at the left of his mouth first, just as hers did? Would I be able to imagine, in my lone-liest moments, that I was looking at her again instead of him?

Could I ask him for forgiveness in a way I never had the chance to with Daisy? I longed for the first pang of labour pains. I wanted to feel each one. I refused medication. I needed to feel my body stretch and open and prepare itself to eject this tiny human in a mess of blood and mucus. I needed to feel the burning and tearing of my flesh. I deserved every ounce of pain.

But the biggest pain came when he was placed in my arms and he was nothing like her. He had the merest wisps of hair. His face was dimple-free. His expression curious, even at a minute old, while Daisy had looked so at peace.

'I know he can't ever replace Daisy,' a well-meaning relative had said. 'But maybe this baby will heal your heart a little.' I suppose I'd hoped that he would too, but as soon as this unfamiliar creature was in my arms, I became acutely aware that he was not her. That moment that should have been the start of a new time for me, a time where I could find some joy again, had instead just reinforced that the life I'd dreamed of for my daughter was gone.

Even as I was trying to coo over this perfect little infant, my heart was breaking all over again in ways I would never have thought possible.

Chapter Twenty-Five

Izzy

When the doorbell rings, Tom gets up to answer it, leaving me with Nora, who seems to be disassociating from reality over and over again – drifting into some world, some memories and coming back with a big jolt each time.

Each time she is back in the room her eyes widen as if she is shocked to be here again. It's as if her mind is struggling to keep up with whatever is going on in its deepest recesses. I can't blame it. I'm struggling to keep up with what's happening myself, and I'm clueless when it comes to what to do to help her.

The best course of action would probably be to contact Brendan. He's bound to have seen Nora in an agitated state like this before and will know how to support her through it. But that weird controlling vibe I get about him stops me – that and Nora's assertion that he will be angry. No doubt he will direct that at me, which I can take, but there's no way Nora is fit for angry confrontation just now. Plus, if I'm being completely honest with myself, I think that if Brendan gets involved he will pull the plug on all of this and I will lose this incredible material.

Tom walks into the room, accompanied by a tall man in a suit. He's in his late forties or early fifties. His hair is sprinkled with flecks of grey and he has a look of Paul Hollywood about him. I'm instantly able to place him as the famous, or infamous, DI Bradley.

We truly are blessed to be granted an audience with the main man himself, I think wryly. But then I remember, he's not here for me. He's here for Nora.

Behind him is a woman with a blonde pixie cut – she looks effortlessly chic in a tailored trouser suit and I wonder if these two think they are the lead characters in a darkly lit, moody cop drama before chiding myself for being a bitch. It doesn't suit me.

Bradley is first to speak, extending his hand to me but all the while making sure his eyes are on Nora, whose gaze is firmly on the floor.

'DI David Bradley,' he says. 'And I assume you're Izzy Devine?'

'You assume correctly,' I say.

'This is my colleague DS Eve King,' he says, nodding his head towards the blonde woman. She doesn't extend her hand, or smile. She simply nods in acknowledgement before sitting herself down on the coffee table directly in front of Nora.

I look at Tom, who nods towards the camera. It's still rolling. Okay, I do want the very best material we can get but is it going too far to surreptitiously film the police? Should I ask Tom to stop recording? Or maybe, I think, just let it roll for now. We can always edit later. You can't edit an empty camera roll, and maybe something will be said here that will be worth taking a risk over.

DS King takes Nora's injured hand in hers. 'How did you do this?' she asks. 'It looks like it's been bleeding a lot.'

'I was up in the attic. At home. Looking for stuff. For Daisy's stuff.'

DS King nods, her head tilted ever so slightly to one side as if she is oozing sympathy and understanding. I'm not convinced she is fully genuine.

'And was this after you posted on the AmateurSleuths website?' DS King asks, head still tilted, voice still soft and caring.

Nora blinks at her then looks at her hand as if she is seeing the injury for the first time. 'I think so. I'm not sure. It's all a bit hazy. This morning . . . I saw the post and I just reacted and I know I'm not supposed to. I know I'm supposed to ignore the trolls but they had a picture of Luca. It must have been taken right under my nose. I was there. Brendan was there. We didn't let him out of our sight, not for a second, never mind a minute. So whoever it was, was right there and they are putting pictures of my child online.' There's an anger in her voice now. Steady and determined. She sounds more lucid than she has since I arrived at her door.

'And you have cause to think this post constituted a genuine threat to Luca's safety?' DS King asks.

'Do I have cause to think there's a genuine threat?' Nora repeats. 'Well, given that I don't know what happened to my daughter, then I'd say yes. I have cause to think it's a genuine threat. And the replies? You saw the replies?'

I can feel the nervous tension start to come off her in waves. Her legs are jiggling up and down, and she has started to scratch at the small daisy tattoo on her wrist, even though it is partially covered by the bandage on her hand.

'Nora has been very distressed this morning,' I interject. I want to tell them that she has been confused and that she has questioned whether or not she's a bad person. I want to tell them how she has been ignoring the persistent calls from Brendan and how she keeps zoning in and out. I want to tell them how she has hit herself around the head and not even remembered doing so. But I don't. Not now, anyway. It would feel like a betrayal of the trust we have just started to build.

And it's not as if I believe Nora is bad, or poses a risk to Luca herself. Or do I?

'I can imagine,' DS King says. 'I imagine it was very distressing to see that image and to read those words. What we have to be careful about is that we manage our response to them. We don't want trolls to get behind these posts. If they get a reaction from you, they are more likely to push for a bigger response next time.'

'Why are you talking to me as if I'm stupid?' Nora says. 'And why are you talking to me as if this indeed is only a "troll" talking? Trolls don't go to the effort to take pictures of other people's children on beaches.'

'And there's no way someone could've accessed a picture of Luca in another way? Perhaps you posted one on social media, or Brendan did? People will lift anything off anyone's accounts these days. It doesn't bother them to do so.'

Nora shakes her head. 'I didn't bring my phone with me. I left it in the car. Brendan may have taken a few pictures. I can't remember. But he most certainly didn't post them on social media. You know how he is about that. He has a very strict rule that we don't share images of Luca anywhere they can be downloaded from. He only sends them via email to the closest family and friends – if at all.'

'Maybe we could start by asking Brendan if he sent that image to anyone? We might be able to solve this before it even really starts,' DS King says and I snort with incredulity. Tom throws me a look as if he is screaming at me to stay professional. I just shake my head at him.

'Before it even really starts?' I ask. 'Nora's right. Have you seen the replies? What has to actually happen before you consider something "really started"?'

As soon as I say it, I know it is one of those things that would be better off not said out loud. I'm not sure who is glaring at me the hardest – DI Bradley or Tom.

'I can assure you, Ms Devine, that we are taking this matter very seriously, as we do any developments surrounding the Daisy Logue case. You have two senior officers with you right now, which is indicative of the robust manner in which we are approaching this situation.'

'This isn't a press conference,' I tell him. 'You can keep your prepared statements. All I'm saying is that perhaps you could put yourself in Nora's shoes in this instance. She knows this isn't a picture someone has downloaded from her social media. She doesn't have any social media accounts for obvious reasons. Nor would Brendan have shared it. And I don't think dismissing these threats as trolls is helpful. She has one child missing and another with his image flashing around the internet. How would you feel if it were you, DI Bradley? I've done my research. It's a daughter you have isn't it? And what age is she? Two or three? The same age as Luca Pryce.'

Emotion flickers across his face. 'My personal life, and my daughter, are not relevant to this matter,' he says. 'But of course I understand your reaction, Nora. It's human to want to lash out. We all do it from time to time.' He has bypassed me now and is crossing the room. DS King budges over on the coffee table to allow room for her colleague to sit down. I want to make a smart comment that we do have armchairs if they would prefer something more comfortable, but I realise I'm probably already at my wisecrack limit for the day and I would do better to keep my trap shut.

Nora doesn't answer him. She just glances down at her bandaged hand.

'Nora, this might seem like a stupid question, but can you think of anyone who would target you in this way? Anyone specific perhaps?'

She looks up. 'DI Bradley, you know as well as I do that there is a long list of people who would target me in this way.

All those who think I hurt Daisy. Or I was a neglectful mother. Or that I must've been off my head on drink or drugs. That's before we even start on the conspiracy theory brigade who think I sold my own child to human traffickers – gave her up to a fate worse than death for the sake of a few pounds.'

'Unfortunately, there are always going to be people who choose to believe the worst,' he says. 'But I do need you to think very carefully now. This is clearly someone local enough to secure a picture of Luca on the beach. Someone who could identify him as your child. Maybe a family member?'

I'm incredulous at this leap to an insane conclusion. 'The world and his mother know Nora's face,' I say. 'It doesn't take a genius to work out the small child she is with is likely to be her own small child.'

If I'm expecting Bradley to be flustered by my outburst, I'm surprised when he nods. 'That's a fair point,' he says. 'And of course it's one we have thought of. But what is also important to remember is that often in cases like this it is someone close to the family who turns out to be involved.'

'Cases like this?' I ask, aware that yes, we are still recording and this is good material. 'Do you mean the internet posts this morning, or Daisy's case in general? Because I'd have thought you'd have already looked at people close to the family.'

'We did our job to the best of our abilities,' he says. 'As we continue to do.' I see that Bradley doesn't miss a beat when it comes to towing the party line. The press office must love him. DS King, however, is glowering at me.

'Miss Devine,' she begins.

'Izzy. You can call me Izzy. No need for formalities.'

'I like to set firm boundaries,' she says. 'And we are here primarily to talk to Ms Logue.' She turns her questions to Nora again. 'Nora, I know this is scary right now. That on top of the picture from Galway it must feel very frightening. We've been doing our best to look into that for you.'

We all sit up a little straighter at this.

'But we've not been able to confirm anything more than you already know,' she says. 'It's highly unlikely, as you know, that this girl will be Daisy. We believe if Daisy is still alive she will not be living in Ireland.'

'So you have evidence that she was shipped out?' I ask.

'No, Miss Devine. We know of trends in human trafficking and the illegal trade in minors but we have no firm reason to suspect this is what happened to Daisy. We can't, however, rule it out, which is why we look to trends and typical behaviours,' DS King says. 'But it's really not why we are here this morning. Nora, I think we really should have your husband here as well for this.'

She shakes her head. 'No. There's no need to involve him.'

'We are talking about his child, and threats you deem legit-imate have been made against his child. I think it's only right that he's involved.' Bradley's voice is gentle but firm. He is not giving Nora a choice here.

'And Luca,' Bradley says. 'Is he with his dad this morning?'

Nora shakes her head. 'No. Brendan's at work and Luca is at creche.'

'And which creche is this?' Bradley asks.

'Bumble Bees,' Nora says. 'They've been minding Luca since he was a year old and I . . . tried . . . to go back to work. They are a good creche. They have strong security measures in place. All staff are carefully vetted. I made sure of that.'

'And did Daisy go to Bumble Bees when she was little?' Bradley asks. 'I forget, refresh my memory.'

Nora shakes her head. 'Daisy didn't go to any creche. She was at home with me.'

'That's right, yes. Sorry. Look. We really do think it would be better if we spoke to you and Brendan together about this.'

Nora shakes her head. 'You don't understand. I'm sorry. I shouldn't have posted. I should've kept quiet. It's just trolls. Izzy is right – everyone knows who I am. Everyone in this part of the world knows especially, and people like to act big and it's nothing . . .'

'Nora,' DI Bradley says, softly but I notice it. I notice the change in his stance. In the way he holds himself. I notice how he looks at DS King and she nods, her expression set like stone.

'Nora, we've asked you if you can think of someone who might want to target you because we have reason to believe that one of these posts in particular is a legitimate threat, and one we should take seriously. We have received communication outside of the AmateurSleuths website that has definitely raised some red flags. We can't categorically say it isn't just some troll, but the manner of this communication seems a little more . . . personal.'

I catch Tom nodding at me and then towards the camera. He is doing his best to hide the glee on his face that this is all now on film.

What little colour had been left on Nora's face drains from it, and she sinks back into the chair.

'What do you mean by threat?' Nora asks, her voice weary.

Bradley clears his throat. 'This one came directly to us. This morning around the same time you posted your response on the website. It was signed off with the same username as one of the posts in AmateurSleuths.'

'Who?' I ask. 'What did they say?'

'I think I'd prefer to discuss that with Nora and Brendan in private,' Bradley says.

'No,' Nora says. 'If there's a threat then you need to let me know and you need to let me know now. It's only fair. I can't be expected to sit here and wait for Brendan. That's cruel. And I don't care if Izzy and Tom hear it as well. They've been helping me too, in a lot of ways.'

I bite back a smug smile and focus on what Nora is saying and the manner in which she is saying it. She is manic. That's the only way to describe it. Her mood and her posture are constantly changing – and I don't know from one minute to the next which version of Nora we will get next.

DI Bradley shifts a little, shuffling over on the coffee table just a smidge.

'I want to stress, strongly, once again that we have been unable to verify the full nature of this threat and don't know for certain if it is genuine. A message was posted this morning on amateursleuths.com from a user identifying themselves as "The Four".'

I freeze, my body stiffening. Shit. I dare not look to Tom. The Four who warned me they were watching 'very closely'. The Four who made the public threat online this morning. Who said they had seen Nora's cruelty first hand.

She barely blinks.

'They sent this email this morning,' Bradley says, and DS King hands Nora a printed-out sheet of paper. Her voice shaking and small, she reads.

'*We are The Four. We are aware that a documentary is being made in which Nora Logue will be featured speaking about the search for her daughter. We had hoped that Nora had learned her lesson, but it seems she can't keep out of the spotlight, not even for the sake of her son.*

'*We have no choice therefore but to take action. No child, not even her own, is safe in her care. If she chooses to keep digging, she may well find her daughter, but she will lose her boy. An eye for an eye and a tooth for a tooth.*'

Chapter Twenty-Six

Nora

The buzzing is back in my ears and it is incessant. It claws at me. Crawls through my brain. I feel as if there is an insect either trying to burrow its way in, or scrape its way out.

I cannot make sense of it. I can't make sense of the words I have just read. Talk of eyes for eyes, and Daisy and finding her but losing Luca, and I don't know what it means or who sent it.

Does it mean Daisy could still be alive? Does it mean I *could* still find her? But why talk of a tooth for a tooth? I know that's a biblical reference – of revenge and blame and guilt. For the longest time I'd have said that couldn't be relevant to me. But this morning's memories, if that's what they are, sit heavy on my shoulders.

I can't escape them. I can't escape any of this. Even if now I decided to call off this stupid documentary. Even if now I did what Brendan always said I should do and kept my head down and my focus on Luca, would it make a difference? Is it too late?

But God forgive me because if there's a chance that I can find her, then I have to take the risk with Luca.

That realisation comes at me like a punch to the stomach,

and I am winded by the force of it. All these words are racing around my head, and I'm aware that DI Bradley and DS King are looking at me for a reaction. I'm aware that Izzy and Tom are looking at me for the same, and I'm aware there is a camera recording these moments. One that I won't be able to run from.

'I should phone Brendan,' I stutter, and as I lift my phone and switch it back on, my hand is shaking. All of me is shaking. This is shock, I think. I can remember it from before. The reality that something is very wrong indeed is sinking in. I can't hide it, or pretend it isn't happening. It's bigger than Brendan being cross with me. He needs to know, and he needs to know now – whatever the consequences.

'Do you want me to speak to him for you?' DS King asks as my hands struggle to scroll to my husband's name. I think it might scare him but I realise he's probably already scared and angry, and I don't want these people gathered to listen to him berate me for not answering before. So I nod and hand my phone to DS King, the movement jolting my sore hand and making me wince.

'Once we speak to Brendan, we'll get that seen to,' DI Bradley says as DS King taps at my phone and I hear the call connect.

I both want and need Brendan to be here. I want the comfort of him, but I realise that comfort is probably lost to me now. Now I will see fear in his eyes that our son could be at risk, perhaps contempt that I'm the person who made that happen. The buzzing in my ears gets louder. Breathe, I remind myself, just breathe.

There's a click, and a moment of silence as Brendan answers the phone, then there is sound all around me.

'Jesus Christ, Nora! I've been trying to get a hold of you for the last hour and a half. I've called you dozens of times, if not hundreds of times and you've not picked up. What in fu—' He is shouting so loudly I wonder if DS King has put him on speakerphone.

'Mr Pryce,' DS King says, her voice stern and authoritative, leaving no room for misunderstanding. 'This is Detective Sergeant Eve King from Strand Road PSNI Station. We've met before.'

'Where's Nora? Is she okay?' I'm relieved to hear concern in his voice.

'Nora is with me. We're at an address in Garden City, an Airbnb property being rented by the production team your wife has been working with on the new documentary. As you can imagine, she is in a distressed state and has also sustained an injury to her hand that isn't serious, but we believe she requires medical attention. Mr Pryce, are you aware of the posts that have appeared on the website amateursleuths.com this morning?'

There's a pause but there's no need for it. By the insistence of his calling, I know that, somehow, he has.

'The link was forwarded to me this morning, maybe about an hour ago,' his tinny voice comes through the phone line. 'DS King, is my son in danger?'

'I think that would be a conversation best had to face to face. Can you come to our address?' DS King says.

All I can do is bury my head in my hands as shame washes over me.

'At this moment, I would prefer to know if I need to be putting measures in place to protect my son,' I hear him say.

There's something in the way he says 'my son' that tells me he has already cut me from the equation. All that matters is his son.

DS King stands up, still talking, but I can't take in what she is saying, and she leaves the room, my phone still held to her ear.

My leg muscles tense, fighting the urge to stand and follow her. To hear whatever she is telling him. Or maybe to hear whatever he is telling her.

'We don't want to worry you unduly,' DI Bradley says, pulling my attention back into this room and away from whatever Brendan is saying. 'This could just be a particularly nasty troll. We've had them in the past, Nora, as you know. These forums just make it so much easier for them to reach out.' I nod, conflicted between wanting it to be someone weaving an elaborate lie and desperate for it to be real – no matter how scary. Because if they are real then the answer to all this is within reach.

There's a cough and Izzy speaks. 'I received a message from an account by the same name yesterday. To my private message folder on AmateurSleuths.'

I must push the panic down. I must stay calm. I must not lose it.

'What did it say?' DI Bradley asks. 'Are you happy to share the content of it with us?' Izzy nods and reaches for her iPad, tapping at the screen before handing it to DI Bradley.

'I screen-shotted it too, and emailed it to myself,' she says. 'Just to make sure I had a copy saved.'

I watch Bradley's face as he reads. He gives a slight nod before handing the iPad back to Izzy. 'Can you email that to me?'

Impatience forces me to talk. 'What does it say? Tell me? Izzy, why didn't you show me this before?'

Izzy has the good grace to colour. 'I received a lot of messages yesterday,' she stutters. 'I was working my way through them. Trying to figure out what might be worth passing on and—'

'It's of a very similar vein to the email we received,' DI Bradley cuts in. 'It makes some vague accusations, and could be seen as a possible threat. So I think it's very important now that we focus on how we move forward with this. Think very carefully about the words that have been used in the message

I showed you. The language. The username. Not just of "The Four" but the person who posted the picture in the first instance. Is there anything there that stands out for you? The biblical reference – does that have any particular meaning? The picture of Luca. Do you know when it could've been taken? Who was with him at the time?'

So many questions. My head is spinning. 'The picture was at the beach. The day before yesterday, I think. I . . .' I realise that everything from the last few days is bleeding into one and I'm not sure of anything anymore. 'I was there, and Brendan too. We were with him. He was never alone. Not even for a second. I swear.'

'Nora,' Izzy says gently, 'maybe you should tell DI Bradley about the nappy, back at your car?'

I nod. 'Yes, of course. When we went back to the car someone had smeared a dirty nappy over our windscreen. We didn't see who it was though.'

'Did you report it to the gardaí?' DI Bradley asks.

'No.' I shake my head. 'We cleaned it up and came home. Respectfully, if we reported every time we were targeted by an angry or suspicious member of the public, we'd need a police force all of our own.'

He doesn't argue, just nods. 'And you didn't notice anyone paying extra attention to you on the beach? Anyone close to Luca at any stage?'

'No,' I say. 'Look, I don't go out and about much. You know that. When I do, I do whatever I can to keep my head down and not get recognised. I especially don't want to get recognised when I'm with Luca. You know I do what I can to ensure his privacy at all times. We made a very conscious decision to keep him out of the public eye and that hasn't changed.'

'But you're making a documentary?' DI Bradley says, side-eyeing Izzy and Tom.

'Which Luca is not a part of,' I tell him. 'He has not been filmed and will not be filmed.'

'And the creche you send him to,' DI Bradley continues. 'Are there any parents there who might recognise him? Or who you know from the past? Someone who would be able to pick him out of a crowd?'

I shake my head and can feel the colour rising in my cheeks. 'I don't do the drop-offs, or the pick-ups,' I tell him. 'I don't interact with the other parents. I only speak with the creche via phone or email. Luca has his father's surname. And as I've said, they take security very seriously. All their staff are vetted.'

Even as I say it, I realise that the staff being vetted is just one very small part of the equation. How many parents, guardians or caregivers also make their way in and out of that building? Brendan has argued that Luca would be more secure at home but . . .

DS King walks back into the room and immediately I abandon my train of thought and focus on her. 'Is he coming here?' I ask. 'Is he angry?'

She gives me a sympathetic look – one that says so much. 'Brendan is on his way to pick Luca up from creche, and then he's going to take him home. He says you should get your hand seen to and that will give him time to think about what to do next.' The 'what to do next' hangs very heavy in the air. I can't speak.

'Look, Nora, I know this is very difficult but we have to do everything we can to make sure Luca is kept safe. At the moment, that has to be our priority.'

My stomach knots as an awful thought strikes me. 'You're not going to take him away from us, are you? Put him in care? He needs us. He needs his family!'

DS King glances to the ground, and I watch as she swallows, desperation rising in me. Christ knows, Brendan would never

166

forgive me. Luca would never forgive me. I'd never forgive myself.

'No,' DS King says eventually. 'At the moment, we don't think we have sufficient cause to remove Luca from the custody of his parents. However, Mr Pryce – Brendan – has said he may look to remove Luca from the family home until the matter is resolved.'

The penny drops and the sound it makes is deafening. He's going to take Luca. They are going to leave me. Instinctively I know that whatever my husband's plans are now, they will not include me. Not while the risk is unknown. I am losing them. Losing Luca. Losing Brendan. And there isn't even a trade-off of getting Daisy back or discovering what happened to her. There is nothing.

Just me. Left on my own. I can't speak. I can't find the words to react. Not now and not here. My head is too full and my heart too sore.

'Nora.' DS King's voice is softer now. There is a sympathy to her tone that wasn't there before. 'I think it's time we went to the hospital about your hand, don't you?'

Chapter Twenty-Seven

Izzy

Tom and I stare at each other. I think we're officially lost for words. The police have taken Nora to the hospital to have her hand looked at. Then, I believe, they are all going to speak to Brendan.

The look on Nora's face as she read the message from 'The Four' will stay with me forever. As will the look on her face as it started to dawn on her that Brendan may want to take Luca away. Of course, I'd assumed when the police had said Brendan may want to make sure that Luca was safe that they'd either be providing some sort of back-up or all three of them would go away to stay with family, or into some form of protective custody or something. It seems I'd way overestimated the resources of the PSNI and such drama only really happens on TV shows or, as DI Bradley says 'when there is a clear threat to life'.

Nora had looked bewildered by it all. She barely spoke and just let Bradley and King lead her from the room, and the house, to go and get her hand seen to. I'd had to remind her to take her bag with her and it was only when she stood that it registered with me that she was still wearing her house slippers – Ugg-like things – and hadn't brought a jacket or cardigan with her. It seemed she'd just about made it out her house with her wits and little else.

'Jesus Christ,' Tom says as he presses some buttons on the camera and sits down opposite me.

'Indeed,' I say, feeling shell-shocked by this morning's events. 'That was intense.' To my self-disgust I feel tears well in my eyes. I'm supposed to remain objective in all this. To remain above the story. I've watched journalists before – serious news reporters and documentary makers – talk of keeping a professional distance even in the most harrowing of circumstances. At the scenes of war crimes, at the uncovering of mass graves, and here I am feeling my heart flutter at this woman in slippers being taken to hospital looking scared and confused. Determined not to cry, I blink them away and take a deep breath.

'And we got it all on film,' Tom says, a hint of glee in his voice. 'You couldn't make that stuff up. Can you say BAFTA?'

'Tom!' I admonish him, a feeling of disquiet washing over me. As documentary makers we are essentially voyeurs but to celebrate such a scary development for Nora seems . . . well . . . a little crass?

'Don't tell me it hasn't crossed your mind too,' he says. 'I saw you glance at the camera a couple of times while she or the police were talking. I can read your body language, Izzy, and I can tell you were feeling it too.'

'Feeling what?'

'Excitement!' he says. 'That buzz that only comes when you know without a shadow of a doubt that you have hit gold. Everything about that – her spacing out, hitting herself on her head, for fuck's sake – it's solid gold.'

I wince a little. 'Tom, there's a threat out there against a young child,' I say. 'Maybe we could dial down the excitement just a little?'

I say it but at the same time I know he's right. This is solid gold. This is what every filmmaker dreams of: a twist in the tale that elevates it to the next level. And catching it on camera is the cherry on top. I bite my lip to force back a smile.

'It's just a damn shame we won't be there to film when she comes face to face with Brendan,' Tom says. 'I think that will make what we caught earlier look like amateur hour. There's something a bit off with that bloke and I don't have a problem saying it out loud. How he spoke when he thought she was on the end of the phone and not that DS King? And how she talks about him telling her what to look at online, and how he'd prefer she kept a low profile? Sounds like a bit of a control freak to me.'

'You feel it too?' I ask. 'I mean, I suppose he could be acting out of concern and love, but there's something there I can't quite put my finger on. For someone who Nora met after Daisy went missing, and who knew exactly what baggage she was carrying, he doesn't seem the most understanding.'

'Probably one of those weirdos who goes for damaged women because he can keep them in their place easier,' Tom says. 'Probably thought he hit the jackpot with Nora. Can you imagine? If you're the kind of guy who needs to be the saviour and you end up with a woman who can't even remember what she was doing when her child went missing? A woman who has been on the front of every newspaper in the western world because of her tragic back-story.'

'Maybe,' I say, my concern turning back to Nora and the lost expression on her face as she was led out to go to the hospital.

Tom is babbling on about Brendan. Wondering aloud if we might be able to change his mind and get him on camera. He seems to think that the threat against Luca might be enough to anger Brendan into speaking to us, but I think the exact opposite is the most likely outcome. He's hardly going to want to court more attention now, and he'll be bringing out the big guns to persuade Nora to back off too.

I excuse myself, lifting the water glasses from the coffee table – they have barely been touched – and bringing them through to the kitchen. The methodical action of pouring the now tepid liquid down the sink, rinsing the glasses and wiping down the work surfaces is enough to take me out of my head for a moment.

That is, until Tom calls to me that my phone is ringing and I rush through to see 'International' written across my phone screen. Could it be that Paddy McGilloway, the photographer from Galway Live, is finally calling me back with news on the picture of the Daisy-a-like?

I've barely said hello, when a gruff voice talks over me. 'How'ya?' he asks in a thick West Coast accent. 'Is that Izzy Devine I'm speaking with? This is Paddy the photographer. Maureen has my heart tortured to call you about a documentary or something?'

'Yes. I'm Izzy. Thanks for getting back to me Paddy.'

'Not a bother,' he says. 'Sorry I've taken a while. I've been flat out here – now tell me this, what can I help you with? It's about fun day pictures or something, is that right?' he asks.

'It is,' I say. 'Look, I was sent a link to your pictures by someone who thinks they recognise one of the people featured. And they'd be very keen to speak to this person, if you could give me any more information about them? There's no names on the captions so I couldn't be sure.'

There's an intake of air, sucked in through his teeth. 'Now, if there's no caption on the picture I can tell you now that it's not one of mine. I always have my captions done. I'm not one of these fly-by-nighters. What use is a photo to anyone without a caption?' he asks.

'Maureen seemed to be quite sure you took it,' I say. 'It was the day at Salthill. Photos went online on Sunday, I think. They've been published since.'

Tom is peering at me, his eyebrows doing all sorts of aerobics on his face, and I know that he'd give his eye teeth to know what Paddy is saying. I put the phone on speaker so he can listen in.

'Right, tell me this. Is there even a code in place of a caption?'

I shrug. 'Hang on, let me check,' I say gesturing to Tom to hand me the iPad. I scroll through the messages Jacqs sent me to find the link and click on it. Sure enough there's a small code under the picture.

'It just says FunDaySub3,' I tell him.

There's another intake of breath. 'Right, so. That makes sense. The thing is, Izzy, GalwayLive is sold now as a "community paper", and it relies on what they call citizen journalism for content creation. Which is just a fancy way of saying they get people to do our work for free and put us out of jobs. You'd be surprised how many people are just happy to have their name in the paper. Except, you know, sometimes whatever poor fecker has been tasked with rifling through all the shite for something worth using sometimes fucks up. Excuse my French. It's probably the case that some young fellah on work experience was told to type out the details and upload the pictures. As well as my photos, we had an open call for photos from the fun-day for our readers. We put those yokes online – not in print. And that code you've just read to me lets me know it was one of them submitted pictures that you saw on our site. That's what "Sub" means – submitted.'

'And is there any way to know who submitted it?' I ask.

'Now there's a question,' Paddy says. 'Lookit, I'm in the office now and I've Maureen here beside me. Let me get her to have a look and I'll ring you back in a minute.' He's gone before I've even had the chance to answer him.

'Fuck,' I can't help but swear. 'I know this story is moving on, but I can't believe that picture might be a dead end.'

'There were always going to be dead ends, Izzy,' Tom says. 'If it was straightforward it would all have been solved years ago.'

I pull a face at him, feeling patronised and more than a little hungover on top of everything else. I need some more paracetamol and something to eat. I take a cold can of Diet Coke from the fridge, crack it open and take a long drink before popping two slices of bread in the toaster. I need carbs and I need them fast. I'm just taking the tub of margarine from the fridge when my phone rings again, flashing up the same 'International Number' display on the screen.

'Paddy,' I say on answering, automatically putting the call on speaker so Tom can listen in. 'That was quick.'

'Maureen here is some worker,' he says. 'I have an email address for you. Do you have a pen handy?'

'I do,' I say, and grab for a pen and paper from the countertop. 'Fire away now and tell me.'

'Grand so,' he says. 'It's a strange one. Right, it's DL180715 . . .' He pauses and repeats what he has just said, enunciating every letter and number perfectly. I'm not shocked to find my hands are shaking as I write.

'So that's at freemail dot com,' he says. 'Bloody odd name to be using to send an email don't you think? Does no one have a proper name these days?' I thank him for his time and end the call as quickly as I can.

Tom is grinning. 'So the person who sent the picture to GalwayLive using the name IrishEyes sent it from an email account with the same username as the person who posted the picture of Luca?'

'Looks like it,' I say, trying to take it all in.

'So it could be the same person?' he asks, his eyes wide.

'Yes. It could be.'

'Jesus Christ,' Tom says and sits down, rubbing his chin, his hand brushing against his stubble making a scraping sound. He shakes his head.

'This is fucking sick, Izzy,' he says, and he doesn't mean sick as in twisted — I know how he speaks. He thinks this is cool.

I just stare, too stunned to speak.

'Solid fucking gold,' he says. 'Never mind BAFTA,' he says. 'Can you say Emmy?'

Chapter Twenty-Eight

Nora

My hand throbs from the four stitches that were needed to piece the cut back together. The painkillers I was given in the hospital have only dulled it the tiniest bit. I think I've long since developed a resistance to many forms of prescription medication. There's always some sort of pain, physical or emotional, bleeding in around the edges.

Brendan's car is outside our house when we get home. There are more cars in the street than usual, ones I don't recognise, and as soon as I get out of DI Bradley's car, I can hear other doors open and the click of heels on the pavement. The press have landed.

'Just keep your head down and walk towards your house,' Bradley says, his hand on the small of my back. 'DS King will deal with matters here.' I don't nod, I just keep walking. I'm afraid to lift my head and look around, and I'm listening for the clicking of cameras as they capture my picture. The noise starts quietly at first. Just one person, a woman, calling my name. Then a man joins in, asking do I want to speak to BBC Northern Ireland. A cacophony of voices follows, male and female, questions and requests to face the camera. DI Bradley guides me onwards to the door, his hand firm enough to keep me moving. 'You're okay. Just keep walking,' he says close enough to my ear that I can hear him over the noise.

With trembling hands I fumble in my bag for my key as I hear DS King start to speak, her voice firm and authoritative. 'Under advisement from the PSNI, Ms Logue will not be talking to the press at this time. If you have any queries about the developments today, please direct them to the police press office. A press release will be issued shortly through the usual channels.'

'What measures are being taken to protect Luca Logue?' a voice calls out. It grates on me that they have his name wrong. They pretend to care but really they don't. He's a headline, just as Daisy was a headline.

My hand is still shaking too much to fit the key in the lock, so DI Bradley gently takes it from me and turns it. Despite being afraid of what mood Brendan might be in, I have never been so relieved to walk into my own house and out of the street.

The house – our home – is in silence. There's no *Paw Patrol* booming from the TV. No sounds of Luca's feet running across the wooden floor, or his sweet voice declaring that his 'tummy is hungry' and begging for a yoghurt or a cheese string. For a moment panic threatens to pull me under again. Is he gone? Has he been taken? Am I too late?

Then Brendan walks out of the kitchen, drying his hands on a towel. He doesn't look angry so much as totally worn out. 'Nora,' he says as he looks me up and down.

'Where's Luca?' I ask, my voice cracking.

'He's not here,' he says.

'Where is he?' I ask, louder, firmer this time. I'm aware of DI Bradley stiffening his stance beside me.

'I left him with Cassie,' he said. 'I thought it better he didn't come home to this circus.' There's the anger. It might have come in a low voice, one that is quiet, but it has come. I see it in how every muscle in his face is contorted with the effort of holding it in.

'And Cassie is?' DI Bradley asks.

'A family friend,' Brendan answers, but he doesn't look at Bradley. He keeps his eyes on me the whole time.

'Cassie used to work for Brendan,' I fill in. 'Now she looks after her grandchildren. She's a good person.'

'Mr Pryce, if you can give her details to my colleague DS King when she comes in that would be helpful,' DI Bradley says.

'It's hardly relevant. Luca won't be there for long,' Brendan says, flicking his eyes in Bradley's direction before returning his gaze to me. 'I'm taking him away until this dies down. I don't want him subjected to the media scrum outside, nor do I want him targeted by people online. I also don't feel it would be a good idea for him to witness his mother in such an . . . unstable . . . frame of mind.'

I wince at his words. I want to defend myself, of course, but I'm aware that I'm the woman standing here in my clothes and slippers, with one hand bandaged. I'm aware that he will have come home to find the study turned upside down, and if he has ventured upstairs he will no doubt have seen the loft ladder still down, perhaps with blood on it . . . signs that all is not well. I'm aware that just hours ago I was hallucinating, hearing voices, either real or imagined memories, and I was hitting myself in the head to try and stop them.

I don't have the mental or emotional energy to be a parent to Luca just now. Brendan knows it and that's why he's taking my boy from me.

I can't speak.

'Where are you proposing to take Luca?' Bradley asks, as I almost drift into the living room and sit down before my legs give way under me. Brendan and DI Bradley follow me into the room, and I hear DS King come through the front door. When she comes into the living room the first thing she does is pull the curtains closed and switch on the light.

'I wouldn't put it past some of those boys to point a camera through a window,' she explains. 'Some of the tabloids are there.'

I mutter a thank you and listen as Brendan says he will be taking Luca to his parents' holiday home on the Antrim Coast. 'This is not a proposition for the record,' he says. 'I am taking him. I've already packed what I need and as soon as I'm finished talking to Nora, we're leaving.'

'He'll be scared,' I mutter, and a tear slides down my cheek. That's what hurts the most. The thought of him, the thought of Daisy, being scared. The voice or the memory from the attic floods my thoughts again. 'No! Don't. I'm frightened.' I feel myself curl up as if I can protect this frightened child – my Daisy – from all bad things. It breaks me that I failed her.

'He's not a bit scared,' Brendan says. 'He thinks we're going on holidays and he gets to go to Nanny and Pop-pop's house near the beach. He has his trucks and his yellow bucket and he's happy as Larry.'

'He needs me,' I say, even though I know that's not true. Luca does not need me – a madwoman who doesn't even know her own mind. From the moment he was born and could breathe independently of me, Luca has always been better off away from me.

Brendan doesn't answer and I understand that. Anything he could say would be little more than a cruel truth.

'We will need those details as well,' DI Bradley says. 'We can inform local police and arrange for extra patrols to be conducted in the area.'

'It's halfway up a hill, overlooking the sea,' Brendan says. 'There are no patrols there to increase.'

'We'll work something out,' DI Bradley says. 'We've had a lengthy conversation with Nora today to try and ascertain if there is anyone who may hold a grudge towards your family and, in particular, if any of the usernames you may have seen on the forum seem to be of any significance.'

He shakes his head. 'We know why this is happening, DI Bradley. We don't need to look beyond Nora. People want to believe the worst, and this documentary involvement is ruffling feathers.'

'Daisy might be alive,' I say, trying to reach him.

He just looks at me for a moment, his expression pitying. 'I truly hope she is, Nora. I hope you find her. But Luca is definitely alive and he's been under your nose for three years and I don't think you see him most of the time.'

'That's not fair!' I say. 'I love him.'

Brendan just nods and the anger is gone and replaced with sadness again. 'You're right,' he says. 'It's not fair. Nothing about this is fair.'

Both DI Bradley and DS King stay with me until Brendan leaves. Both of them try to convince me that it might be an idea for me to stay somewhere else for a couple of nights too. They suggest a hotel, or even the Airbnb with Izzy and Tom, but the latter would cross too many lines and they have seen enough of me as it is. Plus I need time to think. I don't need a camera pointed in my face. As lovely as Izzy and Tom are, I have to remind myself they are not my friends. They are people here to do a job and ultimately their interests are their own.

In the end I'm relieved when the police go, urging me to lock all doors and keep all the curtains closed. They will send extra patrols around this area and I'm to phone 999 if I am concerned for my safety at all. Meanwhile, their tech team are doing their best to track 'The Four' so they can work out how big a threat I'm actually facing.

It would feel surreal if my entire life hadn't been a lesson in surrealism – particularly these last seven years. I wonder what it would be like to surrender to it. To challenge The Four, or DL180715 or any one of the other faceless posters on AmateurSleuths to do their worst. Maybe if they got their literal pound of flesh from me, they would leave Luca alone to get on with his life.

But we'd never know what happened to Daisy then, would we?

I pull the chain across on the front door and take the batteries out of the doorbell, and to my surprise a calmness that I haven't felt in a very long time washes over me. Brendan and Luca are gone. They aren't coming back tonight, or any time soon. I have the time, space and freedom to hunt through Daisy's belongings, and all the clippings and pictures I kept after her disappearance properly without fear that the door will open and my son or my husband will run in. I can be more methodical than I was earlier. I can revel in surrounding myself in traces of her.

Walking towards the study I notice the tsunami trail of papers and cards I had left on the floor and into the hall has gone. Pushing the door open I see that Brendan has obviously tidied up. The file boxes are neatly stacked once more, the drawers closed and the desk clear. Absolutely clear. Gone is my laptop, and the old desktop computer Brendan occasionally uses for work. It's safe to say they've not been stolen and that more than likely Brendan has taken them, or hidden them to leave me a very clear message. I can always access the internet on my phone but nonetheless, I feel my face redden. He is punishing me as if I'm a teenager who has lost her privileges.

A familiar shame envelops me, and I can't help but think of my father and the dictatorial teacher voice he used with me, too often forgetting that I was his daughter and not one of his pupils to be scolded. I shudder. It's a long time since I thought of my father. He may well be still alive but he hasn't factored in my life since I was eighteen when I, in a shaky handwritten letter, informed him I would not be going to university. That was enough for him to cut me off.

I leave thoughts of him and my sense of humiliation at Brendan's act of rebellion, and head for the attic, needing to be near her belongings again.

I stop still when I get to the top of the ladder and see the mess I left earlier is gone – all tidied away, back in boxes, taped up and pushed back in the corner. New boxes, boxes that had never been at this side of the attic before, now form a barrier to where Daisy's belongings are stored. The message is very clear: leave the past where it belongs. Anger surges towards Brendan, growing stronger. The thought of him touching her things, packing them away as if he were packing my grief away with them, makes me want to scream. So I scream, as long and as loud as I can, feeling the muscles in my throat strain with the effort.

There is very little to indicate there had ever been a storm in this room, and I realise that is what Brendan has always wanted. He wanted to be the white knight who rode in and helped me pack away the storm that destroyed my life. Who helped me build a new family. As if a new baby could replace the child I'd lost. Eventually my throat is too sore to scream anymore, my anger is replaced with a deep weariness. I want to cry but I'm spent. Exhaustion takes up residence in my very soul – so much that pulling away the wall of boxes Brendan has placed in front of Daisy's things is too much effort. I have neither the mental nor physical strength in me at this time. Slumping to the floor, I sit on the bare wooden boards and hold the bloodstained T-shirt from earlier to me.

The posts on AmateurSleuths say I don't deserve to be a mother. I was not fit for purpose. They said they'd take Luca from me and keep him safe.

It turns out they didn't have to try so hard. Here I am, alone, in this house with traces of the past hidden in boxes while my daughter is still gone, and her brother is far away with his father. A father who is so angry with me right now that I'm not sure he will ever be able to be anything but angry with me in the future.

I'm too tired to wipe away the tears that are sliding down my face. It's overheated and overly stuffy in this attic – the glare of the hot sun having warmed the slates above me. And in that hot room, against the warmth of cardboard and with my daughter's T-shirt still clasped in my hands, I feel myself start to drift off. It crosses my mind that it would be blissful to just drift off forever right now. I wonder if there are enough of the painkillers the doctor gave me to help me slide over into a sweet nothingness.

I wonder if any of our shared memories would still exist within her. I was told once that lasting memories are not really formed before the age of six. Everything before then can fade away. Even if Daisy is alive, so much of what we were to each other will have faded away into the dim past. That is the thought that breaks me as I start to drift off in my attic. In this moment the worst could happen – vigilantes could burn down my home with me in it for all I cared – and it would be a blessed relief.

I am in darkness but beneath me there aren't hard floorboards. I'm not cushioned by cardboard and as much as I reach my hands around I cannot find the T-shirt I had been cradling. There is noise, the same buzzing that has been pinching at me over the last few days. Is it inside me? Or is it real? I can't locate it or feel it. All I can feel is something cold and wet below me. For a moment I wonder if I have wet myself, having woken from an exhaustion – and painkiller – induced slumber to find I've lost my dignity. But it's not that. It's different.

In the darkness, shapes start to come into focus and it's the smell that strikes me first. Damp. Earthy. A mixture of something pure and something putrid. Looking down, I see it all over my hands, under my nails, ingrained into the whorls and swirls of my fingerprints. Claggy and dark.

I shiver, wondering how it is suddenly so cold when I had been lulled to sleep by the warmth in the attic. Not only is it bitterly cold, but it is also wet, the kind of wet that seeps into your very bones – and the ground is heavy with mud. That's the smell. A heady aroma of grass and bark mixed with the putrid smell of rotting fungus and animal excrement. I take a moment to register that my hand no longer seems bandaged, but it is still cut. It still aches. There is blood. Both my hands, in fact, are raw, my fingernails torn below their beds, my knuckles scraped. Rain, thick and heavy – what I always call fat rain – falls without taking its time to hit the ground. Tiny icy missiles of water bombing the unsettled earth, sending dirt and damp into the air and into my face.

I can taste the moisture in the air, and the dirt and the blood, and my throat is sore. So sore. Everything around me comes into focus now, the ground below me and how I have been digging and burrowing. Scraping and screaming. Terrified but unable to stop. I know I will see her face. I know I will find her. Or what is left of her. I know she is below the ground and the only way I can bring her home is to find her – whatever it takes. I cannot bear what awaits me but I can't leave her here. In the cold and the dark and the blood-slick mud. 'No! Don't. I'm frightened. Please! Please don't,' rings in my ears, along with a man's voice. Talking, talking, always talking and never listening.

He said she was here. That comes to me now. He said if I looked I would find her. He said it. And then he left me alone in the dark and the rain.

Scrabbling through the dirt, both craving and dreading, my hand brushing against something cold and rotted, I scream again but no one comes. No one helps. And then there it is, the soft flesh, just a glimpse of it. Stark white even in the darkness. My heart thudding, my stomach *sick to its very core, I start to brush away the dirt, and the twigs and the mud — desperation clawing at me in the same way I'm clawing at the ground. Even though I know it is too late. Even though I know she is gone.*

A face emerges. Young, beautiful, even in death. As pale as the moon. Eyes clouded. As the shocking reality of what I'm seeing settles in my very bones, I open my mouth and scream for help at the top of my lungs.

But all my scream does is wake me up and put me back in my attic and in the heat and the dark.

But I know it wasn't just a dream. I know it in a way I have never known anything before. It wasn't a dream. It was a memory. It happened. It really happened.

And the face in the dirt — it wasn't Daisy.

Chapter Twenty-Nine

Izzy

'Do you think I should call round to see if she is okay?' I ask Tom after I've tried to call Nora for the eighth time in two hours. I'm worried about her and, if I'm being honest with myself, worried about the possible impact on the documentary. But definitely more worried about her – given the pitiful state she was in when she left and how Brendan had spoken on the phone.

I'd tried to get an update of sorts from DI Bradley when I'd called him to pass on what Paddy McGilloway had told me about the DL180715 email address. He's playing his cards close to his chest though. When I'd asked if Nora was doing okay, he'd simply told me in a very efficient police officer way that she had received medical treatment for the injury sustained to her hand but it wasn't appropriate for him to comment further on her personal circumstances.

'She might not be at home,' Tom says. 'If I was her, I'd be doing whatever I could to get away from that house. The press are going to keep coming. I'd be moving out for the foreseeable. Especially if Brendan has taken Luca somewhere – which sounds like it was the plan. I'm not sure she should be on her own.'

'You don't think she's likely to have gone with Brendan and Luca?' I ask, even though I sort of know the answer to this already.

Tom raises an eyebrow at me. 'I really don't think so,' he says, before looking back at his computer screen.

I'm on edge though. Nora needs a support network around now – and I'm really not sure she has one.

'I think I might call round, just in case,' I say.

'Up to you,' Tom sniffs, and I wonder how he can seem so casual about it. Or maybe I'm just being too uptight about everything. Maybe I'm too invested and I need to remind myself that I'm not here to drive the narrative, simply to record it. I try calling her one more time, telling myself that if she doesn't answer I will back off until the morning and let this story play out with Tom and I as observers, even though I suspect we're now up to our necks in it.

As expected there's no answer and I regret my decision to let it play out, but I will stick to that. Instead, I'll throw myself and my ongoing hangover back into my work. It's hard though. I want to email the DL180715 account but I also know Maureen and Paddy shouldn't really have passed on that information (cheers GDPR) and I don't want to get them in trouble. DI Bradley has also advised me to let the police deal with the situation. I'm restless and my car keys glint in the evening sunlight, tempting me to get out of this house for a little while.

'Tom,' I say. 'Did that girl in the café ever call you?'

'Erm, what? No. Not yet,' he says. 'Why?'

'Because we have anonymous people claiming to know bad things that Daisy did and this girl also claims to have worked with her and she made that freaky "not the first" comment. I'd say it's worth looking at in more detail.'

'Hmmm,' he says, his eyes still stuck fast on his computer screen. 'If she doesn't call back I can maybe call into the café again tomorrow? It's a bit late in the afternoon now . . .'

He might think so, but my restlessness won't let me sit still and get on with the pile of research I should be doing.

'Are we still okay for the interviews tomorrow?' Tom asks. 'I have journalist Ingrid Devlin pencilled in at Shipquay Street for two and Sammy Harkin, the community volunteer from the initial search, pencilled in for four. Have you had time to refresh your research on both of them?'

'Yes,' I say, knowing I could definitely do with looking over that material again. 'I have it covered. But you know, I think I'm going to go out and about for a bit. Get a bit of fresh air. I need to blow away the cobwebs of this hangover.'

'What you need,' Tom says, finally turning to look at me, 'is some hair of the dog that bit you.'

'More alcohol?' I say, my stomach turning at the very thought. 'I can't think of anything less appealing. I'll opt for some fresh air.'

He shrugs. 'Lightweight. Look, it doesn't have to be a session but maybe we should have a glass or two tonight to celebrate another day well done.'

I normally drink maybe once a week at most. This would make three nights on the trot and I need to have a clear mind. 'I think I'd rather just get on with work,' I tell him.

'After you clear your head?' he says, his expression cynical at best.

'Needs must,' I tell him, lifting my keys and telling him I won't be long.

'Where are you going?' he asks as I head for the door.

'Just a drive,' I tell him, knowing even as I say it, that it's a lie.

The café is quiet by the time I reach it. It's almost five o'clock and when I push the door open to walk in a tired-looking woman with a ruddy complexion tells me they're closing soon and the best she can do me is a takeaway tea or coffee.

'We've a couple of scones there you're welcome to take with

you if you're not fussy,' she says with a smile. 'They'll be going in the bin otherwise. Everyone likes a fresh bake in the morning.'

'That's very kind,' I tell her. I had just been meaning to ask about Tom's mystery woman but I feel as if I have to at least order a takeaway coffee, and take some of the free scones in case refusal offends.

'Busy day?' I ask her as she sets to work on my latte.

'Always busy this time of year. Actually, it's always busy all year round. I shouldn't complain. Sure the days go faster when you're kept busy.'

'True,' I say with a smile. 'You'll be ready to sit down though. Must be hard being on your feet all day.'

'You get used to it,' she says. 'But still you're right, I'm looking forward to getting my shoes off and my feet up this evening. Just need to lock up first.'

I glance around and there doesn't seem to be anyone else here. I wonder if she's locking up all on her own. 'What has you in Derry anyway?' she asks, then pauses. 'Naw, hang on. I saw you talking to that big handsome English man in the street? The one making the documentary. He was telling me about it yesterday when he was in. Nora Logue. Awful business. Are you working on that film too or are you two doing a line?'

I choke. Doing a line? Is she asking me if we're on cocaine? She must notice the confusion on my face. 'Jesus.' She laughs. 'Derryism – I keep forgetting that means different things in different places. Are you a couple is what I meant?'

For some reason I blush, and shake my head. So Tom was talking to this woman – but he said the woman he was talking to had worked with Nora part-time when she first moved to Derry. This woman has a good twenty years on Nora – but I suppose it's still possible.

'Oh no. No. We're just colleagues. Are you the woman who worked with Nora when she was a teenager?'

She looks at me strangely. 'God no. I've never even met her.'

'But there's a girl who works here who did work with her?' I say. 'My colleague, Tom, said he was speaking to someone who worked here who told him they knew her from a Saturday job.'

She looks at me as if I'm speaking a different language. 'Naw, love. There's no one here who worked with that one. We all know each other well, and no one has ever mentioned it to me – and it wouldn't be like the other girls to keep secrets. Especially not when the bars are as juicy as that.'

'The bars?' I ask, this being my turn to look at her as if she is the one speaking the foreign language.

'The scandal. The craic, you know. The gossip?'

I nod thinking it's sad that this massive tragedy in Nora's life can be reduced to someone else's craic or gossip. 'That's strange,' I say. 'I could've sworn he said it was here he spoke to someone. When he came in for teas yesterday morning.'

'Oh he was in here all right,' she says. 'I served him myself. The other girls were jealous. We don't often get such a fine thing through our doors. Now, you will take a couple of scones won't you? You can share them with your . . . colleague.' She smiles and winks, mutters something about him not staying a colleague for long if she was working with him.

Me? I take my coffee and my scones and leave the café feeling more confused than when I arrived. Surely Tom hasn't lied to me? Why would he? There has to be a logical explanation.

Chapter Thirty

Nora

After scrambling down from the attic, I grab a piece of paper to write down what has come back to me, even though it is already starting to blur around the edges. My brain, rushing ahead of itself in a way that frustrates and annoys me, was filling in the blanks with unreliable details.

Already the face I saw is distorting and morphing into Daisy, when I'm sure – well, mostly sure – it was not Daisy I saw. But even now, moments later, that face is blurring and I can't seem to hold onto the details of her features. Apart from her eyes. Wide open, opaque in death, as if an internal light had been turned off. There's a familiar something there but I can't think why. I have never, to my memory, seen a dead person with their eyes still open.

Of course I've attended wakes, seen the dead laid out in their coffins, eyes closed and hands clasped in repose. I saw my own mother that way. Is this my brain's way of telling me I saw Daisy like this? Fear clutches at me now in a way unlike any other. Are these snapshots of memories that have been locked away or my mind playing tricks on me?

All these details that I don't know whether to trust or not.

Our brains do that, you know. They colour outside the lines, fill in details so we can make some sort of sense of things. Even if our memories are unreliable. They lift memories, stories we've heard, and bit parts of experiences we've had or been told about and splice them all together to help us try and make sense of something that is utterly disjointed. But it doesn't work. It doesn't fit right. It's like trying to fit the wrong-shaped jigsaw piece into a puzzle. You might achieve it, by cutting and squashing and reshaping, but step back from the table and the bigger picture is always going to be flawed.

But for now, flawed is all I have and I can't get the idea from my head that this might somehow be real.

Parts of it are. Something tells me that my digging in the dirt is real. Since waking it's almost like I can smell the earthy tones, the warm rain. I can feel the sticks and leaves and stones under my hands as I scrabbled through the topsoil. Behind the mundane sounds of my empty house — the ticking of a clock, the hum of the fridge — I can also hear echoes of noises that I have heard in another place and time. The distant hum of traffic. The thumping of my heart. My sobbing; pleading. A dog somewhere, barking. The splatter of the rain, growing heavier, against the ground, and pummelling the leaves on the trees above me.

Closing my eyes even now I can see my hands, and my arms and the ground, and I will my brain to bring more details to the surface. In my dream — no, in my memory — I was sure there was a man and he had told me she was here. But who is he? Did I know him before? Do I know him now? I will my brain to bring back to me the tone and cadence in his voice so I can identify him. The harder I try, the more impossible it gets. All I get for my effort are more faces swimming in front of me. Daisy's father Conal, Brendan — both men I know it can't be. God, I didn't even *know* Brendan then. My head hurts and I'm questioning myself and my memories again. What if I did know Brendan? What if I blocked him out? No. That's too crazy even for me.

There's only one thing I think that might help me to bring these voices into focus, and that's to go back to the woods, but the press are still outside and the last thing I want is for them to follow me. Maybe if I wait until later, they'll have gone. I can sneak out. This is not a big enough story for them to be here all night. They will have families, children of their own to go home to. Children they'll hold a wee bit closer, maybe.

I make myself a cup of coffee. Its taste is bitter on my tongue but I drink it anyway. As my hand starts to throb again, I eye the painkillers the doctors at the hospital gave. I can't think with the constant throb as the nerves in my hands protest at the stitches pulling my skin back together, but these painkillers are so lightweight I know they'll be worse than useless. I remember the co-codamol that are stashed at the back of the bathroom cabinet, left over from when Brendan hurt his back. If I take one, maybe two, I can clear my head and wait it out until the street outside goes quiet.

It's an easy decision to make.

Chapter Thirty-One

Izzy

There absolutely and categorically has to be a rational explanation for this. There's some legitimate mix-up because it's impossible that it could be anything but. Tom wouldn't lie. He has no reason to. But the woman in the café seemed pretty sure of her stuff as well and as far as I know she has no reason to fib either.

My hangover is now presenting as a constant pressure behind my eyes and it actually hurts to try and think about this too much, so I decide to come right out and ask him, then quickly decide that maybe I should be a bit more subtle. What will he think if I tell him I went to the café because I felt frustrated that this particular puzzle piece hadn't slotted into place yet? He hadn't seemed bothered not to have been called back. Would he think I was stepping on his toes? Or that I don't trust him?

But I don't want to piss him off. Not at the moment when this is all moving at a breakneck speed and when I need us to be working well together. I leave my free scones in the car in case he asks where they came from and go into the house, trying to decide how to slip the topic of the mystery café woman into conversation without letting him know I was snooping or making him feel as if I'm accusing him of something.

Tom is sitting, feet up, on the sofa, laptop on his knees, but he is staring into space. For once he doesn't have his earphones in.

'Penny for them?' I ask and he startles.

'Christ, I think I had totally zoned out there,' he says, shutting his laptop and swinging his long legs so he's sitting with his feet on the floor. 'I didn't hear you come in. Did your escape do you any good? You feeling any more refreshed?'

I grimace. 'I need carbs. And cheese, I think.'

'Pizza?' he says.

'Perfect. And this one is on me.'

'About time you put your hand in your pocket.' He grins, standing up. He's close to me now, standing in front of me, and suddenly I'm just really tired and more than a bit weepy, and I find myself imagining what it would be like to just let him hug me. That's what I want just now, a hug. Some hangover curing comfort. Not to have to ask this man who I thought I understood if he is lying to me.

But a hug wouldn't be the right move either. Not with Tom, so I decide to just go and get a shower instead. I rushed out of the house this morning without getting one, and I probably look like a hot mess – which is exactly how I feel. A good shower will allow me the peace and quiet to have the sob that I absolutely need, and hopefully will also wash away the hangover fear and allow me to emerge feeling human again, ready to ask awkward questions as we push forward with this incredible documentary. 'I'm going to go and stand under a hot shower for half an hour first,' I tell him.

'I was wondering where that smell was coming from,' Tom teases, but he doesn't step back from me. We exist in each other's space for a moment or two too long before I break away, and go and cry in the shower.

Three hours and four slices of pizza later, I am feeling much more like myself. I've avoided alcohol and settled for an ice-cold Diet Coke, which absolutely hits the spot. Rather than dissolve into self-pity, I refocused and threw myself into work. Tom and I have been working across the table from each other while we eat our pizza, bouncing ideas around, cross-checking our research for tomorrow's interviews and doing our best to try and find any mention or link to the number four, or four people close to Nora, or anything that might help solve the mystery.

The thread on AmateurSleuths with Luca's picture has been removed. Jacqs messaged to say it had been archived and simply hidden from public view. The moderators have been working with the police. They've also posted a pinned thread at the top of the board asking users not to speculate at this time as to identity of the posters. Accounts belonging to both The Four and DL180715 have not been suspended at the request of the police – who want to keep as many lines of communication as possible open.

Tom has suggested we get a moderator or two from the boards to speak on camera and we're currently trying to arrange that.

Even though I've yet to ask him about the café, because I'm still trying to think of a logical explanation, it has been a very constructive evening and the pizza has definitely made me feel better, if a little stuffed.

'I'm going to crack open a beer,' Tom says. 'Are you sure I can't tempt you?'

I laugh. 'I am sure. Beyond sure. I'm perfectly content right now in my little carb-induced endorphin bubble.'

He smiles. 'Well at least let's call it a night workwise. We've been on the go since the crack of dawn and if tomorrow is anything like today, we'll be grateful for some kind of rest.'

I nod. I'm tired anyway, and even if my head is full of ideas and thoughts, my body is definitely flagging a bit. I need to kick back, watch some rubbish on the TV that maybe distracts me from worrying about Nora and how she's doing.

We clear away the pizza boxes before relocating to the sofa. 'Netflix and chill?' Tom says with a wink.

'Can we just do the Netflix bit?' I ask him with a smile.

'You wound me, Izzy,' he says, his tone light, but there's something in his expression that makes the very pit of my stomach tighten. 'I'll have you know I am very skilled in the art of chilling.' His eyes darken just a little, or maybe I'm reading something into his teasing that isn't there.

'Tell me that isn't a line you've used before because, seriously, Tom. That's not going to cut it.' I smile again, but I can feel a blush rising in my chest.

'How do you know I don't just mean the regular, old-fashioned meaning of "chill"?' he asks. 'Izzy Devine, is your mind in the gutter?'

'Tom Walker, did you mean the regular, old-fashioned meaning of "chill"?' I ask, wondering if we are playing some kind of flirtation chicken.

He looks at me as if he's trying to decide just what exactly he does mean, but he doesn't speak.

'Netflix it is then,' I say, reaching for the television remote, but as I do, I feel his hand wrap around my wrist, stopping me. The warmth of his touch shocks me, as does the force of it. It's not just his strength – but suddenly there is no denying the charge of electricity between us. The feeling of his skin on mine sends prickles of desire through my body. It is completely unexpected and yet it feels absolutely as if this is how it should be in this moment.

'I think we should skip the Netflix and go straight to the chill. The newer meaning,' he says, his voice low and husky. I know enough about Tom to know he is a player. He has left a trail of smashed hearts and dropped knickers in his wake. He could charm the knickers off a nun. His free and easy way of talking to people, engaging with them, is irresistible. How he reveals just enough of himself to pull people in but not enough that anyone ever feels as if they really, truly know him. And when it comes to feelings – to any interactions above the physical – he isn't one to ever let his guard down. He's a closed book for all his apparent openness. But right now, with his skin warm on mine, his hand wrapped around my wrist creating the most intoxicating friction, and after the stress of the last few days, I don't care if this is the worst idea in the world.

'What do you think?' he says, looking directly into my eyes and holding my gaze. His grasp tightens a little and he pauses for a beat. It's long enough to allow the gasp of breath I have just taken to settle low in my lungs, the pulsing in the very pit of my stomach to send ripples of expectation and longing through the rest of my body. 'I think we could really do with chilling the fuck out,' he says as his grasp loosens, his thumb grazing across the pulse point in my wrist.

I need to feel his lips on mine, his hands in my hair. I need to feel his warm breath on my skin, as he whispers in my ear exactly what he will do to me. How he will take control. How he will own me. How I will take all of him, over and over again until he has had enough. I need to feel the trace of his tongue on my body, on my neck, my breasts . . . between my thighs. I want his hands on me, pulling me to him – caressing, groping and pinching me until I gasp. I want to feel the taut-ness of his skin. To feel his hardness. To hear his groans of pleasure. And in this moment, to my complete surprise, I want it all like I have never wanted anything before in my life.

If there is a part of me that knows I am crossing a line and letting my professional persona down, that knows I am breaking all my own rules about mixing business with pleasure, then it is silenced the very moment he kisses me. There is nothing wrong with wanting that bit of delicious, forbidden and dangerous pleasure.

I need it.

Fuck it, I deserve it.

We allow the stress of the job and the heightened emotions it has brought us to slip away as we lose ourselves in uninhibited, passionate sex until I'm not sure I can even remember my own name. It is raw and it is risky and we throw caution to the wind. I tell myself there is always the morning-after pill, but even if there wasn't I don't think I'd be able to stop myself from doing this. It's completely outside of my control.

It is everything I am not.

It is everything I need, that I hadn't even realised I needed, and neither of us wants to stop. But eventually – exhausted and sated – we fall asleep still tangled around each other, slick with sweat, in my bed.

Chapter Thirty-Two

Nora

I fell asleep while I waited for the journalists to leave, waking in pitch darkness to the silence of my house. It was too early, and too dark to go to the woods so I decided to wait it out until the first sliver of light drew itself across the sky.

Now, with the rest of the world still asleep, I find myself walking through the old wooden gate into the woodland. The only sound I can hear is my trainers crunching on the parched soil and twigs beneath my feet. It hasn't rained in at least ten days – nothing short of a miracle for these parts, even in summer. The ground is crying out for a good soaking, not knowing how to behave in such unfamiliar conditions.

This is the place that has haunted my dreams for seven years, but I haven't been here in almost as long – not since the last fingertip search. This is the place that brought me the most unbearable pain, when it used to bring Daisy and me so much joy. These woods were one of our favourite places to walk. They brought as much wonder to me as they did to Daisy and that's what brought us back here time and again.

I used to tell her they were magic and they changed shape every day. If I'm honest, there was a part of me that believed just that. There always seemed to be something new to discover that we'd never managed to find before. A little bridge over the smallest of streams, a half-built hut of sticks and twine that someone had clearly spent hours on. A new pathway we'd never found ourselves on before, winding to a new clearing that was unfamiliar to us. These paths, weaving their way between tall willow branches, seemed to me as if they appeared out of nowhere and no matter how often we thought we were following the same path, we always seemed to find our way out of the woods in a different place than where we had walked in.

I'd told Daisy it was a magical, fairy-inhabited space because I always believed childhood should be filled with mystery, wonder and a belief in the power of make-believe. Those times were so incredibly special to us. They were everything I thought childhood should be.

With a pang, I realise that Luca's childhood has been so very different. I've tried, God knows I have tried, but I've never told him of fairies and legends and portals to other realms. I no longer think magic makes childhood more special; it just makes it dangerous.

And now, thanks to me, he's in danger anyway. It feels as if I am cursed.

I shiver in the half-light, realising that I am at the tall concrete water tower not far from the entrance to the woods. At first glance you'd be forgiven for thinking it is just another tree reaching up towards the sky. The tall narrow concrete structure is no wider than the trunks of the ancient trees in the woods, and ivy winds its way around it as if trying to claim it for nature. It's only the presence of a padlocked door that forces your brain to adjust, to see it for what it is. I remember the first time I looked up and could see where the giant bowl mushrooms over the top of it.

'It looks like Rapunzel's tower,' I'd told Daisy, who was obsessed with the Disney movie *Tangled* and yearned for hair as long and strong as her heroine's. She'd begged me to go inside and had been so upset when I told her no, that it wasn't a safe place for little girls. She'd promised me she'd be very careful.

'Nothing bad is gonna happen, Mammy,' she'd said with the authority of someone ten times her age.

Oh, how I wish she'd been right.

Determination is set in my bones as I walk on. These memories are mine and I want them back. 'C'mon, Daisy,' I plead. 'Come back to me.' My frustration rises the more I walk, around and around in ever-decreasing circles. There are no secret hiding spots here anymore. No new paths emerging. Or new bridges over streams. There is what there always was, a few abandoned picnic sites, and a few discarded crisp bags that stick out like sore thumbs even in the half-light of the early morning sun. They are not of this place and they shouldn't be here.

I should not be here.

Daisy should not be here.

But something claws at my mind, making my head spin. As I try to walk on, I feel a wrench on my cardigan and I'm back seven years ago, and there is a tugging and a crying and a 'Mammy! No.' In the here and now, I flip around, sure that I'll see her, so sure in fact that I reach my hand out, certain I'll feel hers in mine. But she's not here, of course, and it's just a branch that my cardigan has snagged on but the memory – that's real. I know that's real. Her pulling at me, or being pulled from me? And the 'Mammy! No' and the dirt on the ground, the rain and the mud, and blood – my blood. 'You should've been more careful,' a voice echoes. A woman's voice this time. 'You brought it on yourself.'

'Maybe you didn't look hard enough. She's there. Where you

left her. You know that. You were always careless and clueless,' a man's voice chimes in.

'But I didn't leave her,' I shout into the open space. No one answers for a moment, then the chorus of blame and threat and 'Mammy! No' starts up again.

I can't place these voices, these people, but I know – just like Daisy – they are not here now. They are from then. A sea of faces swim in front of my eyes and I can't tell if any of them are real or if I am surrounded by ghosts. I shiver, remembering how these woods are in the grounds of the old mental hospital. We're all a little closer to crazy than we may care to admit.

Wishing the voices would quieten down, I try to focus on what feels most vivid. If only I could pull the real memories from the insanity. Slumping to the ground, I press my hands into the dry dirt again. If I can immerse myself in the sounds and textures, I figure I've a chance. Closing my eyes, I focus on what is real – adapt a technique I was given to help combat panic attacks. Things I can feel – the cool soil beneath my hands. The grit of stones and twigs. The silky smoothness of a leaf. Things I can smell – the morning dew, fresh air, the unique smells that come from nature, floral and woody mixed together. And what can I hear – the rustle of leaves against the slightest of breezes. A scampering – probably a squirrel running for cover. I am here. I am present. I am ready.

The ringing of my phone startles me, making me swear. I answer without looking at the screen first, figuring it's probably Brendan: no one else would call me this early in the morning. If he's calling at this time then he must be angry or worried about something. Most likely Luca has had a bad night. No matter how much he loves his daddy, and how this will have been pitched to him as a big adventure, he will have found the events of the last twenty-hours unsettling. He'll be wondering why I'm not there with him.

I startle when an unfamiliar male voice starts to speak. 'You're out on your own very early this morning, Nora.'

Pulling my phone from my ear, I glance at the screen and see the words 'Unknown Caller'.

'Who is this?' I ask, trying to keep my voice light, but I feel a lead weight settle in my stomach. Whoever it is somehow knows I'm not at home. I glance around me. Am I not alone here?

'Very foolish to be out walking in the woods when it's still so early. No one much around. No one who can hear you, anyway. Bad things happen in the woods in the early hours, Nora. Don't you remember?'

Scrambling to my feet, I look around. 'Who is this?' I ask again. I curse the panic that is leaking into my voice, giving him all the power.

'Ach, Nora, you know who I am. We go way back, don't we? Way, way back.'

'You'll have to give me more than that to go on,' I say, and the tremor in my voice is even more obvious now. I peer around, but I can't see anyone past the ghosts that are back swimming in front of my eyes.

'I'm hurt, Nora. Did we mean so little to each other?' The voice is low and gravelly. Muffled a little. Maybe even intentionally distorted in some way.

'It's not a good line,' I say. 'I can't hear you properly.'

'I thought, given what we've been through, we'd be unforgettable to you. We've been through so much together. It hurts me that you don't remember us.'

We? Us? What is this man talking about? I am not in the mood for game-playing, for whoever this is to be getting his kicks from my pain and confusion. That's when it comes to me.

'The Four,' I mutter.

203

'Oh, you're quick,' he says. 'I'm impressed. Then again, you always were a smart one.'

'Just tell me what you want,' I say. 'And if you have my girl, tell me. Tell me where she is!'

'Now, Nora, patience really is a virtue. We've waited all this time, what's a little bit longer among friends?'

'I don't know who you are, but I can assure you that you are not my friend,' I snap. 'I don't know what sick game you're playing but you're playing with the wrong person. You can't break me any more than I've already been broken.'

There's a sniff that might be a snort. 'I think we both know that's not true,' he says. 'People can always be broken just a little bit more. We thought, years ago, that we had been broken too but you know what? There was more to come. That's the thing with trauma, Nora. It doesn't go away, it just goes into hiding for a bit.'

'Just tell me where she is,' I plead, my voice cracking. Desperation is digging its claws into me. 'I'm sorry for whatever trauma befell you, but I can assure you it was nothing to do with me. I've led a quiet life. I've not hurt anyone. I just want my girl back, and if you can't give her back to me then please just tell me where she is. Let me find her.'

The image flashes across my eyes of my child, alone some-where. In some shallow grave. I think of the unthinkable cruelty of killers who have refused to reveal where they buried their victims. Killers who have denied families a proper burial, a final resting place to visit. It twists something inside me and I can't help but think of the mother of Keith Bennett – one of five children murdered by the Moors Murderers – and how she went to her grave never knowing where he was. And of the families of the disappeared here in Northern Ireland, never knowing where their loved ones met their end at the hands of the IRA during the worst of the Troubles. Although I can't bear to think of her as dead, I could at least find some comfort in knowing I had laid her to rest properly.

'You know where she is, Nora. You were there with us that day. We know you told everyone you can't remember what happened, but we've never bought that. You just wanted to absolve yourself of all blame. You like doing that, don't you, Nora? You like letting others face the consequences of your actions.'

Doubt creeps in again.

'I don't know what you're talking about,' I sob. 'I don't remember. If I did she would be with me. I don't know what you think you will achieve but I don't deserve this,' I blurt, the unfairness and pain erupting from me. 'No mother deserves this and Daisy doesn't deserve this. She was just a child. Just four. I wouldn't have hurt her. I wouldn't have it in me.' I say it loud and strong, and part of me wonders if I truly believe it or am just trying to convince myself.

'Come on,' he says, with a derisive laugh, and I think I can hear footsteps crunch through the dried detritus on the woodland grounds. 'You know you don't truly believe that. We've all seen how it's well within your power to hurt people. Given the right circumstances, we can all do the unthinkable. And some of us, Nora, are just programmed wrong, aren't we?'

I continue to look around me, my head spinning now. Swaying, I lean against a tree to steady myself. I'm hyperventilating now, my breath coming in small, shallow gasps. I can't breathe. I didn't hurt anyone. I know I didn't hurt anyone. My knees are starting to buckle under the weight of these accusations. I cannot live like this anymore. I can't endure it.

'Please,' I beg, tired to my very bones. 'If you know where she is then just tell me. That's all I want. I don't need your name. I don't need revenge. I don't want to talk good and bad with you, I just want her.' I'm sobbing now. Huge racking sobs, bending me in two. A convulsion of grief. 'You're cruel. This is cruel.'

There's a pause and I wonder whether this bastard has gone, leaving me here scared and broken, but just as I'm about to take my phone from my ear to check if the call is still connected I hear his voice again.

'You would know all about cruelty, wouldn't you, Nora? You saw it every day and you turned a blind eye. As long as it didn't affect you, you didn't give two damns. How many people, Nora, did your silence hurt?'

I have rattled him now. I can hear it in his voice, even though it is distorted and the line is poor. I can hear his cool superiority has gone, replaced by anger and something else – something I'm only too familiar with.

Pain. But I honestly, in my heart, have no idea what this man is talking about.

'I don't know what you think I did wrong to you, but I have never intentionally hurt anyone in my life and I'm sorry if you feel I did. Please, I just need my girl. You don't understand—'

'No!' His voice is loud, authoritative and I swear I hear it not only through the phone but booming through the forest. He is near. Within shouting distance. My heart beats faster, my body pulsing with grief and adrenaline and fear.

'It's not me who doesn't understand, Nora!' he shouts, dropping the us now – this is his anger and it is terrifying. I can hear the echo of an undistorted voice bounce off the nearby trees. Feeling as if I am surrounded, I try to follow the sound but it is nowhere and everywhere all at once. 'You stand there giving me an insincere half-apology,' he bellows. 'You're sorry if *I feel like* you did something wrong! I don't just feel it. I know it. I've lived with it every day. And it's a burden that has destroyed me.'

The playfulness and control is gone from his voice. His pain is fuelling his anger. 'You court a TV production company. You want to benefit from your loss? To play the victim again? How dare you! How fucking dare you!' It has moved beyond shouting to roaring. I can feel the force of it even through the phone, and I pull my head away from the earpiece, wincing at the volume of his voice.

'It's ironic that you of all people have never learned her lesson,' he says. 'And it's up to us to drill that lesson into you. You tell me that you aren't capable of hurting people – not intentionally . . .' There's a beat, and an inhalation of breath. I know before he speaks that what he will say next will forever change my life. I feel it in me as much as I feel the dirt beneath my feet and the splinter in my hand from scrabbling in the twigs and detritus to stand up.

'You have to choose, Nora. It's as simple as that. Who will it be? Daisy or Luca?'

My stomach twists. 'What? What do you mean? I don't underst—'

'Daisy or Luca?' he asks again. 'Who do you think should live?'

A force akin to a blow to my chest knocks the air from me. Who should live?

'You can't ask me to make that choice,' I blurt. 'How can I make that choice? How could any mother?'

'Terrible isn't it?' he says, sardonically. 'But you already have the answer, even if you are too much of a coward to admit it to yourself.'

'No,' I stutter. 'That's not true.'

'It is, and you know it. Do you really think you haven't been watched this whole time? That it's not been clear that poor little Luca could never measure up to his big sister?'

'I love my son,' I say, even though I know that while that's not a lie, it's not the whole truth either. I love my son but, and

God forgive me for saying this, a part of me hates him too. The realisation hits me like a tonne of bricks. I love him for who he is but I hate that he is not her. I hate that I have to mother him when I can no longer mother the first baby I gave birth to. The one who made me a mother in the first place. I hate that I have to relive all those firsts and special occasions with him when all they do is remind me of when it was with her – and each one reminds me that sometime, not that far away – their lives will diverge completely. He will do new things – big things. He will go to school and learn to read and write. He will make friends and go to sleepovers and move on to big school. He'll sit exams, fall in love, learn to drive and travel the world – but she is frozen as a four-year-old. Forever.

'If you love him, then choose him.'

I can only answer with a sob. 'I can't. I need them both.'

'We don't always get what we want, Nora. Sometimes we have to trust that what we get is what the Lord wants for us.'

'God has nothing to do with this. There is no God in you. Only the devil,' I spit.

'Each of us has God in us. You of all people must remember that. So be not afraid in making your choice. God will not forsake you.' His voice is thick with sarcasm and I don't know how to take him. I don't understand any of it.

'Just give me my child back!' I scream, so loudly and with such force that I can feel the soft tissue of my throat stretch and tear. A metallic taste – blood – fills my mouth and I retch onto the arid ground.

I have dropped my phone now but it's not far enough away that I don't hear him speak. 'You have to decide, or we can decide for you. Choose one or lose both.'

As the full horror of his words hits me like a punch to my stomach I want to scream at him to take me instead. But he has ended the call already and I am screaming into the void. I can't even call back. I have no one to turn to. But at least, I think, at least Brendan and Luca aren't here. They aren't at home. They are safe, miles away. Except, of course, I've not heard from them since they left and this man, this man who isn't working alone, has been watching. If he saw me leave the house, and was able to follow me here then maybe he saw Brendan and Luca leave too. And if he saw them leave, could he have followed them as well?

Chapter Thirty-Three

Izzy

When I wake in the morning, I am alone. The sheets are cold and the house is quiet. I allow myself a minute or two to replay the events of the previous evening. To allow myself to savour the rawness of my skin where his stubble rubbed against my face when we kissed. To explore the delicious aches that exist within me. To curse myself for being so fucking careless with contraception. Jesus, the risks we take when we're horny.

Lifting my phone, I see it's not long after seven. So I've got time to get up, have a long, hot shower, get some breakfast and make myself look like a totally in-control professional before the chemist opens and I can get my hands on the morning after pill.

After getting dressed, I go into the kitchen and peer around, beginning to feel confused. The room is empty. Gently, I tap on Tom's bedroom door and expect to hear him, his voice thick with sleep, call back to me. But there's silence. I pause for a moment, wondering whether to just leave him, but it's now past eight and we really should be making moves to see what is going on with Nora.

Maybe it would be okay to wake him to ask if he wants a

coffee or tea, I reason, before tapping on the door and calling his name again. Once more there's no answer. Frig it, I think. Throwing caution to the wind I turn the handle and push open the door. It surprises me to see light when I fully expected the room to be in darkness. Pushing the door wider, I see that his bed is not only empty, but neatly made, too.

I check the living room and kitchen again and even the garden for traces of him. Perhaps he has made a coffee and is sitting out enjoying the morning sun.

But the back step is clear, as is the little bistro set on the patio. He must've gone out for milk, or croissants or something like that, I tell myself, but an uneasy feeling is washing over me.

I tell myself I need to wise up. That I'm a woman in my thirties and not a lovesick schoolgirl and sex is sometimes just sex – no matter how good it is. He won't have done a runner as if I'm a silly one-night stand. We're working together for God's sake. Up to our eyes in the project Tom thinks will win him his BAFTA, no . . . win him an Emmy.

I decide to distract myself by doing some work. I'll call Jacqs and then Nora. I'll leave a message for DI Bradley or DS King to call me back and let me know if either of them is now willing to go on camera to discuss the threat. I wonder if and when they will be releasing that information to the media at large. No doubt the baying crowds of eager hacks will have been torturing the press office since Nora's post yesterday. If the threat the police received gets out, I can only imagine the media scrum that will ensue. It will make yesterday look like a walk in the park. Part of me hopes Nora is indeed packed away somewhere safe with Brendan and Luca.

But maybe I should phone Tom just to check all is okay, or would that be too needy? It's closer to eight thirty now and it seems strange that he's still out. Would he think I'm being clingy because we slept together or would he be okay with it? Because I'm absolutely not being clingy. I know what this is.

Damn it! I hate that I'm questioning myself now because we threw caution to the wind. I'm about to launch into a prolonged period of self-loathing when I hear a key turn in the door and there he is with the milk I suspected he had gone out for.

I smile at him – a small awkward smile that screams 'we had sex last night and we're work colleagues and I've no fucking idea what this means for us'.

'Morning,' he says, with his usual cockiness. 'I trust you slept well? And are ready for another day hard at it?'

He must know there could be a double meaning to his words. I sense he is trying to unnerve or embarrass me. The cockiness that I found so irresistible last night is less than desirable now. Well, I won't let him win at this.

'Yes, I slept well and yes I'm ready for another busy day of work. I'm going to check in with both Nora and DI Bradley, and I think that will colour the day for us.'

He nods. 'Good plan. You want a brew?' he says, switching the kettle on.

'I think I'll call round to Nora's, actually, rather than phone. Just in case she has her phone off, you know.'

'Give me fifteen minutes and I'll come with you,' he says, 'bring the camera. If there's a crowd there . . .'

I feel a flicker of frustration. I want to also use it as an opportunity to nip to the chemist without him knowing. For some stupid reason, I feel a bit embarrassed about it. 'I don't want to overwhelm her,' I lie. 'So, what if I go and get the lay of the land first. If I think there's footage outside her house, I'll call you. She might respond better if it's just me at the door, you know?'

'If you really think so,' he says. 'You're the boss. Right, well, I'll go and get set up at the townhouse then.'

'Why don't you call into the café again?' I say innocently. 'See if that girl who you were talking to is working today. It would be nice to get some more information from her, especially in light of everything that happened yesterday?'

'Great idea,' he says without even a moment's hesitation. 'Maybe if I'm there in person I can use the old Walker charm to get her to open up without waiting for a phone call that might never come.'

'What café was it again?' I ask. 'The one just next door to the townhouse? Wee Buns, or whatever it's called?'

'That's the very one,' he says. 'Actually I might pick up some buns while I'm there. I need to work out this Derry obsession with baked goods.' He's grinning and in a great mood even though I know now, without a shadow of a doubt, he is lying to me.

Chapter Thirty-Four

Nora

I clamber to my feet, try desperately to hit Brendan's number on my phone, but my hands are shaking so much I can barely breathe, let alone hit the screen in the exact right place to make a call connect. Cursing, I try my best to catch my breath and steady myself, while at the same time fighting off a rising panic.

Is this mystery man still watching me? Who is he? And who are the others he has mentioned? His 'we'. And could he or they really, truly hurt Luca or take him from me? Seven years ago I'd have told you these things don't happen, not in real life. But I've learned that the monsters under the bed are real, and life has never been the same since and it never will be again. The fear is always, always here and this proves I have been right to be on my guard.

I walk, then break into a run, moving through the forest and waiting for the call to Brendan to connect. I just want to hear his voice. I want to talk to Luca. I want to know they are okay. Why in God's name did I not call them both last night to check they were settled and safe? The pause between my finally managing to hit the right number and it connecting seems interminable. I want to scream in frustration but something deep inside tells me I need to save my strength. A storm is coming. I can feel it building, not only in the heat around me but in the burning rage inside me.

How dare this man come into my life and try to force me to choose. I'm not a monster. Or at least, I don't think I'm a monster. The image of blood on my hands and the sound of my daughter's cries tears at me again. I want to pull it from my head, rewind seven years, more even. To wrap Daisy in cotton wool and keep us safe and secure in our home. As I step on a mound of twigs, my ankle twists and I stumble, swearing, loudly, drowning out the first ring of my phone connecting with Brendan's. Despite the pain rippling through my foot, I stop dead in my tracks, force myself into silence. The phone rings. And rings. And rings.

But there's no answer before it switches over to his voicemail message.

'Fuuuuuuck!' I shout, hitting redial and listening to the same rhythmic trill of his unanswered phone, followed by the same click and connection to his cheery voicemail.

'Hi, this is Brendan . . .'

I want to weep with frustration until I think of the time and it crosses my mind that maybe, just maybe, he's still asleep and his phone is on silent or Do Not Disturb and I'm panicking too much.

But there is no such thing as panicking too much. Panicking too little, yes. That's a thing. With just that thought I'm spun back in time to seven years before. To a memory of my walking through the woods, alone. The sun warm on my face. A smile playing across my lips as I sing-songed 'Daisy! Come out, come out wherever you are,' popping my head around trees, looking down into the hollow below. There was no panic then. Not at first. It was a game. At first it was a game.

Hide-and-seek.

Is that what this sick bastard was playing with me now? 'WHO ARE YOU? SHOW YOURSELF!' I scream, my voice cracking with the effort. I want him in front of me, to tear into his skin with my fingernails. I want to tell him he's a fucking monster. Ask him why. Ask him where my daughter is. Hit and kick and score my pain into his face with my nails until he tells me. Hell may have no fury like a woman scorned, but that fury is only multiplied when it belongs to a wronged mother.

There's no response from the man who has been taunting me. Of course there isn't. He's probably someone utterly content to hide in the shadows. A pervasive, disgusting evil person who is ultimately a coward. My fear pulses in my veins now, fighting with anger for first place.

The only sound I hear is the useless ringing on Brendan's phone as I try to call him one more time, only for it once again to go through to his voicemail. Unable to hide the fear in my voice, I sob a garbled message down the line. I don't want to scare him unduly, but I need to warn him. 'Brendan, please. I need you to call me as soon as you get this. I know you're mad at me but it's really important we talk. I need to know you are both okay and I need you to be careful. Don't let Luca out of your sight. Not even for one second. I don't want to scare you, Brendan, but this is important. Please, call me.'

I hang up, deciding to go to my car and drive straight to Brendan's parents' holiday home. It's on the Causeway Coast, between Portrush and Portstewart. If I hurry I can be there in maybe ninety minutes. I can keep trying to get through while I drive. He has to pick up.

My ankle still throbbing, I hobble back out through the clearing. Looking all around I see no sign of anyone else. No car. No lone walkers. No one to scream at or chase after, even though I'm not sure I could run if I wanted to. I've only thought I've been broken before, but the truth is I am in pieces now in a way I never even thought would be possible. If it wasn't for my need to find Daisy, and my fear for Luca, I would give up.

'If it's me you want to hurt, then take me! Hurt me! Do whatever you want to me. They're just children!' I scream, my legs finally giving way under me as grief fells me. 'They're just children!'

I don't know if what flashes in my brain is real, or a memory, or an exhausted mind trying to make sense of what is utterly incomprehensible, but I'm sure in that moment I hear a voice – the man from the phone, though his tone is still distorted – say very calmly in my ear: 'We were all children once.'

Chapter Thirty-Five

Izzy

As I'm queuing to speak to the pharmacist, I send a quick WhatsApp to Nora.

'Hey Nora, could you let me know how things are? I hope you are doing okay, and Brendan and Luca too of course. I don't want to overstep, but am worried about you.'

I can't help but watch my screen, waiting for the two blue ticks to appear to let me know she has seen and read my message, but they stay unlit and the queue slowly moves on. Until I'm forced to put my phone back into my bag to sort out my own business.

It's just after half nine when I get back to the car, and my message remains unread. I can't help but feel deeply uneasy about it all. Coverage has started to hit the internet – reports of Nora's angry post. Rumours that this could be a strong indication that Daisy may actually still be alive. Or, if you believe Nora's haters, just another attempt at grabbing attention. I see my documentary mentioned on one news site, the comments providing in-depth judgement on the 'ghoulish nature' of true crime documentary makers.

'I bet they are paying Nora a fortune. They're probably paying her to stir this all up now. Makes for a better end product for them, doesn't it?'

I click out of the site before I'm tempted to do a Nora myself and write an angry response. I call her number again and this time it switches to answerphone after just four rings. She must have rejected my call.

Deciding to call Jacqs, I tap her name and wait for the call to connect. If this one goes straight to answerphone then I'm going to start to take all this rejection personally. Thankfully, Jacqs answers on the second ring, her breathing heavy.

'I'm just out walking the dog,' she starts. 'Well, not exactly walking. He's dragging me up this fecking hill. If I have a heart attack and die I give you full permission to make a "When Pets Become Killers" style documentary about it all.'

I laugh, my heart immediately just a little lighter to hear someone sound so normal. Well, normal for Jacqueline, anyway.

'Hey, Jacqs,' I say. 'Are you okay to talk then? I don't want to contribute to your respiratory distress.'

'Hang on,' she says, and I hear her call Bonnie, her beloved Lab, and promise her a treat if she's a very good girl. There is some muffled background noise and then I hear a sigh of relief. 'Right. Grand so. We're in the dog park so she can run around to her heart's content now without me getting the evils from the anti-dog brigade. You'd think she was a sabre-toothed tiger the way some people react to her coming within ten foot of them. But anyway, fill me in. What's the latest?'

For the first time since I've known Jacqs, I hesitate. I'm not sure what it is that is holding me back but suddenly it all feels a little sensitive to be blurting out everything that has happened since yesterday morning to someone I've never actually met in real life.

'Well, it's all a bit full on,' I tell her. 'As you can imagine yesterday's post was like kicking a hornets' nest. The media have been all over it.'

'The cops too, I imagine?' Jacqs says and I know I should tell her about the threat. Before the last few days there is no doubt in my mind that telling her about the message received by the police, Nora's disjointed memory and Brendan's anger is exactly what I would've done. In fact, I'd have done it as soon as Nora left with the police yesterday, but there is something holding me back even now.

'You know the police; they don't seem to want to tell me anything,' I say, feeling bad for keeping the juiciest elements back from her. 'But yes, they were with Nora yesterday. I think they spoke to both Nora and Brendan.'

'And you saw her too? How is she? Don't hold out on me, Izzy! It's amazing to have the goss direct from the horse's mouth. Not that I'm saying you're a horse, of course.' She laughs a little and I see this for what it is to Jacqs, and to the people on AmateurSleuths. This is entertainment. Livestreaming of real drama right in front of their eyes.

This is the kind of adrenaline kick that has me so addicted to true crime documentaries and podcasts. It's the story, the drama, the twists and turns. We all kid ourselves that it's because we care about the real people behind the scenes, but the truth is, we rarely do. Not to any meaningful extent anyway. And it's not because we're bad people – it's just that it's hard to think of the true, horrific reality of these situations. Most true crime addicts will never have to sit and look Nora Logue in the eyes, or bear witness on any real level to her unspeakable pain. It's different then.

At least that's what I tell myself as I answer Jacqs. 'Well, she's as you would expect her to be. Unsettled and angry.'

I don't mention the cut on her hand, or the worry she'd 'done something bad'. I don't say how angry Nora thinks Brendan will be. I keep all of this to myself.

'Do you think,' Jacqs says, 'that rant she posted shows she has the potential to become totally irrational about it all? Like, actually lose the plot?'

There is a tone to Jacqueline's voice that lets me know this is exactly what she would like to hear. Of course she would. It would make for a killer twist in the story. Or it would feed the belief that Nora might actually have lost the plot a long time ago – and lost it enough to have indeed done something bad.

'God, I don't know,' I say, which is true. 'But I don't think anything about how she would or could behave at the moment could be deemed irrational. She's under intolerable scrutiny.' Guilt pulls at my conscience, given that I'm one of the people holding her under that scrutiny.

'I suppose,' Jacqs says and she sounds deflated. 'No one on the boards seems to have a clue what or who "The Four" is or what it could mean. They are looking though – not that there is a lot to go through. You know as well as I do Nora led a very unremarkable life – never in trouble, flew under the radar. She just got on with things. Boring really.'

'We have to be missing something,' I say. 'If Nora herself knows what this is about, she's hiding it well and that would make her a complete sociopath. I get a lot of different vibes from her, but sociopath isn't one of them. If whoever is behind this is a troll, they are putting extreme effort into their trolling. But if it's someone who really knows what became of Daisy, what reason would they have for risking their identity becoming known now? Why after seven years?'

'I could ask some of the tech geeks in the groups to look into VPNs and ISPs. They have ways of doing things that maybe aren't strictly legit, but you never know, they might trace something?' Jacqs muses, and I suppose it's an option. AmateurSleuths attracts a fair number of computer nerds who claim to have the power to hack sites and untangle web code. But that still brings us back to why whoever is doing this is doing it now of all times.

I tell Jacqs that would be great and I'd appreciate it, before lying that I've another call coming through and ending our chat. I don't feel good about keeping information from a friend but I don't want everyone to know just how fragile Nora is right now. At least that's how I justify it to myself and when my conscience nags at me again, telling me that my documentary might just be what has dragged the bad guys out of the woodwork in the first place, I shake it off.

One last glance at my phone shows me Nora still hasn't picked up my message. Maybe she's deliberately keeping me at a distance like I'm now doing with Jacqs. Maybe Brendan has forbidden her from talking to me again. My chest tightens at the thought. Okay. I told Tom I was calling round there and that is exactly what I'm going to do. It's much easier to switch your phone off or ignore a message than it is to ignore an actual real-life person standing at your own front door.

When I turn into the cul-de-sac where Nora and Brendan live, I see further evidence that the world is waking up to this story. It's crazy that just a few feet away, there is nothing to indicate a massive breaking story involving one of the most talked about missing child cases in recent years is happening right here. But one turn of a corner and everything is different. I park and get out of my car, taking in what's in front of me. It's not quite a media scrum – but it's one in training. Cars are parking all along the footpaths, some half on the kerb. Journalists stand in huddled groups. Men in suit jackets, casting withering glances at the sun, hoping for once that the weather eases. Women in neat dresses and tailored trouser suits. Hair perfectly coiffed. Ears to phones chatting animatedly.

Close by, less groomed and less constrained by the formal wear required for on-camera chat, are the photographers and camera people. A few of them are eating ice lollies, enjoying the sunshine and the atmosphere that only ever comes with a big story. I watch as they all swarm around an older woman, two young children in tow, as she walks out of the garden of a neighbouring house. A cacophony of camera clicks and questions. The woman putting her hand in front of her face. One of the children crying. She says something, shaking her head and then hurrying the children – her grandchildren maybe – along.

Watching from this distance I see how the feeding frenzy looks. It makes me feel deeply uncomfortable. Again a part of me hopes that Nora is nowhere near this place, and is off somewhere with her family getting the support she needs.

The street goes quiet. The media resuming their original positions and their small talk.

'They've been there since nine,' a voice from behind me grabs my attention. I turn back to see the same neighbour from yesterday standing, hands in his pockets watching the scene. 'The neighbours don't like it. The footpaths being blocked. Not being able to nip out to the shops or the park without being set on.'

I nod to acknowledge that he is talking to me, just as I remember my last interaction with him was to tell him to fuck right off. I blush a little.

'I suppose you're one of the them,' he says. 'I know you said you were her friend, but really . . . I know what goes on in this street and I've never seen you before yesterday and here you are again today. Snooping about.'

'I'm not snooping,' I say defensively. 'I'm here to check on Nora and see how she is. You can see why I'd be concerned.'

He sniffs. 'She's not in. Went out early, when it was still dark. Hasn't come home.'

'And Brendan?' I ask, figuring in for a penny in for a pound.

'Took the wee man and off they went yesterday. He didn't look happy. Face on him like a slapped arse.' He recounts his story with enthusiasm.

I nod again, but feel a stirring of unease. I'm getting all the shitty vibes from him, but I can't quite pinpoint why. Maybe it's because he's standing in judgement of the media, when he seems to spend his life watching the comings and goings on this street and making note of all the details.

'I might go and knock on the door, just in case,' I say.

'Good luck. You'll not get through. There's a cop down there. In the unmarked car. Can you not see it? He's been chasing away anyone coming near the door.'

I'm not sure how I'm supposed to recognise an unmarked police car, but I look down the street anyway.

'Look,' he says. 'I'm only telling you this so you're not wasting your time. The Logues are gone and given all this carry-on, I wouldn't guarantee they'll be back. It'll be no bad thing in my book.'

'And you are?' I ask again, hoping he might just give something more away today than he did yesterday.

'I told you, I'm a neighbour. That's all you need to know, Izzy. Now, if you don't mind, I've things to do.'

He nods a curt goodbye and turns, walking in the opposite direction away from the crowd.

He's just turning at the top of the street when it hits me that he said my name. I never told him my name.

Chapter Thirty-Six

Nora

I dial through to DI Bradley's office, my heart thumping so hard I'm afraid it will burst right from my chest. I'm going to drive to Brendan and Luca, of course, but I need to get the police there first just to make sure they are okay and to warn them. They need to know now. Luca needs to be safe now.

I can't believe I was so blasé yesterday. How had I not insisted that Brendan and Luca were properly protected? I'd broken my own rule. Never let them out of your sight. Don't ever close your eyes, even for a second. Even without me caring for him, my son is in danger and I am still to blame. '*Choose one or lose both.*' It screams in my head over and over.

The call connects and I listen to it ring through the Bluetooth connection in my car as I swing out of the Gransha Park grounds and turn left onto the Clooney Road towards Limavady. Thank God for school summer holidays and lighter traffic. If I break a few speed limits I might get there in just over an hour. I don't care if I get a ticket. I don't care if I get pulled over – it could be one way of drumming into the cops just how serious this is.

DI Bradley's phone has rung three times and I can feel tension pulsing behind my eyes. My injured hand hurts on the steering wheel and my ankle screams every time I hit the clutch but I have to push through.

'We were all children once.' Did I really hear that? Did he really say it? Was it his voice or someone else's. What did it mean? We were all children once?

The phone has now rung five times and I'm expecting it to go to voicemail any second.

'Chose one or lose both.' The words echo in my ear as bile rises in my stomach, its acidity burning at my throat. I think I might throw up but if I do, I'll just keep driving anyway. I can't allow anything to stop me.

The phone has rung seven times and hope drains from me, but just then there is a click, a short pause and not the sound of an automated message.

'Good morning,' a chirpy female voice pips in my ear.

'This is Nora Logue,' I stutter. 'And I need to speak to DI Bradley urgently. It's an emergency.'

'In an emergency we advise that members of the public call 999 and ask your call handler to direct your call to the police,' she says and I wonder if she is new to the job, an insufferable jobsworth or both.

'This is Nora Logue,' I repeat. 'And I need to speak to DI Bradley right now. There are people in danger and he is the man leading my case. He needs to know what has just happened. He needs to know that the threat against me and my family is real. Do you understand?' I am hysterical by now, but I don't care. If I could reach down the phone line and shake this woman I would and I wouldn't think twice.

There is a muffled sound before I hear DI Bradley speak. 'Nora, how can I help you?'

'You need to send someone to Brendan and Luca right now. You need to check they're okay,' I blurt.

'One of our officers on the Causeway Coast is due to call out to your husband this morning to discuss safety precautions.'

'No,' I say, my voice cracking. 'They need to go now. They are in real danger. Luca is in real danger.'

'Nora, slow down. Hang on. Are you driving? You sound like you're driving.'

'Yes, I'm driving! I'm driving up to Brendan and Luca right now. I'll be with them as soon as I can. Please, you have to get someone there before something happens!'

I don't know how to get it through to him that this is absolutely serious. I am not crying wolf. I am not overreacting to some trolling.

There's a beat before DI Bradley speaks. 'Nora, are you telling me you are going to harm your family?'

Wait . . . what? The shock of his words causes me to almost lose control of the car, swerving into oncoming traffic but thankfully I right myself just as an approaching lorry blares its horn at me. 'No! Jesus Christ, no! How could you think that? I'm telling you I was followed this morning. I went down to the woods and there was a call on my phone – an unknown caller – and he was watching me. I could hear him move about but I couldn't see him.'

'You were in the woods? What woods?' DI Bradley asks and I'm starting to think he's not quite picking on all the right areas of concern here.

'Gransha Woods – where Daisy went missing. I'm remembering things, just flashes and I went there to see if I could make sense of it and what I'm telling you is that I was followed, and this man, he said that I had to choose between Daisy and Luca and if I didn't choose one of them, I would lose them both. He said he'd been watching. What if he was watching the house when they left yesterday? I've not heard from them and I've been trying to get Brendan on the phone but it's just ringing out . . .'

I hear an intake of breath. 'Okay, Nora. Did he say who he was? Did you recognise his voice?'

'No, I didn't recognise it. It sounded distorted or muffled in some way.' I try to pull anything from my mind that might help identify him. 'The Four,' I say. 'He said he was part of The Four . . . said I knew him. Knew them all. Really well. But I don't . . . I can't think and you just need to get Luca. You need to make sure he's safe. Brendan isn't answering the phone and I can't—'

'Nora,' DI Bradley cuts in. 'We'll get someone around there right away, but you really shouldn't be driving. The hospital gave you some pretty heavy-duty medication and I'm not sure what else you are on. I'm going to need you to pull over, and I can arrange for a car to come and get you.'

'I'm perfectly fit to drive,' I snap, knowing full well that I am not. Medication aside, the pain in my hand and my ankle renders my driving dangerous at best and then, of course, there are all these voices buzzing around me, deafening me. I don't know if they are memories, or ghosts, or the madness in my own brain. At times I think I see someone in the passenger seat, or feel a brush of a hand from behind me, but I know it can't be real. I'm not going to tell DI Bradley that. I just have to get to my family and make sure they're safe. We can go somewhere. Then it strikes me, of course, that this mystery man might be following me now. If he doesn't already know where my boy is then I could be leading him directly to Luca.

'That's not a matter for you to decide,' DI Bradley says. 'I'm saying this as kindly as I can: Nora, pull over safely to the side of the road. Tell me where you are and I'll have a patrol car with you shortly. We will get someone out to Brendan immediately. You're only risking yourself and others by driving in this state.'

I know he's right but . . .

'*You'd know all about cruelty,*' the distorted voice whispers in my ear again. '*We were all children once.*' The chorus of voices is now louder, more insistent. Daisy calling '*Mammy, no!*' The taunts of the mystery man. The '*are you telling me you're going to harm your family?*' that DI Bradley said only moments ago. And those opaque eyes, dead and staring, and I know in that moment that the '*No! Don't. I'm frightened*' is that pale-faced child in the dirt and I know that's real. I know there's something in that, which is very, very real. A new voice now, crashes above the others, loud, booming. '*You choose, Nora. You choose. Spare the rod and spoil the child.*'

All these voices. The accusations. The abuse. The headlines. The lack of time and opportunity to grieve. Trusting no one. Not even myself. Everyone is a suspect. Everyone shifts about on a chessboard as I try to work out who to trust and who to run faster from. Maybe I shouldn't even trust DI David Bradley. He's asking me to pull over, telling me he'll get someone to check on Brendan and Luca. He'll have someone come and get me. What if it's just a ploy to keep me from them? Has he been part of a cover-up? Is he part of this plot to send me tumbling over the edge?

I slam my foot to the accelerator. No. They won't win. The bastards won't win. They can continue to shout in my ear from now until eternity but it won't make a difference. I can ignore them. I can file their bile and their hate away. Just as I have filed so much away from my past.

Faster and faster my car goes as I slap the side of my head to dislodge the voices that continue to taunt me. 'Stop it,' I scream. 'Stop it!'

I only close my eyes for a second. Just enough to push away the images dancing before me now.

'Spare the rod, spoil the child.'
'We were all children once.'
'You'd know all about cruelty.'
'Are you telling me you're going to harm your family?'
'Choose or lose them both.'

Just one second. But a second is enough. The impact is bone-shattering. I feel broken glass glance across my face like confetti, specks of clear light, turning to pink then red. I hear, then smell the screech of tyres. There is a car horn blaring. Air is forcibly pushed from my lungs, through my throat and out in a gasp that preludes blackness.

Chapter Thirty-Seven

Izzy

My first thought is to call after him, but of course I don't know his name. I can't let him just walk away without knowing how he knows my name, so I turn on my heel, leaving the media circus of Nora's house behind, and run up the street after him. I can only assume he hears the slapping of my sandalled feet on the pavement because he speeds up without even looking back.

'Excuse me!' I call. 'Excuse me! I need to talk to you!'

He does not stop or slow his pace even for a moment.

'Excuse me!' I shout again, louder this time and this time he does pause, for just a second. He pauses and turns to look at me, but it's clear he's not willing to give me time to speak. He simply shakes his head, before unlocking a silver Volkswagen and climbing inside. I reach the door just as he is turning the key in the engine, and he wastes no time in pulling away, leaving me shouting after him.

With my phone still in my hand, I try and snap a picture of his car registration as he powers down the street, his engine roaring as he crunches through the gears. I just about manage before he turns the corner but between the glare of the sun and the speed at which he is travelling, the picture isn't the clearest. Even zooming in, I can only make out a partial plate. 'Fuck this shit,' I mutter under my breath and turn to head back to Nora's house.

I've only just got as far as putting my hand on the gate when I feel an arm on my shoulder.

'You can't go in there,' a male voice says. I turn to see a baby-faced uniformed police officer, looking for all intents and purposes as if he might just shit himself at the seriousness of the job he is undertaking.

'I know Nora. I'm working with her.' I realise that sounds sort of cold, so I try again. 'She's a friend and I know what's going on. I just want to check if she's okay. My name's Izzy Devine. You can check I'm telling you the truth with DI Bradley or DS King.'

He raises one eyebrow. The mention of his superiors clearly rattles him. He's lifting his radio to his ear to, I assume, check in with them when a well-dressed woman who I vaguely recognise as a lesser-known news reporter steps in front of him as if he is invisible.

'Did I hear you say you were Izzy Devine? Izzy Devine of Devine Productions? The same Izzy Devine who is behind the documentary on Daisy that started all this?'

I blink as I try and think of a response that says everything I want it to say as quickly as I want to say it, aware that this journalist and her perfectly pronounced accusation has attracted the attention of her fellow media members.

How does one say this is indeed who I am, but I didn't start anything and really I need to speak to Nora to find out if she is okay and to ask how a neighbour might know my name.

If I'm thinking the young police officer will intervene on my behalf and shoo her away, I'm mistaken. He gives me a look that lets me know he's as interested in the response as the woman asking the question.

'Yes, I'm the producer of the new documentary. But I'm not here in that capacity right now. I'm here to see Nora. As a friend.'

'As a friend,' the young officer scoffs, his voice laced with cynicism.

'Well, she's not here,' the journalist says snootily. 'She went out early this morning, I'm told, and no one seems to know where she is.' She gives what can only be described as a withering look at the police officer. It takes the smugness off his face.

I decide not to bring any more unwanted attention to either me or the story by asking any more questions. Instead, I just nod before asking the officer if DI Bradley is at the station.

'I believe so, yes,' he says, before immediately remembering there is a party line to follow here. 'But my advice to you would be to contact the press office for any media-related queries.' He parrots the line so formally it is clear he has said it already one hundred times or more today.

'Cheers,' I tell him, the sarcasm heavy in my voice.

'You're no better than the rest of us just because you're making a documentary,' the snooty journalist says. 'You don't get special access to the cops. Any truth to the rumour you've stirred all this internet drama up to make for a more exciting TV show? Sure beats chasing a cold case that hasn't had any new leads in years. Go on, tell me, off the record even. Is Nora in on it too? Are you paying her a fortune to up the dramatics? Like one of those phony reality shows? Go on, you can tell me.'

At this stage, she has the attention of nearly all the assembled media and all of them are looking at me for a response. I should of course retain my dignity but I'm about all out of tolerance for arseholes at this stage. 'Oh, go fuck yourself,' I tell her, making sure to enunciate it carefully before turning on my heel and walking away.

'Have I touched a nerve?' she shouts as I walk away and I resist the urge to raise my middle finger to her in salute.

As I drive back to the city centre I try Nora's phone once more and I want to cry when again it goes directly to her voicemail. But I don't cry, I bite back the tears and call the police instead. When a female constable tells me DI Bradley isn't available and nor is DS King, my patience is finally done. I am tired of not being taken seriously or being seen as the villain in the piece when there is very clearly an actual villain at play here.

'This is Izzy Devine. I need to talk to DI Bradley with the utmost urgency,' I say, my voice strong and determined. 'I'd prefer you didn't fob me off. There's something really bad going on with this case and I'm starting to get worried, not only for Nora but also for myself. There's a man who says he is a neighbour of Ms Logue, but he knew my name and—'

'I'm sure that's unsettling but I don't think it warrants an immediate conversation with a senior officer. Unless you have more information to offer, I will be sure to inform the team and someone will come back to you in due course. As you can imagine, in a case as high-profile as this, which is attracting increased public attention, we are receiving a large number of calls, so we do ask for your patience.'

'I'm not some crackpot caller. I'm the producer of the documentary on Daisy Logue,' I say, frustration coursing through me.

'We are well aware of who you are, Ms Devine, and I will be sure to get an officer to call you back when they are free to do so. Of course, if you receive any further information on this case that you think may be helpful then you can call us back.'

She is gone before I have time to say another word.

I decide the only thing I can do is reach out to DI Bradley personally. I have his email address – I will get in touch with him that way, send him the picture of the partial plate and a description of the man who was hanging out these last two mornings and tell him I have a really bad feeling about things. Even as I think it, I realise I sound utterly ridiculous expecting anyone to take my 'really bad feeling about things' seriously, but I just know something is badly wrong. I feel it in the very pit of my stomach and I have always believed in trusting my gut feelings.

I'm about to start the car to drive back to the townhouse when my phone rings and Jacqs' name flashes across the screen. I'm tempted to ignore the call, but my (stupid) gut tells me to answer it.

'Izzy,' she says, breathlessly. 'Are you at a computer? Get on AmateurSleuths right now. Jesus Christ, this is unreal.' And for the first time, Jacqs does not sound breathless with excitement at how juicy this story is becoming. She sounds shaken to her very core.

'I'm in the car, Jacqs,' I tell her. 'I'm not at a computer to look at the site. What is it?'

'Can you get to a computer? Because you need to see this. I've never seen the like of it before,' Jacqs says, and the tremor in her voice is unmistakable.

'I can be at our base in about five minutes,' I say. 'But since you're on the line, why not just tell me? I assume this is about Nora?'

'Christ. Right. Okay. I'm sorry, my head is all over the place. The site is going mad. I'd say it'll not stay up for long.'

'What won't stay up for long?' I ask, exasperated.

'Well the post, and maybe even the site. The mods were telling me all the extra traffic is hammering their bandwidth and—'

'Jacqs, what is the post?'

'Will I read it to you?'

I almost swear that she better bloody read it now, but I don't.

'Okay, so it appeared this morning around nine. "The Four" have/has posted again. I don't know if it's one person or a group or . . .'

'Jacqs, what did they say?' I cut in. I can tell she is on edge and floundering but I want her to get to the point.

'Right, sorry. Okay. The title of the thread is, let me read this right – *The monster responsible for Daisy Logue's disappearance.*'

As I feel my chest tighten, I hear Jacqs take a long, slow breath in.

'Before I start to read, Izzy, you should know there's a picture of a man here. Well dressed, in his forties or early fifties maybe, surrounded by school children in uniform. It's an old picture – from the Eighties maybe? I'm just trying to guess by the haircuts and the colours. The children are sat in rows, legs crossed, fingers on lips.'

'A teacher,' I say.

'Yes. Though it must be a small school. There are only twelve pupils in the picture. Primary school age. Not infants but definitely primary school.'

'Nora's father was a teacher,' I say as the knot in my chest tightens further.

'Yes. That's who it says it is. Percy Logue,' she says.

'But how is he supposed to be tied up in all this? Percy Logue has been in a nursing home since his wife died – and that was before Daisy was even born. He can't possibly be connected in any way to her disappearance or to what's going on now.'

'Well, exactly. But reading this post . . . he might not have done it, but according to The Four, he was the reason behind it.'

My brain is desperately trying to do all sorts of mental gymnastics to figure this one out but I'm not having much luck. 'But how?' I ask. 'Nora hasn't even spoken to him in years as far as anyone is aware?'

'Let me read you the post,' Jacqs says, and this time it is she who is sounding frustrated.

'Okay,' I say. 'Okay, you go.'

Chapter Thirty-Eight

The Four

We don't hate Nora Logue. We have never hated Nora Logue. Our teacher, Mr Percy Logue, Nora's father, used to tell us that hate is a very powerful word and it should only be used with extreme caution, lest we devalue the true meaning of it.

Hate, he argued, is best reserved for those to whom redemption is impossible. For the Hitlers of this world. For the Myra Hindleys and Ian Bradys. For those truly evil.

We don't think Nora Logue is evil. We don't even think she is bad. But she did a bad thing and there have to be consequences. Her father taught us that. He taught us that lesson at a great cost – a cost that has been covered up to protect his reputation, to protect Nora, and so that our parents could sleep at night.

All we are doing, and all we have done over the last seven years, is to balance the books a little.

It may have been reported that Percy Logue was a respected educator – but he was not a respected human being. At least not in the eyes of any of the children who endured time in his tutelage.

Percy Logue, for all his love of the Bible, was not a Christian man. He ruled his domain with fear. He did not command respect, he demanded it. When he believed he was not given enough of it, he took it with brute force. He was a tyrant, but one who was tolerated because he got results. He created winners. For our parents that was enough to ensure we were placed under his private tuition in what was referred to as a 'school' but which in fact was little more than a private arrangement among parents who tolerated nothing less than perfection from their children. And we were just children when we were boarded out to his 'school' to be hot-housed for greater things.

It would be understandable for you to pity the young Nora Logue. Her home life was not anywhere near normal. She was not allowed the childhood that each and every child deserves. She was not encouraged to mix with her classmates. Lunch breaks, for her, were spent in quiet contemplation. Fun was absent from her life. We saw that. We tried to reach out to her. We tried to be her friend. With her as our 'friend' we became our own little gang.

But Nora was never really our friend. She was not just a child who needed a friend, a child, who – like us – was not shown enough love and told that her academic achievements were all that would define her.

You should not pity Nora. She was a player in her father's games, and the apple did not fall far from the tree. She wielded what little authority she had with scant regard for the safety or mental wellbeing of her peers.

When we learned she had become a mother, we were immediately concerned. We did not want a child growing up under the poisonous influence of someone raised by Percy Logue. That was and is our primary motivation.

We know, more than most, that it's impossible to escape your past – yet Nora Logue seemed intent on trying to escape hers and to deny what she had played a part in.

And we also wanted revenge. Percy Logue, a man so arrogant as to believe he was a worker for God, often quoted the Bible. He often told us 'Vengeance is mine, sayeth the Lord' in spite of his own predilection for enacting vengeance. We wanted revenge because no one has ever paid for what happened that night in the woods. And someone needed to pay for it.

We waited a long time before we acted. God was not forthcoming, so it was up to us. It was up to us seven years ago and it's up to us again now as Nora Logue prepares to sell her story, begging for sympathy from countless TV viewers, once again. We've seen the picture from the beach of Luca Pryce. We've seen that for all her claims of being a good and loving mother, she is not. Nor is she the victim here.

The victim is a girl you'll never have heard of but she was our friend. Our sister. One of our gang of four. We were too young to save her, but we were not too young to take Daisy and we are not too young to take Luca too.

We are doing this for Catherine. She is who you should be holding in your heart and your prayers. She is the real victim.

Chapter Thirty-Nine

Izzy

'Who the fuck is Catherine?' I blurt, trying to wrap my head around what she has just read out to me. 'Is that name familiar to you at all?'

'I've never heard it before,' Jacqs said. 'Never heard anyone talk about her. I've never read about her. I'm googling her name now but it's not throwing up anything obvious. I'm sure half the forum are running the same searches right now. Maybe they'll come up with something?'

'We can't have missed something this big though? Can we? Although the girl in the café said it wasn't the first . . . but the girl in the café doesn't exist . . . and I . . .'

'Izzy, are you okay? What girl in what café?' Jacqs cuts through my thoughts.

'Oh, nothing. It's nothing,' I say, my head spinning. Does Tom know about this 'Catherine'? Surely he'd have told me? But I think of the café and the lie, and I just can't wrap my head around it.

'What do you think he – or they, or she, whoever the fuck it is – is going to do?' Jacqs cuts in. 'This isn't some troll, is it? This doesn't feel like a troll.'

Shaking my head even though she can't see me, I stutter, 'The police . . . consider them a legitimate threat.'

'So are the police looking out for Nora then? What's going on, Izzy?' Jacqs sounds frustrated now, no doubt aware there is information I've not passed on to her.

'Nora isn't at home and she's not with the police,' I say. 'I called round to her house to check on her. She's not answering her phone either. There were loads of people there – media and the like. And this creepy guy I'd seen the day before – who said he was a neighbour – told me that he'd seen her go out earlier, when it was still dark.'

'And this creepy guy – you don't think he's an *actual* neighbour?' Jacqs asks.

'No. No I don't. There was something about him that gave me very bad vibes. And he knew my name, Jacqs. How would he know my name? I know I never told him what it was.'

'If he's a true crime fan he might be on the site. He might know it from there?'

I consider her point for a moment, before shaking my head. 'No. I can't really explain it but my gut is telling me there's something not right with him. When I described him to Nora yesterday she didn't recognise him. That was my first red flag. Surely she would know her neighbours. It's a small enough cul-de-sac. And if he was just a Sleuth member he'd have told me that, surely? Wouldn't he have said hello? Our community has a strong bond. I can't think of any other obvious local members, either.' Certainly no one apart from Jacqs had identified themselves as local on the Daisy Logue subforum.

'Do you think he's lying to you about her going out early then?' she asks.

'I honestly don't know. No, I think . . . There was a police officer at the house who said she wasn't in,' I say, trying to make sense of the jumbled collection of information in front of me. 'I'm scared for Nora,' I say, and my voice is small. Tears prick at my eyes. 'And for Luca and Brendan too, but especially Luca.'

'Me too,' Jacqs says. 'We're in over our heads here, aren't we?'

'And it's my fault,' I say, realisation washing over me like a wave. 'If I hadn't pushed Nora to make this documentary—'

'Then someone else would've,' Jacqs cuts in. 'You can't blame yourself. And certainly not without the full facts. It seems there is a lot going on here. This stuff about her father is wild. How did we not know all that before?'

'We knew he was strict . . . but that's all anyone knew. And he's been in a home all these years, there was no reason to look into him,' I say, 'but we should've anyway.'

'By the sounds of it, you'd have been met with a wall of silence,' Jacqs says.

'You can't silence a dead child, though. This Catherine? If she was hurt . . . killed even by Percy and Nora, then surely that information would be out there? Surely that can't be covered up? And that's what The Four are implying, isn't it? That this little girl is dead and the Logues are to blame?'

There's a pause as both Jacqs and I try to take on board what has emerged. As we try and balance our fear for Nora with our questions about what happened to a child called Catherine. As we try and process all that we've heard.

'She didn't hurt Daisy,' I say, this key detail somehow being lost among everything else.

'What?' Jacqs asks.

'Read the post again,' I say, a sense of hope or relief or maybe even excitement rising in me. 'Whoever this was, if they're genuine, said they wanted to teach Nora a lesson. They very clearly said they took her, or did something to her. They very clearly point the finger in their own direction.'

'Christ,' is all Jacqs replies.

But of course that would also mean they know what they are doing. If they have taken one child and gotten away with it for seven years, then they are more than capable of taking another. My blood runs cold.

Chapter Forty

Nora

'Wake up, Mammy!' a voice, sweet as a bell, is trying to rouse me. I can feel her soft, warm breath close to my ear. I can feel the gentle touch of her hand on my chest as she tries to shake me awake.

'The sun is shining. It's wake-up time!' There is a lilt to her voice. A lightness to it. I'm trying to open my eyes. Really I am, but it's so warm and my eyelids are so heavy, and the effort required seems insurmountable.

I feel the gentle touch of her lips on my cheek and I can smell the soft lavender scent of her bubble bath. She's right here with me. I want to see her. I want to wrap my arms around her.

'Mammy, it's a sunny day! Time for rise and shine!'

I'm trying, I think. I really am. I'm trying to say the words out loud too but my tongue feels too thick in my mouth.

'I'm here, Mammy,' I hear her say. ''S'okay.' And I feel the weight of her head on my chest, the tickle of her curls on my bare skin. Her body against mine. A perfect fit. No matter how she grew, she has always been a perfect fit. Our two bodies able to snuggle together as if we are pieces of a jigsaw.

Suddenly, I don't want to open my eyes anymore. I don't want to wake up because I know, as pain starts to rack through my body — my legs at first, feeling as if they are on fire, the pain so intense I can feel a scream start to grow from the very pit of my stomach — I know if I open my eyes she will be gone.

I lost her once and I can't lose her again. If I just stay here with my eyes closed, where I can feel her touch and hear her voice, then that's all I could ever want in the world. Right here. With her. The pain won't matter. I can manage the pain as long as she's here. I can endure anything as long as I can hear her, feel her and know she is with me.

I allow myself to sink away from the pain, further into a sleep where I can see a wee girl under the dappled light of the trees, twirling and singing in front of me — a smile broad and beautiful drawn across her face.

Chapter Forty-One

Izzy

I am breathless with the exertion of getting back to the town-house on Shipquay Street. My mind is running wild, jumping between everything that I have learned. Everything that has been said. I am desperate to read that post on AmateurSleuths again myself. Desperate to see if any more updates have been posted and to read the responses that might have come in. Desperate to search for this Catherine child myself.

My phone has already started to blow up with calls and messages and not a one of them from Nora or DI Bradley or any of his cohorts. I've been rejecting every call that comes in, keeping my phone clear for the calls that really matter.

Pushing the door open, I see Tom sitting in front of his own laptop, with his phone in his hand.

'Jesus Christ, Izzy! I've been trying to get through to you but your phone keeps going directly to voicemail,' he says. He looks genuinely annoyed – no, not annoyed. Annoyed isn't it. Worried. He looks worried. His face is pale and tired, his expression gaunt.

'My phone has been blowing up with calls, I'm sorry,' I say. 'I've just been ignoring them so I'd get here as fast as I could.'

'So you've heard then?' he says, his expression grim. I should've known he would have already seen the post, or been directed to it by someone else. There is no doubt that if my phone is blowing up then so is his.

'About the post? Yes. Jacqs called me. Wild stuff.'

He looks at me as if I'm speaking a different language. 'The crash, Izzy. I'm talking about the crash. What are you talking about?'

'What crash?' I ask him, moving almost instinctively to sit down because I know what is coming next will have the power to fell me.

'Nora Logue's car was involved in a serious crash this morning. Between here and Limavady. It's all over Facebook.' He pauses. 'When you were taking your time getting back here, well, part of me thought – worried – you might have been in the car with her.'

I shake my head slowly, trying to take in yet more information. 'No. I went to her house like I said I would, but she wasn't there. And I was caught up on the phone with Jacqs. Is . . . is Nora okay? Is she alive?'

Tom pinches the bridge of his nose and rubs his eyes as if he is the kind of tired that comes only from intense worry.

'I don't know. Last I heard, via Twitter of all places, is that an ambulance is still at the scene. The fire service too.'

'Well that's a positive. The ambulance wouldn't be there if . . .' I begin but even as I speak I see a flaw in my theory. The ambulance would be there regardless of her condition. There's nothing definitively positive to be read from its presence. If she's alive it will be to treat her at the scene, then convey her to hospital.

If she's dead, her body will still have to be recovered from the site and taken to the morgue for a post-mortem.

I stop talking. Tom doesn't speak. He just looks at me for a minute and we both sit in silence. The sound of the traffic on the street, the chatter of people walking below the open window the only noise.

'Do we know what happened?' I ask, the words on the forum running through my head, as well as how disturbed Nora was yesterday.

He shakes his head. 'I've told you everything I know. I suppose we should be grateful that Luca wasn't with her. There is that.'

Oh God, yes. It would be unthinkable if something happened to Luca too. 'Thank God,' I say, suddenly tearful again. This was all too much to take in and I couldn't help but think, again, that it was all because we had kicked the hornets' nest. If I hadn't chased this documentary, if I hadn't been so set on getting an interview with Nora and having her break her silence.

There's a pause as Tom looks at his phone again. 'Hang on,' he says. 'There's more on Twitter. A witness saying the car was being driven erratically and at speed when it crashed. That was about two hours ago, from what I can see.'

'And they're sure it's Nora? How do they know?'

'Someone recognised the car,' he says. 'I suppose she's quite well known.'

'Christ, Tom, what have we done?' I stutter, my stomach churning.

'We've done our job, Izzy. Nothing more or less. Don't be giving yourself too much credit for something that is beyond our control. Nothing about this is our fault or our responsibility for that matter.' There's a coldness to his voice that seems alien, and I don't like it. It makes me feel like I don't really know him as well as I thought I did.

And of course, he has lied about the woman in the café.

'Tom, I need to ask you about something,' I say, and I know I should've asked him this last night before I jumped into bed with him. *Should've* seems to be factoring a lot in my thought process today. 'The woman at the café . . .'

He rolls his eyes. 'Jesus Christ, Izzy. You're like a dog with a bone. The story has moved on from some rando in a café mouthing off. We don't even need her.'

'But we do, don't we? Didn't she say Daisy wasn't the first and now with this Catherine stuff . . .'

'Catherine?' There's a pause. He's not making eye contact with me. 'Who's Catherine?'

'Tom! Have you not seen the forum this morning? That's what I thought you wanted to talk to me about. Jesus, look at the forum!'

'I'll do that now,' he says and sets to work while I resolve to try and speak to DI Bradley again myself. I might be on a hiding to nothing but just maybe I'll be able to find out how Nora is. As expected I am passed from desk to desk with each of them telling me that DI Bradley is busy.

'Look, this is Izzy Devine from Devine Productions. I've been working with Nora Logue these last few days. She was with me yesterday when DI Bradley came to see her – in the Airbnb I'm renting as it happens. I'm not just some stranger, or a random journalist. I'm up to my eyes in this and I just want to know how Nora is, and if you all know about the new posts on AmateurSleuths. What I'm trying to do is help.'

My voice is pleading and I'm not going to apologise for that. I *am* trying to help. And I *do* care. For all my bloody sins, I have to concede that all remaining pretences of objectivity are gone for good.

Chapter Forty-Two

Izzy

After hitting a dead end with the police, I want to cry. Moments later, my mobile, which is still in my hand, rings and I answer it instinctively.

'Hello,' a female voice that sounds vaguely familiar says. 'Izzy, you just spoke to me on the phone? I'm from Strand Road PSNI station. If you don't mind, I won't give you my name. I'm calling you from my private mobile.'

'Okay,' I say, not sure exactly what's going on, meanwhile I watch, confused, as Tom starts to pack up his camera bag with the smaller camera he normally reserves for outside shots or location pieces.

'Officially, you know that the PSNI cannot comment on the status of victims of road traffic collisions unless you are next of kin, or until next of kin have been informed,' the unnamed officer continues. 'But off the record—' her voice drops to little more than a whisper '—Nora has been conveyed to hospital. I know she was alive at the scene but I'm told her injuries are severe. Potentially life-threatening. You did not hear this from me and I will deny all knowledge of this conversation. And yes, we are aware of the post on AmateurSleuths. I've been following your work there for a while, Izzy, in a personal capacity, and that is the only reason I'm risking my job to tell you this. I hope I've not been wrong in putting my faith in you.'

With that she is gone and I have no number to call back. But she has told me what I need to know for now.

The relief at knowing Nora has made it this far comes at me in a huge wave – and a burst of incredible emotion explodes from me in a giant sob.

'What is it?' Tom asks, darting across the room to me. 'Is she okay? What did they say?'

I nod through my tears. 'I spoke to an officer who told me, off the record, that she was alive at the scene. That's absolutely confidential information, Tom. That officer was risking her job to tell me that much.'

'That's good news, isn't it? That she's alive? Do you think I should go to the scene of the accident, see if I can get any footage of the wreckage? Or would I be better placed at the hospital? Although, obviously, I won't be able to go inside the hospital so the wreckage is probably better.'

'Tom, what is wrong with you?' I cry. 'She's in a bad way. I don't think she's out of the woods by any stretch of the imagination. We don't need to be ghoulishly recording the wreckage of her car. Jesus.'

He smirks his usual cheeky smirk. 'Interesting choice of words there, Izzy. "Out of the woods". No pun intended!'

He playfully punches the side of my arm but it's not endearing this time. This is as far from endearing as it gets. The subject of our documentary is potentially fighting for her life in hospital and Tom thinks it's okay to banter about it. He must feel my disdain, and notice my expression, how I pull back from him.

'What?' he says. 'You think I'm being too insensitive? Izzy, I'm glad she's alive, but I've just read that post on Amateur-Sleuths and I'm going to be real, it doesn't paint her in a good light. I'm not saying she deserves to be in a car crash but I'm not sure she's worth getting this upset about either. That post made for grim reading.'

'That post said a lot but said nothing at the same time,' I say, suddenly angry at how flippant he is. 'There is a lot of dancing around the edges but nothing substantial. No actual concrete allegations of anything. There's the first name of a child that no one seems to have any knowledge of before now. Don't you think people would know something if there was another child that had been hurt? The only child we know for a fact that has been hurt in some way is Daisy Logue. Where is she? Why was she taken from her mother and how? The Four – and we'll not even get started on the fact they're anonymous – say they wanted to "protect" Daisy. Yet, everyone who knew how Daisy and Nora were together spoke of a really loving mother and daughter bond – certainly not anything anyone would need to be protected from. And they've let the world think that Nora was capable of hurting her own child for seven years? Jesus, Tom!'

He scoffs and I'm taken aback. This is not the Tom I know. This is not the man who has been gentle with Nora and understanding towards her. This is someone who is hard-nosed, angry and unrecognisable to me.

'You'd do anything to think the best of her, wouldn't you?' he continues. 'You are so happy to skirt over everything that provides any kind of a challenge to your narrative that she is an innocent, wronged mother in all of this.'

His tone is light, but there's no doubt there is a harsher note behind it. It's a jab and it hits the right spot.

'I don't think that's very fair, Tom,' I say. 'I've been objective through this.' He snorts in a derisory manner but I continue anyway. 'And that objectivity requires that I ask why, if these four are so sure they're right about her being the devil incarnate, aren't they outing themselves? Why haven't they gone to the police with their accusations? Do you know of any young girl called Catherine involved in a murder or mysterious death? Children's deaths don't tend to stay quiet. Why don't they have the balls to tell the world just who they are? Because from where I see it, these are people who have made Nora's life hell – and not just recently, but for the last seven years. They took her child for Christ's sake! They've threatened Luca.'

'Well that's not exactly true,' Tom counters. 'Threat is a very strong word to use. They said they would take Luca, they didn't say they would hurt him. It mightn't be a bad thing if they do take him. She's unhinged!'

His voice is louder now, angry even. But I'll be damned if he is the only one getting angry. 'You'd be unhinged if you'd endured what she has!' I shout. 'The psychological torture of not knowing what happened to your own child! Everyone watching you and judging you. Not being able to do anything without someone, somewhere having an opinion on it and then, to top it all off, some fucking psychopath decides to start threatening you and your family. Drip-feeding their threats out online and stirring up a hornets' nest that brings the media to your door in droves? So much so that your husband no longer trusts that your son is safe and takes him away from you.'

Tom blinks at me and there is something in that motion, and in where he is standing, that draws me to a blinking light. Small and red, it flashes rhythmically on top of his camera. Is Tom filming this? Why the hell would Tom be filming this? He wasn't recording set-up shots when I got back. He didn't need to record set-up shots anyway – all that has been done. We've interviewed in here before. Unless . . . no. A thought strikes me that is so ridiculous, but also all too believable as well.

'You wanted to capture my reaction on camera,' I say, slowly, as things very gradually start to fall into place.

'What are you going on about now?' he says, and there is disgust and disappointment in his voice.

'You're filming,' I say, nodding to the camera. 'You've been filming me since I walked in this door.'

'Oh for fuck's sake, Izzy. That's what I do. You hired me to do this. To film things.' He waves his hands around the room, indicating his domain. 'So I was testing the camera out before the interviews this afternoon. It's part of my job,' he hisses.

But I know it's more than that. Now it seems so incredibly obvious. 'You've been recording a lot,' I say and am rewarded with a massive roll of his eyes. He slams his laptop closed and says he's had enough.

'Cameraman in films-a-lot-of-things shocker,' he drawls.

'Even when I've expressed concern, you've insisted on running the camera anyway, like when Nora was first here . . . and the police were at the Airbnb . . .'

'And you've been more than happy to let me!' he says. 'You know I've got amazing material because I've pushed the boundaries a little and recorded around the edges. You didn't have the balls to do it yourself so I've been doing you a favour. I've been making this bloody documentary better than you ever could on your own!'

'Whoa,' I say, feeling the full punch of his words. 'I've got this documentary this far and I know what I'm doing. I was the one who secured Nora for interview in the first place.'

'And yet you're accusing me of . . . of what . . . exploitation? For filming for you?' he snaps.

I do not recognise this man in front of me. This angry, smug, arrogant arsehole of a man.

'You are filming ME!' I say. 'I am not the subject of this documentary, Tom. Why are you filming me at all? What the hell are you at? The only time I should be on camera at all is while interviewing someone else – and even then you know my preference is that I am off camera. My voice shouldn't even be heard. Ever.'

'Half the appeal of this story comes from personalising it. People want to see someone on a journey – so why not let the viewer see who is sailing the ship. You're the true crime addict; let them see you go full amateur sleuth.' He says the words 'amateur sleuth' with such patronising disdain, my desire to slap him only grows.

'Oh go fuck yourself, you arrogant prick!'

'There's no need to become a hysterical diva about it all,' he continues. 'Or maybe this is your way of trying to make me regret what happened last night – well, let me assure you there's no need. Because believe me, *that* particular ship has already sailed.'

A younger me, a different me, may have felt mortally wounded by this barb but this me, who has had the absolute fucking morning from hell and is suddenly having her eyes opened to the truth of this man standing in front of her, is just angry.

'For you and me both, babe,' I drawl, trying to replicate the same level of disdain in my voice as his. 'But that's irrelevant to this moment and this conversation. Don't try and distract me from what you've been up to. What else have you been doing behind my back?'

'I've been doing your job for you!' he says.

I can't help but roll my eyes. 'I don't need you to do my job for me. I know how to do my job, thank you very much. I've been doing it just fine. You, on the other hand, have been crossing every line. How dare you set up a camera to film my reaction to you telling me Nora had been in a crash! This is not some reality TV show. That is not what I set out to do and I don't care what you *think* I should be doing. I know what my goal is and I have made that very clear to you at all times.'

'Christ,' he says, exasperated. He's standing now, his arms crossed defensively, his dark eyes blazing. 'You are so naive, Izzy. You want this to be a success, don't you? You have been banging on about how you need this to be huge. That you need it to be snapped up by one of the big streamers. You want it to be the talk of social media, a trending topic on TikTok like the fucking *Tiger King*. Do you really think your "easy does it" way of approaching it was going to make that happen? You need me. You've needed me all along to make this what you need it to be to have people sit up and take notice. I know how to tell a story. In fact, I know how to *make* a story.'

I shake my head, not quite able to believe what he is saying. I never wanted to cross ethical lines, but then again he's right. I didn't stop him filming those times when I knew the camera was running when maybe it shouldn't have been. Have I unwittingly given him carte blanche to colour outside the lines, to manipulate the story? Had I, on some level, hired him to work with me because I knew he would push me outside of my comfort zone? Tom's reputation as a player stretched beyond the bedroom, after all.

'These are the big leagues, Iz. When you jump in the water with the sharks you have to fucking learn to swim like a shark, otherwise you'll end up swallowed up in minutes. You should be grateful. I've got you what you need to make this stand out from the crowd. True crime documentaries are ten a penny these days – even on cases as high-profile as Daisy Logue. We needed something different. Something raw and powerful. Not your airy-fairy nonsense. That was never going to cut it.'

Had he known from the start he was going to cross lines? I realise with such ruthless ambition driving him, recording when people weren't aware wasn't likely to be his only tactic in getting his big story. What else could he have done?

It's then that it clicks that what he had said to me, just minutes before, didn't fit with his narrative. When we had been discussing the crash, he'd told me that Luca had not been in the car. Of course, I knew that to be true because I'd only just come from Nora's house where I'd been told how Luca had left with his dad the day before.

But Tom *couldn't* have known. I certainly hadn't filled him in after leaving Nora's house – and he's been here on his own. He'd known about the crash through social media, because Nora's car had been recognised at the scene. But he'd been very clear that he knew nothing else. All he knew was that emergency services were still at the roadside. So how did he know Luca wasn't in the car?

A cold feeling washes over me as I look at Tom, who is glaring at me, waiting for my response.

'How did you know?' I blurt.

'That your softly-softly approach wasn't going to work? Because I'm a professional. I'm great at my job.'

I shake my head. 'No. That's not what I mean. How did you know Luca wasn't in the car with Nora?'

He pauses and blinks back at me. It's enough of a delay to know that he has to think of an answer and whatever he is going to say now is a lie. I'm not going to give him the chance.

'You had no way of knowing who was in that car. You didn't know that Brendan and Luca had left yesterday. I only found it out myself in the last hour and I most certainly hadn't mentioned it to you yet.'

'I . . . must've read it online or something.'

'There's nothing official online. The road is closed. No one will be near the accident site. Certainly not close enough to see who is in the car. So how did you know?'

'Well, I guess I just assumed. Brendan wasn't happy yesterday . . .'

'Well which was it, Tom, you read it online or you assumed or what?'

A beat. He blinks at me, gathering his thoughts, and his face is hard and certain once more. 'You wanted a good story,' he finally says. 'I've given you a good story.'

Chapter Forty-Three

Nora

'Nora! Nora! Can you open your eyes for me! C'mon, Nora. There's a girl. Open your eyes and give my hand a squeeze.'

The voice isn't Daisy's. It's not one I recognise at all. It's loud and urgent and brash and the pain in my legs that I tried to escape from is back, but worse now. I don't want to open my eyes. I don't want to be here, to be feeling these things. I just want to go. I want to go back to the woods where Daisy is waiting. Where she is dancing in her leggings and T-shirt, her dark hair glossy in the dappled sunlight.

It's too bright here. And cold. And loud. Other voices chime in now along with beeps and bangs and the ringing of a phone, and all I can think is that it's not my phone. Not my ringtone and why won't the pain stop?

'Nora, you've been in an accident. You're at Altnagelvin Hospital. Can you open your eyes for me, please?' I try to find Daisy in my own darkness but I can't. Wherever she is, it is not here. There is no comfort of her here, only all the voices. I hear a countdown from three to one and then the pain intensifies. I feel as if I am being lifted but not all of me is where it should be. Like I am twisted and broken. The pain is enough to force my eyes open and for me to emit a scream so shrill that it hurts my own ears. My face feels as if someone has taken a sledgehammer to it and I'm shocked to find that I can't seem to close my mouth and it hurts to try and swallow.

A nurse, a blur of dark hair and warm hands, tells me I've dislocated my jaw. It may well be fractured. She tells me not to panic and that I am in safe hands.

I don't feel safe. I have a feeling there is something I should be doing or saying but I can't latch onto a fully cognisant thought. There is only pain and a vague memory of Daisy holding my hand. Now it's the nurse who is speaking gently to me while she mentions pain relief. Urgent voices surround me. I feel pokes and prods and waves of pain so fierce I feel I'm going to be sick and I know that if I am, lying as I am on my back with my jaw slack and out of place, I will choke on my own vomit.

My eyes wide, I try to talk, try to turn my head, and panic rises up in me along with the bile and vomit that I need rid of. I want to turn my head, but I can't. I'm strapped down so all I can do is let out an inhuman howl that releases from me at the same time as I vomit.

'Turn her on her side,' I hear the nice, blurry nurse shout. 'She'll aspirate.'

A world of pain washes over me as I am turned, still strapped to a board on my side, and vomit slides from my mouth.

'Have we informed her family?' I hear a voice above the melee. 'They should be here. We need to try and get them here.'

As pain drags me back under I think of my family, of Brendan and Luca, and I wonder if they are okay. I remember then where I had been driving to and I want to scream more but of course I can't because I'm already slipping under and the nice, blurry nurse is telling me it will be okay.

I wake to darkness and silence. There is no chatter. No

beeping. No bright lights or dull lights or any light. I can't move. I'm trying – trying my very, very best to move my arms, even my hand but I can't. My head feels like it is full of cotton wool. And it is so dark. I think my eyes are open. I'm sure they are but I don't understand why it's so dark.

'Do you want to play?' a voice, small and sweet but not Daisy calls out in the darkness. I know this voice, I'm sure of it, but it's too dark to see anything and I still can't move.

'I can't see you,' I croak. 'It's too dark.'

'I don't like the dark,' the voice says. There's a shake to it now. She sounds scared and I feel a deep sense of dread. I can't move my head even. I don't know where the voice is coming from. It feels like it's everywhere and nowhere all at the same time. Echoing off the walls, which seem to be closing in around me.

A scratch and a flare of light. A match igniting and a candle flickering. I can see it now and the vague outline of a person. A child I once knew passes in front of my now open eyes.

'Will we go into the woods?' she asks, her voice tinkling like a bell, enough to send shivers into my very core. 'You like the woods.'

I can't speak. Fear clutches at me because I know who this is. I know this child.

'I didn't like them,' she says. 'I was so scared. You left me there and I was so scared. And it was so dark, Nora. Like now. Are you scared, Nora?'

I feel an icy breath on my face and it's as if the air has been sucked from my body. I can't breathe and still I can't move. But what I can see in the flickering of the candlelight is Catherine Simms, sitting with her eyes closed and legs crossed on my bed, almost blue with the cold, her hair lank and wet around her face, her clothes streaked with mud. Tilting her head to look at me, leaning towards me, she opens her eyes until I see the cold, cloudy stare of death in them. And still I cannot breathe in and I cannot fill my lungs with air to scream. I am suffocating here in this darkness and I remember it all now – what became of Catherine. What happened to Daisy that day in the woods. It floods back in.

If your life flashes past your eyes before death then that includes all your sins and all your failings and mine are here now as vivid as if I am still in that moment, as crystal clear as if I never blocked them out in the first place.

Chapter Forty-Four

Izzy

'What have you done, Tom?' I ask as he stands across the room from me, the assuredness I'd so admired before now unbearably cocky and arrogant.

'I've not done anything you need to worry about,' he says. 'The less I tell you, the better.'

'That's not how it works,' I snap. 'This is my project and I want to know what the hell you've done. How did you know Luca wasn't in the car? What do you mean exactly by saying you gave me a story?'

'What do you *think* I mean?' he asks, and I swear I want to launch at him and pummel him with my fists. He is standing here in front of me playing some sort of stupid little mind game, and there are people whose lives are in real danger. God only knows if Nora is still alive or not. Someone is threatening Luca, no matter how he wants to look at it. And now . . . now he is telling me he has been manipulating this all along – I just don't know to what extent. My stomach twists.

'How wrapped up in all this are you?' I ask even though I'm afraid of what his reply might be. 'Everything was quiet in this case until we arrived and now it's one giant fucking mess. This is not what I set out to do.'

'You just wanted to be the big hero. You wanted to be everybody's friend. Because you don't have the balls to really rattle some cages to get the truth. The reality is you backed the wrong horse. You backed Nora fucking Logue. Daughter of a psychopath. You bought into her story entirely. Your lack of critical thinking is unforgivable.'

My head spins, trying to make sense of what this person in front of me is saying. This person who I thought I knew so well. This person who I trusted implicitly, for God's sake. 'Tom, we both came into this with open minds. We've had this chat before, you and me. Many times. Christ, we've had it in the last few days. How we don't know who or what to believe. We're learning too.'

'You're not really that naive, are you?' he asks, a smile playing across his lips. 'No one is that open-minded, Izzy. We all have our prejudices. We all have our beliefs and our gut feelings. Yours were either way off, or you ignored them altogether. You just didn't want to see beyond a possible happy ending. That's your end goal.'

'That's a load of shit,' I spit at him. Anger is pulsing in me now. My heart thudding, my skin fizzing with a build-up of pure rage. 'We're talking about a missing child. She's been missing seven years. Do you really think there's a hope of a happy ending? Did you think I am really that naive or stupid? Because I have never believed we'd find her, and certainly not alive. I may have allowed myself a moment of hope with the Galway picture – but I've always believed this was about finding a body, not a child.'

He smirks. 'It wasn't though, not for you. Your interest was in solving the mystery and not telling the story the way it should've been told. You wanted to be the hero who brings the dead back to life. The very arrogance of you, Izzy! You didn't even do your research properly. A proper deep dive, one in which you actually wanted to find the truth and not just some sanitised version of it.' He is shouting now. His voice terse, loud, angry. Spittle shooting from his mouth. But his anger is nothing compared to mine.

'Of course I did my research! I've been researching this for two years. I have read everything that there is to be read. I have spoken to everyone who wanted to talk, no matter what it was they wanted to say. You know that. You've been with me through that.'

'Ha,' he spits. 'Your little website with all your little Scooby-Doo gang friends doesn't count as proper research. You're delusional. There are people who are angry that you are giving her the time of day and they weren't afraid to do whatever it took to try and stop it. These people are not hard to find. And I don't just mean the baying mobs of conspiracy theorists and smug parents. None of this had to happen, but you made sure it did.'

'Tom, for fuck's sake. Stop talking in riddles. What do you mean? What people? The anonymous Four? Whoever sent the Galway picture? The trolls on AmateurSleuths? Who thinks I shouldn't have given this story the time of day?' It's my turn to sound borderline hysterical now. I'm starting to question myself and everything about me, and how I've approached this project. But more than that I am now just completely floored by the fact Tom seems to hold me in such genuine disdain. Tom who I have laughed with and chatted with into the night; Tom who I had sex with last night. Who I felt a genuine connection with. I thought we were on the same page. And now he's mocking me and has been talking to people about me behind my back. Mocking my work.

I watch him and for a second I think he's just going to walk out. It's like he's holding back from saying something. Maybe he realises he's gone too far, but he can't take it back now. It's out there.

'Who?' I ask him again, quieter this time, the feeling of being defeated washing over me. 'Who has been trying to stop this?'

'Well, Brendan for one,' he says.

I stare at him blankly. Surely he didn't just say Brendan was caught up in this – not any more than I already knew? He didn't want Nora to be involved in the documentary, but surely he wouldn't have done anything to make his own wife feel threatened. Or his own child, for that matter. Wasn't the entire crux of his objection that he didn't want to risk Luca being negatively affected by it all?

'Oh come on!' I say rolling my eyes. 'If that's all you've got, Tom, then just stop now because this is really quite pathetic. Brendan's objections are hardly a secret. It doesn't mean—'

'Did the police, or even Jacqueline for that matter, ever come back to you about that account on AmateurSleuths?' he cuts in. 'The DL180715 one? The one that posted the picture of Luca, and said they'd take care of him?' Tom asks, leaning back against the table now, arms crossed in a pose that screams smugness.

'No. Not yet. The poster used a VPN – as you well know.'

'Did it not ever cross your mind that the poster was significantly closer to home than you could've imagined? I mean, Brendan was at the beach the day the picture was taken . . .'

Surely not. Surely this is just Tom off on one of his flights of fantasy. 'That's ridiculous,' I say, shaking my head.

'Is it really that ridiculous, though? He sees his wife disappear back into whatever happened that day and he sees her withdraw even more than usual from their child. He wants to make sure Luca is never put in a position where, God forbid, he becomes a target.'

I'm about to tell him that was never going to happen. Luca wouldn't have become a target – but I remember The Four and their threats. But Jesus Christ, surely there were other ways for Brendan to get to his message through to Nora without posting that picture online – without drawing more hate towards her?

'I don't buy it,' I tell him. 'It's too cruel.'

'You really don't have a clue, do you?'

I want to fight back, say that I know more than he thinks but the reality is, I don't. Right now, in this moment – my head spinning – I really don't have a clue. Not a single one. There's a second or two while I struggle to find the right response. As I struggle to make sense of the changing picture.

'Brendan came to me last week, after you'd arranged the meeting with Nora.'

'Hang on, why did he go to you? I'm the producer.'

He shrugs. 'My guess is that this project is your baby. You're the person driving the whole thing. I imagine he felt he had a better chance of a fair hearing if he came to me. And there's probably a bit of sexism thrown in there too. He wanted to chat to me "man to man".'

I can't actually believe I'm hearing this.

'Anyway, he pleaded with me to try and get the documentary cancelled or at least to limit or stop Nora's involvement. I obviously wasn't going to do that. I wanted to do the project, for you and for me. I believe in it. But I'm not a total bastard.'

'That's debatable,' I snap but Tom ignores me and just keeps talking.

'He made a very convincing case about his worries for Luca. It wasn't enough to make Nora fear she'd be hurt herself, he said. But he hoped that she'd slip back out of the public eye if she thought Luca was in danger. My first thought was to tell him to get lost but then the idea came to me that we could use this approach of his to the advantage of the documentary. I thought it could be the perfect way to add some drama to the whole thing – something outside the same old going over of information that has been dissected a million times before. So, together we hatched the plan about the beach picture.'

'What are you saying?'

He sighs impatiently. 'Brendan posted that picture. Or at least Brendan sent the picture to me, and I posted it from the DL180715 account.'

I sit down, trying to take in what he has told me. This goes against everything – every little thing – I want to do in film-making. Rogue accounts, manipulating the story, taking advantage of vulnerable people. Not this. Not making people scared and, Christ, it dawns on me that he has done so much worse than that.

'The Galway picture,' I say, feeling every part of me want to be sick. 'That was the same username. On the email. They both came from the same username.'

I don't know if I expect him to look ashamed, or hope that he will deny it and offer a plausible alternative explanation but he doesn't do either. He doesn't look one bit contrite.

'Brendan didn't have anything to do with that. I had to shake it up a bit,' he says with a small shrug. 'I figured I might as well add extra drama into the mix – so a bit of Photoshop, an email to a small-fry newspaper who wouldn't have the time to look too closely at it. It was fairly easy, to be honest. A quick search of a Facebook page, five minutes' work on Photoshop and we had it. I didn't expect them to publish it so quickly but it definitely ensured we got things off to a cracking start, didn't it?' He is absolutely without any sense of remorse or regret.

My head hurts, and my heart aches for Nora.

'You are both total and unspeakably cruel bastards,' I mutter. 'How could you?'

'Because it makes for great TV, that's how.' He is so matter-of-fact that I want to shake him. 'Look, you're fairly new to this, Izzy. You're so full of all your ideals and ambitions and you haven't realised yet that's not what commissioners or viewers want. They want drama and tension and peril. If you want a success, you need to work at it. You need to make it happen. Well, that's what I was doing – for you, yes but for me too. I'm tired of being an also-ran. I needed this for me and I knew you'd never go for it if I told you, so I didn't.'

'But what you did brought The Four, whoever the fuck they are, out of hiding and they have threatened Luca anyway! Nora is in hospital. She might be dead for all we know. What if Luca had been in the car with her then? Could you have lived with yourself?'

'Brendan is never going to let that happen. He has Luca in his sights at all times. Why do you think he insisted on taking him away yesterday?' he says, smugness radiating from every pore.

'Nora had Daisy in her sights all that time and they still took her. They aren't some opportunists by the sounds of things, Tom. They know what they're doing. They could get that little boy and they could hurt him and it will be your fault. It will be our fault.' I feel too hot and dizzy and utterly sickened that this man in front of me is not the man I thought he was. Most of all I feel responsible for this awful mess now, for whatever condition Nora is in physically and emotionally. Dropping my head in my hands I try to breathe deeply.

'We're here to observe,' Tom says, without a hint of self-awareness. 'We're not responsible.'

'But *you* are! You have lied and schemed and now there's a woman critically ill or worse, and a second child in danger. And need I remind you, the lead we thought we had in finding out where Daisy was – if she is even alive – was one you mocked up in five minutes in Photoshop!'

'There's no need to get hysterical,' he says, and I have to resist the urge to go completely bat-shit hysterical right here and now.

'Isn't there? The girl in the café too – that was all bullshit, wasn't it?'

For a moment he is quiet. Glancing up I can see a flash of something in his eyes. Is it too much to hope it's regret? Or remorse? Or just humanity?

'You wanted a story,' he says.

'But not at this cost!' I shout back. Everything we have done in the last week flashes through my mind as I try to pick the lies from the truth, and sift through this massive web of manipulation.

Then it strikes me. The girl in the café may not have been real – but Tom said she warned that Daisy had not been the first and now, according to 'The Four' there *was* another girl in the mix here in the form of Catherine Simms. So how did Tom know that particular accusation? It's too much to even pretend to believe it was a mere coincidence.

'You know who they are, don't you?' I ask him.

'Oh for fuck's sake, Izzy. If you're going to ask a question, ask it right! Who are "they"?' His tone is sneering now and I have never felt such a strong urge to smack someone hard across the face.

'The Four. You know more about them than you're letting on. Or are they are a figment of your imagination too? Something else created to add a little drama.'

'No,' he says. 'They are not some made-up figment of my imagination. They are one hundred per cent for real. Well, three of them are anyway. The fourth was Catherine Simms, and she's long dead.'

'You know who they are? Tom, you have to tell the police. You have to tell them now! For Luca if for no one else.'

He shakes his head. 'That's not going to happen. Not yet anyway. They'll out themselves soon enough.'

'If you won't call them, I will. Maybe having a police officer here will compel you to do the decent thing,' I say.

I pull my phone from my pocket, pressing my finger against the screen to unlock it.

The first thing I'm aware of is the noise that comes with the movement of air. A swooshing, a whistle almost. Then I sense the air around me shift just that little bit before I feel the impact that knocks the phone from my hand and sends it hurtling towards the wall.

'What the fuck?' I exclaim, looking up to where Tom is now just inches from my face, his expression set like stone.

'You're not calling the police,' he says, his voice chillingly calm.

'I. Am. Calling. The. Police,' I say with as much authority as I can muster, given the thudding of my heart and the shake in my voice. I raise my hands to push him away from me so that I can retrieve my phone from the floor, but before I can get any leverage, he grabs my wrists, twisting the skin so tightly it hurts. I gasp with the pain and shock of it, looking him directly in the eyes. 'What the fuck?'

'You. Aren't. Calling. The. Police,' he spits back, twisting my arms, turning me away from him and pressing himself against me, his breath hot in my ear. 'Don't make me hurt you. I'm doing this for us. For our careers. You'll see that, Izzy, and you'll thank me for it.'

'No I fucking won't.' I try my hardest to wrestle myself free from his grasp.

'This is my project too,' he hisses. 'It's my BAFTA in the making. Don't fuck it up.'

Unable to free myself, I open my mouth and start to scream, sure that someone in the busy street below will hear me. The windows are open to let fresh air in. There's no way I won't be heard. As soon as the first hint of a scream leaves my mouth I feel Tom's hand clamp across my face, silencing me.

'Don't push me, Izzy. You've no idea what I'm capable of.'

Chapter Forty-Five

Nora

I know the voice beside me now. I can't quite open my eyes, not yet, heavy as they are with sleep or pain or both. But I know who is talking to me. I know who is saying my name gently, giving my hand the softest of squeezes.

It takes a herculean effort to try and open my eyes – and there is pain and a blinding light. I try to open my mouth to talk but it feels as if I am encased in something, unable to move. My instinct is to panic, and I squeeze as tight as I can on the hand that is holding mine.

A different voice now. Female. Calm. 'Nora, don't try to speak. You've had some surgery to repair a pretty serious facial injury. Your jaw has been wired in place and your face is very swollen. We have a tube in your nose to help with your breathing. You are doing well, all things considered.'

My eyesight is still hazy and the nurse's face blurs in front of me. I blink, that solitary action sending waves of pain through my body. A gurgled cry I don't recognise escapes from my throat. 'We'll give you a little more pain medication,' she says. 'It will make you more comfortable and the doctor will see you shortly. Don't be afraid to rest if that's what you need to do.' Her kindness is almost too much, and I know I am crying.

It's then I hear the familiar voice again. 'It's okay,' Brendan says, leaning over so I can just about make out the outline of his face amid my tears. 'You're safe, love. It's okay.'

But I'm not okay. I don't know where Luca is or if he is safe. Did help get to them in time or has Brendan just endured the same nightmare I once did? Because I remember it now – or at least enough of it to feel as if I am back, stuck in that awful, awful moment.

We had been playing. Having the most fun. My face was sore from smiling so widely and I felt as if my heart would burst with love. It was one of those wonderful, incredible days where all seems right with the world. Contentment is so underrated. It was all I'd ever wanted – the contentment of loving someone and being loved back. It didn't have to be romantic love. I had all I could ever ask for with my child. It was a pure love. Unconditional. So much of my life had been subject to the strictest conditions. Even friendship had come on its own terms.

But Daisy and I – we shared a bond no one else was a part of. It was as if we existed in our own bubble. We spoke the same language. She was the very air I breathed.

And that day we were ridiculously silly and full of mischief. It had been enough to distract me from the funny phone calls I'd been getting at all hours of the day and night. The hang-ups. Prank calls that were becoming so frequent I'd ended up changing my number the day before. I'd slept so well knowing my phone wouldn't ring that I'd felt ready to take on the world.

So we walked into the woods, and we smelled the flowers. We let the leaves of the bushes tickle our legs and arms as we walked past. We sang and marched and told each other stories. We'd found the tree where someone had tied a swing and she had held on so tightly as I pushed her – not too high.

And then we had played hide-and-seek. I'd felt uneasy about it. Something in the very pit of my stomach told me something was off. And I'd called her and called her, and she hadn't answered. That was when panic started to set in. It didn't take long to overwhelm me. My gut was telling me something was badly wrong.

'Come out now, Daisy!' I called, over and over until I was screaming her name. Images started to flash into my head unbidden. Day seemed to merge with night then seemed to merge with day again. I'd hear voices only to look around and see that no one else was there – but surely I wasn't just hearing things?

'Daisy!' I'd screamed, my voice cracking, my entire body electric with adrenaline. I'd looked around; there had to be someone here. There was always someone here in one little corner or another. A dog walker, or some teenagers or someone – anyone – who could help me.

I'd screamed her name again and again, and when no one replied I'd screamed for help. I'd expected someone to come running, but no one did. I hadn't known whether to stay in the spot I was in, in case she returned, or to look everywhere. Maybe she'd fallen and hurt herself. Maybe she was just taking this game of hide-and-seek too seriously, but even as I thought that I'd known it wasn't true. She would've come to me when I called her, if she was able to. She would've come.

So I started running down those twisting pathways – some carved out of the ground by the forestry service, some manmade as frequent visitors chose their own pathways. But there was no Daisy. I'd scrambled through bushes. Looked in the small shack by the bridge. Panic had already taken what was left of my senses when I ran into a man. Tall. With a beard. About my age.

'Have you seen a little girl? Tell me you've seen a little girl. She's four. She has long, dark hair and she was wearing leggings and a T-shirt with daisies on. And she's only four and I can't find her.'

He'd looked at me with a strange expression. One I couldn't put a name to straight away.

'Please!' I begged. 'Can you help me look?'

He'd just stood and stared some more until I'd wanted to shake him. I don't think I've ever felt so frustrated in my entire life.

'Please!' I'd begged again. 'She's only four.'

He'd kept staring, his eyes cold, and that's when I'd noticed something familiar about him. It was his eyes, I think. Wide. Blue. I couldn't help but feel I'd seen them before but panic clouded my brain.

Then he'd shook his head and turned his back to me, walking out of the woods. I didn't understand. I couldn't understand.

'Please!' I'd begged again. 'Don't go! Please I need help.'

I'd followed him, howling and screeching, hoping we'd find someone else but there was no one.

I was sobbing, my ribs aching from the fierceness of my crying. I swore I was feeling my heart shatter bit by bit. When we'd reached the edge of the woods, he stopped. Finally. My legs almost went from under me, relieved that he might be listening.

'Thank you,' I sobbed as he turned back and looked at me. 'Please. Do you have a phone? Can I phone the police? My battery . . .'

'That's a shame,' he said, just shaking his head.

'I . . . I don't understand,' I'd stuttered.

'You don't remember me, do you, Nora?' he'd asked and I wished I did. I wished I could place those blue eyes but I couldn't and there was no use in my lying. I didn't have time for games.

I shook my head.

'Do you remember her? Do you remember Catherine?'

Ice flooded my veins. Yes, I remembered Catherine. I remembered the horror of that night and the days that followed.

'She was left in the woods, in the dark, too,' he said. 'Daisy's gone, Nora. She's gone. She might be in there somewhere.' He'd gestured towards the woods. 'Or she might not be. But you won't see her again. For Catherine's sake.'

And he had turned on his heel and stalked off and I stood, frozen, not knowing whether to go after him or to run back into the woods. If it was for Catherine, then it stood to reason Daisy would be still in the woods and he could be wrong. If I found her, I'd see her again.

I'd run back into the woods hoping to find my daughter, but instead I'd lost everything. My contentment. My joy. My mind.

I want to speak. I want to tell them that I remember. That I know she had been taken and I know it was for Catherine and that there are only a handful of people in this world who know the truth of what happened that night in the woods when we were children but of course, I can't. My head is too heavy. My jaw wired. My consciousness slipping away and coming into focus just for brief moments.

'And you're not to worry about Luca,' he says. 'He's happy as Larry. No idea about the drama at all,' Brendan says with a smile, adding, 'He's with my parents.'

My stomach churns. No, he can't be with Brendan's parents. He needs to be here. I need to know he is here and safe. I never got to warn Brendan about the choice, that I was told to choose one or lose both. That's where I was going, wasn't it? When it happened. The crash. I was going to warn them. Wasn't I? Or was the man in the woods right? Had I already chosen Daisy? Is she really still out there?

I feel panic start to rise in me again, hear Brendan try to

soothe me but he doesn't understand. If he knew what I do, he would be panicking as much, if not more, than I am.

'This will help,' the blurry-faced nurse says as she approaches with a syringe. Try as I might to shake my head, I of course can't. The vice-like grip has me immobilised. I make what noise I can – another low, guttural moan, which is met only with soothing reassurances that everything is going to be okay. I'm going to be okay. But it's not me I'm worried about. It's impossible to make myself understood before I'm aware of a tugging at my arm. The nurse is telling me not to fight her, and explaining to Brendan how the anaesthetic combined with shock from a serious accident can make patients agitated. It could also be the head injuries I sustained.

I want to scream, of course, but what noise I can make fades away as my body is flooded with morphine. My last conscious thought is that Luca is out there and there is no one to save him. I'm going to lose him just as I lost Daisy.

Chapter Forty-Six

Izzy

'You can't keep me here all day,' I spit, as Tom pulls his hand from my mouth only after I promise him I won't try to scream again. 'And do you really think with everything that is happening today people won't try and get in touch with us? We have people coming here to be interviewed this afternoon, for God's sake.'

'We don't,' he says, matter-of-factly. 'I've already cancelled them. In light of what has been happening today.' There's a smugness to him that makes my skin crawl. 'Funnily enough they were understanding about it. That journalist woman said she wants to be able to see any more updates on AmateurSleuths as they come in, so she was going to cancel on us anyway.'

'We're in a busy city centre. It won't take much for me to attract attention,' I say.

'It wouldn't take much for me to make sure you aren't able to,' he says and my eyes widen as fear claws at me. Just how far is this man willing to go? Just how little did I actually know the person I was working with? The person I had sex with . . .

He has been involved in damaging Nora Logue more than she is already damaged. To think he is capable of actual physical

278

violence makes my entire body tense – ready to adopt a fight-or-flight approach. Ready to do the things that he has warned me not to.

Tears, shamefully, prick at my eyes and I bite them back. I will not cry in front of this man. I will not show any more weakness.

'You just have to trust me,' he says and I almost laugh.

'Are you for real? How can you expect me to ever trust you again?' One horrible, lonely traitor of a tear falls when I blink and hastily I wipe it away. I know he sees it and I wait for his response – wait for him to mock me in some way. But he doesn't.

He sits down, gestures for me to sit, just feet from him. I see the tension in his body too, feel it crackle in the air. He is not as comfortable with this as he is pretending to be.

'Look, Izzy. When you know the truth, you'll think differently. I promise you that.'

'So, tell me the truth,' I say. 'Tell me exactly what is going on here. These allegations, whatever they may be, against Nora – what are they? Surely she was just a child in any case – and by the sounds of it a child in a really fucked-up place. That doesn't justify the hurt that will be caused to Luca, or whatever has happened to Daisy.'

He glances to the clock by the old marble fireplace – a mahogany grandfather clock that stands guard over the room, its rhythmic ticking reminding us to breathe. It's not as easy as you'd think when every part of you is screaming to get away from where you are and who you are with.

'The Four are posting more information in five minutes,' he says. 'If you read that and still want to call the police, then you can. But I guarantee that you will feel differently.'

'Five minutes could be the difference between Luca being safe and him being dead,' I say, frustration making me want to scream. 'Do you really want to live with that on your conscience?

If you know who they are, you can stop this before anyone else is hurt!'

He simply shakes his head. 'They have to be allowed to tell their story, Izzy. They've not come this far to stop now.'

Desperation forms a knot in my throat. This is madness but how do I make him see that this cannot end well for anyone? That's when I see the flashing of the small, red light on top of his camera. It is still recording. We're not in its eyeline anymore but we are still close enough that any audio will be picked up. If I can't realistically get out of here, I can at least make sure to gather as much evidence as I can on camera. Tom can hang himself with his own devious methods.

'How do you know what their plan is?' I ask. 'How do you know when they will be posting?'

'Well, I contacted them through AmateurSleuths – using the DL180715 account after they replied to the picture of Luca on the beach. Told them I was interested in what they had to say. That I believed Nora was a danger to Luca . . .'

I gasp. 'You had no right to do that. You had nothing to back that up! Jesus Christ – what have you done?'

For the briefest of moments there's something in his eyes that makes me think he is realising that he has gone too far, but it's gone as quick as it arrives. 'I'm going to read what they post now,' he says. 'Do the same. Then you'll understand.' He clicks on his keyboard before turning to me with a grave expression on his face. 'There it is. There it all is.'

Chapter Forty-Seven

The Four

Daisy Logue was four years old when she went missing. Catherine was just ten – the youngest of our group – when she was lost in the woods. You probably won't have heard of Catherine. In fact, I'd pretty much guarantee you haven't.

Because Catherine turned up again the next day. But she was never the same. For the brief amount of time she remained with us, she was not the same child who learned alongside us, played with us and had been our friend.

It wasn't a beautiful summer's day when Catherine went into the woods. We had not been going on a picnic. We were not, as Nora Logue has recalled of her last day with Daisy, singing as we marched. We were cold and wet and miserable. We were also silent. There was rarely any childish banter when Mr Percy Logue was leading an excursion. Even though we were all young and full of childish enthusiasm, we were told we should walk in quiet contemplation. We were told of the benefits of silent intentions, internalised prayer.

It's a hard task to kill the spirit of children eager to learn, but Percy Logue was adept at just that. We'd long known it was best never to step out of line. To do as we were told or risk retribution. That was the word he used. One most of us couldn't say, never mind spell.

Initially it was Nora who bore the brunt of her father's authoritarianism. We're not sure if it was because he felt he could be tougher with his own child, or because he hoped it would show our parents there was no favouritism at play. Maybe it was just that it was in his interest to break her first. For this, we had extreme amounts of pity for Nora. Her life was regimented, almost military. Her father was cold and cruel. Her mother, not that we saw much of her, was meek and quiet. As children we didn't understand these things. We didn't understand these relationships, or what they signified. We weren't worldly like other children. We didn't spend hours watching TV or mixing with others. We took life for what it was. We assumed this was how all people behaved. We didn't question it. Even the cruelty. We knew little different.

Percy Logue was an inventive man in his time. His punishments stretched beyond the cane and the strap. For example, he would force Nora to stand, toes to the wall, arms stretched wide in what we now know was called a stress position for hours. It was a method of torture used to punish and break those accused of terrorism charges in Northern Ireland. The realisation, watching a documentary in adulthood, that this is what was done to us was beyond upsetting.

This man was not a person who should have been allowed anywhere near children. He was a monster who used the stress position punishment often and in response to minor transgressions. A forgotten line in a poem that should have been known by rote. A loss of concentration. An unkempt appearance – hair that had fallen loose of its bobble.

Nora for her part initially responded with the right amount of penitence to please her father but there was a spark in her – a 'badness' he called it – and she soon came to mock his punishments. By the age of twelve, she would taunt him that he would not break her. She didn't care what he did to her. She would laugh in his face. But she had one flaw that he soon realised he could use to his advantage.

He had realised that Nora was fiercely protective of us, her friends. There were times when she would take the blame for things we knew were not of her doing because she swore the punishments no longer bothered her.

And that's when he changed. He knew that the one way to bring Nora into line was to target her weak spot, and we were exactly that. It wasn't enough to simply turn his attentions to us, though – no, he wasn't going to let Nora escape the repercussions of her actions.

If she did something wrong, he would force her to choose which of us would be punished for it and he would force her to watch.

It was with extreme pity and horror that we watched these punishments meted out. We lived in fear of her stepping out of line and God knows she tried her best not to. But that spark of wilful rebellion that had ignited inside her was extinguished, and in its place was only darkness.

When you are without power, you will cling onto any semblance of it that you have. Even if it involves turning your anger against those people you used to protect.

Nora changed. There must have been something of her father in her, because it seemed as though she started to enjoy pointing the finger and watching us, those who were her friends, suffer. After a while, we came to suspect there were times when she deliberately acted out. Her father took some perverse pleasure from her increasing willingness to point the finger. Perhaps it was just that he saw his own cruelty reflected in her and that pleased him.

So on that day in the woods – in the cold and the wet –

when Nora slipped and covered her pristine uniform in mud, and several of us laughed at the sight in front of us, Mr Logue was ready to inflict his ire with gusto.

As had become his habit, he asked Nora to choose between two of her classmates as to which would take her punishment for her. She wasted no time at all in calling out Catherine's name. We have no idea why Catherine was chosen over the rest of us.

Mr Logue decided that if his pupils were content to look like animals and behave like animals then Catherine could live like an animal. He told her she would spend the night in the woods, and use that time to reflect on what it is to live a good life.

Catherine – Cathy to us – was terrified of the dark. We all knew it.

Breaking all the rules, we pleaded with Mr Logue to rethink his punishment. I think we hoped he'd leave us all there – at least there would be safety in numbers. We knew that Catherine would not be able to endure this punishment.

Mr Logue silenced our pleading and turned to Nora. He gave her another choice right there and then – should Catherine face the punishment he had decided on, or would Nora be willing to take the punishment in her place?

Without hesitation, Nora said no. Catherine should face it.

The horror on Catherine's face as we were marched away from her will haunt us to our graves, but it did not appear to haunt Nora. In fact, as we marched back to the school, she walked hand in hand with her father.

We had been marched back out, none of us daring to make a sound and watching every step lest we slip and dirty our uniforms too. Lest we make this worse than it already was.

Percy Logue gave us a sermon – and that's what it was – about how us modern children had it too easy. Every child should be skilled enough to know to find shelter, and drinking water, to survive a night in the woods. Catherine would be fine and stronger for it. I remember him saying with glee: 'Imagine how emboldened she will feel to have survived a night in the woods – how empowered she will feel to have conquered her fear of the dark.'

I wasn't convinced and I don't think the others were either. I don't think any of us slept.

By the time morning came we were all exhausted but impatient to get back to the woods to get our friend back. But Catherine wasn't where we had left her, of course. I remember even Percy Logue seemed worried. He was shouting: 'She has to be here. The stupid girl! Where has she gone? She has to be here where we left her,' and we were tasked with searching. I remember the dread in the pit of my stomach, the fear that I would find her but it would be too late.

When she was found, she was curled under some hedges, knees to her chest, knuckles white with fear, eyes pressed closed. We tried to coax her out of the hollow but she didn't, or couldn't speak. We said it was okay, we were taking her home. Still she didn't speak, but she did cry.

I remember Percy Logue finding us children trying to coax her out and he ordered us out of the way, before reaching in with one of his big, bony hands and dragging her by the coat out of the hollow. 'Right, young lady. I think it's time we went back to school.'

He didn't acknowledge her fear. Her exhaustion. The way she shivered so violently that her teeth chattered. He just marched her back to his home – our makeshift school house – and ordered his wife to run her a bath. Catherine was put to bed after that. She never made it to the classroom again. She never spoke again either. We don't know what she saw, what she experienced, but we knew it destroyed her. She was just a child.

When she became ill, when she spiked a fever, we watched as she lay as pale as a ghost in her bed, still silent. After a day or two, her parents came and collected her, their faces gaunt with worry. When they asked us what happened, Percy Logue had shooed us from the room before we could answer. Only Nora stayed – Nora, who told them Catherine had simply taken ill in the middle of class.

Catherine never came back. A few days later we were asked to pray for her eternal repose.

Catherine did not die in the woods, but she might as well have. That was Nora's fault. She could've stopped it. She could've taken Catherine's place. She could've told Catherine's parents the truth of what had happened. But she didn't. And a child died.

Chapter Forty-Eight

Izzy

'You can't tell me you've read that and still feel like the world should be on Nora's side?' Tom asks, almost triumphant as if he has presented me with a slam dunk.

'You're talking about a child,' I say. 'She was a child who was being horrendously abused and manipulated by a monster of a man and she acted in a way that preserved her own safety. She was given an impossible choice. No child is unbreakable, no matter how strong they seem. They're still just children.'

I'm looking directly at Tom trying to find a hint of understanding or compassion under all his bullshit bravado. Surely he must realise she was just a child! And now there are more children whose lives are being turned upside down. Daisy, and Luca. Where will it end? 'Nora isn't responsible for what happened to Catherine Simms. That blame lies solely with Percy Logue!'

Tom blinks. 'But if she was capable of being so cold, then what right has she to be a mother?'

'And what right have you to stop her? Or what right do "The Four" have to stop her?' I ask, and I'm shouting now because I'm so fucking angry. If they took her child as an act of revenge, when they were adults and knew better, does not that make them worse than Nora? Indeed worse than even Percy Logue.

'Is Daisy alive?' I ask Tom. 'If you know them so well, have they told you what they did to her?'

'Would you keep your fucking voice down,' Tom hisses.

'No! I absolutely won't keep my fucking voi—'

He's on his feet, gripping my arm again, bending it backwards so that I am forced to kneel to stop it from breaking. The pain is excruciating – a burning, tearing flood of pain and then a crack and I think I'm going to pass out. At that noise, at the breaking or fracturing of my wrist, he lets go, tossing me aside like I am nothing. Like I am less than nothing.

'I was giving it all to you on a fucking plate!' he shouts, but he's upset now. I swear he's on the brink of crying. Well, I'll be damned if I'm going to feel sorry for him. He can cry all he wants.

'All you could've wanted,' he says. 'The fame and recognition. This will win awards. Your career will be made. You will be made and all you can do is tell me I'm wrong?'

'I didn't want success on these terms,' I cry out, my wrist now throbbing so much my head is light. It's too warm and the pain and the heat are making me nauseous. 'How could you ever think I would? You're the one who is messed up. Not Nora, or Brendan or whoever your secret school friends are.' I can't hide the scorn in my voice. Because truly he is worse than all of them because they were all acting out of pain or fear. He was acting out of ambition. 'You've ruined it all,' I shout.

He storms to the window but doesn't keep his back to me for long. Maybe he is afraid I will make a run for it after all. If I could get ahead of him, even by ten seconds, I could be out on the street before he could catch me.

Just as I'm trying to figure out how to get to my feet and get to the door, he is back towering over me again. 'I didn't ruin this, Izzy. You are the one who seems set on doing that. I don't think I can let that happen.'

With a bravado I most certainly am not feeling I force myself to laugh. 'Ha! How deluded are you? Everyone is going to know what you did. And I'm pretty sure DI Bradley and his crew will want to have a chat as well.'

'Be careful, Izzy,' he warns. 'I have friends now, after all, who are very good at making people disappear without a trace.'

Maybe he intends those words to terrify me, and I'd be lying if I said a cold shiver hasn't just run up and down my spine – but pain and anger are motivating forces and I'll be damned if I'm going to let this go on for a moment longer. I need to de-escalate this and fast.

Fighting through the pain in my arm, ignoring the strange way in which my hand now hangs limply, and how swollen my wrist is already, I get to my feet. It doesn't take much effort for me to feign sickness – to look as if I'm going to faint. To be honest, I'm starting to think I actually might faint but I have to push on.

'I need air,' I gasp. 'Please, Tom. Let me get some fresh air. Even from the window.'

There's a beat while he tries to decide if he should let me or not. I can see him measuring the risks – wondering if I have the balls to take him on. Wondering just how scared of him I really am.

'I know you're not this person. I know you're a good man,' I tell him. 'And I get it. You acted in the best interests of the documentary. You've only done this to make sure we get the audience we want and deserve. I get that your intentions have been good ones.' As I speak, I inch over to the window, allowing the soft breeze from outside to wash over me and help stem the wave of nausea that threatens to engulf me.

'They have been!' he says. 'So you see that? I need you to see it.'

'I do,' I say. It's not a lie. He did do it for the documentary. That doesn't make it right of course, but if I can get him to calm down. If I can get him onside . . . then I have a chance. And everyone else has a chance too. Nora, Luca . . . even Daisy if she's still alive. God knows threatening him with the police isn't working.

'Look,' I say, 'it's just a shock. It's a lot to get my head around.' He nods.

'It's been a whirlwind few days. Very emotional and I've been chasing my tail trying to keep up with it all. I'd have been lost without you helping me.' That part, of course, is a lie. I know that now more than ever.

I nurse my poor broken and swollen arm, wincing as I try to elevate it, to rest it against my chest. If I can fashion some sort of makeshift sling it might help.

'I'm sorry,' he says, looking at my arm. 'I didn't mean to. I'm not like this. This is not me. You know that, don't you? You know me, Izzy. I'm not someone who hurts people.'

'It's okay, I know,' I say, even though I want to tell him this is exactly who he is.

Very gently, he guides me closer to the window, fetches a chair and helps me sit down.

'Is it very sore?' he asks and I can't lie anymore, so I nod and that action in itself releases the tears that I swore I'd swallow back.

He crouches on the floor beside me, his head in his hands. 'This is a mess, isn't it?' he asks.

'It is,' I tell him, reaching out with my good hand and gently stroking his hair as if he is a child who needs comforting.

'I just wanted to make sure we smashed this. And then when I spoke to Paul . . .'

'Paul?' I ask, hoping my voice doesn't belie my surprise at him having said a name.

'One of The Four,' he says. 'He's the main guy, by all accounts. Then there's another bloke, and a woman. Catherine Simms was the fourth person in their gang. When I spoke to him he was so convincing. I could sense the horror in those woods that night poor Catherine was left there and I felt for them all. What a thing to have witnessed. But it wasn't meant to go this far. No one was meant to get hurt.'

I want to scream at him that people have already been hurt, but I don't. Now is not the time to lose my cool. Not when I'm capturing this all on film.

'It doesn't need to go any further,' I say, gently. 'You can stop it. You have that power. Get these four to back off from Luca. Tell them they've made their point. Stop this and we'll move on from here like none of this – between us – ever happened. We'll wrap up the project and say no more about it.'

He looks up at me and I cannot tell from his expression what he is going to do next.

The anger that was in him just minutes before is gone, but I know that I am walking a very fine line here. One wrong word, one wrong look, one wrong gesture and it will be back. And if it comes back, I fear it will be worse.

But he just nods. It seems that, for now anyway, he believes me. 'You have a good heart, Tom. I know you did this mostly because you felt sorry for those children. For Catherine. Maybe you even believed Luca would have a better life away from his mother. Maybe that's what they've done for Daisy too. You were doing a good thing,' I say.

He is lapping up my soothing words, which have largely been playing to his ego. Each is sticking in my throat. I have to swallow back my anger and my disgust and struggle against the pain that seems to grow stronger and stronger. I have to do it because I know it's my only way to get out of this room without him hurting me even more – and if he can break a wrist with a simple twist, I dread to think what else he can do.

'Please,' I beg. 'Be the guy I know you are. End this.'

I'm still sitting on the chair beside the window, people walking below that I dare not call out to. I watch as he picks up his phone and makes a call. I can't control what they will say back to him, of course. They may convince him I'm wrong but I have to at least try and stop this before it goes any further.

'We've fucked up,' I hear Tom say. 'I think we've played it all wrong.'

My heart in my mouth, I watch as Tom paces across the room. He is speaking so quietly into the phone, his back to me so I can't hear what he is saying or read his lips.

Then he turns and looks at me, just stares for seconds that feel like minutes and I think I might have an actual heart attack but I don't want to push him. He needs to feel he is in control, that he is driving this.

'They are stopping. They never wanted this to happen. They wanted to scare her − to punish her, but they didn't want her to end up like this,' he says. 'They thought they were doing the right thing. They thought she was a different person − more like her father.

'Izzy,' he says slowly, and his voice is breaking. 'He tells me they gave her a choice. He spoke to her this morning in the woods, followed her there, and told her she had to choose which of her children to save.'

Bile rises in my now empty stomach as I imagine the horror Nora must have gone through.

Tom speaks again. 'She refused. Even though she is desperate to know about Daisy, she refused and said no mother could make that choice. He told her she had to choose one or lose both. That's when she got in her car. He said they knew they had fucked up then, when she refused to make a choice. They knew she wasn't the monster they had remembered.'

Chapter Forty-Nine

Izzy

These are the kind of moments you expect to be really dramatic. It's what the movies promise. Flashing blue lights. Armed police. Drama. A gunfight. That's how the bad guys get caught.

There is nothing dramatic about this. We, Tom and I, are sitting in A&E and we are waiting for the police to arrive to talk to us. Tom knows they're coming. He doesn't know I will be pressing charges for my broken wrist but I imagine I am the least of his worries now. He has made a mess and no one can hide it for him. From issuing anonymous threats, to wasting police time and resources, and aiding in the planned abduction of Luca Pryce he is up to his eyes in it. And once that's all done and dusted, he knows he will never work in this industry again.

I can't bring myself to speak to him just now. I'm half expecting him to bolt for the door and that would be the very worst thing he could do. He knows who the remaining 'three' of The Four are. He has the key to finding out what happened to Daisy Logue after all this time.

If they claimed they weren't going to hurt Luca, simply to make sure he led a full life away from Nora's influence, do we dare to hope that Daisy could still be alive? If they asked Nora to choose between her two children, surely this means she must still be out there? She may just think she's like every other eleven-year-old child and unaware of who she really is and the anguish her disappearance has caused.

Or was their choice a lie too? Just another cruelty?

If I was still planning on finishing this documentary, it would make for a cracking ending. But I don't think I have the stomach for it anymore. This may have been my dream project – the one I desperately felt connected to. The one I was sure would lead to me being taken seriously as a film-maker and which would open so many doors for me . . . but it would be tainted now. Much too tainted. And I feel Nora has been used enough. I shudder when I think of her being asked to choose between her children.

Tom has said he will give what details he has to the police. He has a phone number. A name. An email chain. It's a concrete lead. It's not enough to make me want to forgive him, or ever see him again, but it's enough to make me think there is still the trace of a decent human being inside him.

I've already sent Jacqs a text. Given her some scant details. Sworn her to secrecy. She is currently on her way to Derry and she has vowed to look after me. It's not how we planned to meet, but it will be so good to see her. God knows I'll need a friend after this. I can't believe I distrusted her of all people when the real liar was under my roof.

'I am sorry,' Tom says, his voice small – all his usual bravado gone.

'You and me both,' I tell him, just as DI Bradley walks through the double doors followed by two uniformed police officers. I brace myself.

Chapter Fifty

Nora

'You're safe,' a soft voice in my ear comforts me as I swim out of unconsciousness. It takes a moment, and the awareness of pain for me to remember where I am. Then it hits me – the fear that I have to make a choice or the worst will happen. But of course I can't speak.

The voice is close by again and I force my eyes open, to see who I assume to be the blurry-faced nurse. Forgetting that I cannot speak I try, and am rewarded with an electric shock of pain in my jaw that almost blinds me.

'Nora, I'm told you shouldn't try to speak.' I blink my eyes and try to focus. Doesn't the blurry-faced nurse know that I need to speak? I need to make sure my boy is safe. I need to tell her I know why this has happened. I remember what my father did. Catherine. The children that we were. What I did, may God forgive me. I need to know if they have Daisy.

Panic threatens to set in until I feel a gentle hand on mine.

'Nora, everyone is safe. We know what happened this morning. We know what you were asked to do and we're so sorry about that.'

I blink again, look at the nurse as she comes into focus, but it's not a nurse. It's DS Eve King. Is she here for me? Has the man in the woods told her about Catherine? All those voices and faces in the car with me – all those children he hurt while I let him. I chose her that night because I desperately wanted to please him and I was so scared of the dark too. So scared of the woods. He'd told me once he would take me out there and leave me – and no one would find me. The nightmares I had . . . My body rotting in the mulch, animals gnawing at my hands – blood and twigs and stones. I try to catch my breath, my heart ready to explode. I may not have hurt Daisy, but that doesn't mean I wasn't responsible.

'You're safe,' she says again. 'We know it all. We know you did nothing wrong.' She encourages me to breathe slowly, and I hear a voice – a nurse I assume – in the background coaching her. My breath begins to settle. I am safe. I am safe.

I need to make sure Brendan knows I did nothing wrong. I need him to know Luca is safe. Is he with Luca now? I try and look over DS King's shoulder to see if I can spot him but I don't. The only voice I hear in the room is the nurse, now telling DS King it's better not to upset me. But I need to know.

'Luca is with his grandparents. I'm told he's been watching *Paw Patrol* on a loop all day,' DS King says with warmth, as if she can read my thoughts. 'Brendan is talking with DI Bradley right now. We know who has been sending the messages. We know why. And we know they will no longer be posing any threat to you or your family.'

All I can do is blink. I have so many questions but I can't speak. I don't even know where to start.

There is some muttering that I can't tune in to, before DS King is back beside me. 'Heather is here. You know Heather? Your family liaison officer? She'll stay with you for now. There's a lot to take in.'

I try and nod but the slightest movement hurts.

'We know they wanted you to choose,' DS King says softly and despite the pain I can't stop a guttural cry escaping from my throat.

'Nora, we have news for you. Daisy's alive. We know where she is. We know who took her. She's safe and well. She has been looked after. Do you understand what I'm telling you?'

I try to nod again and this time I don't care about the pain. The sob that gurgles from the back of my throat is one of guilt, and joy, and pain, and hope.

I feel the darkness of exhaustion, of pain-relief-induced sleep, wash over me again but when I close my eyes this time, I'm not afraid to fall asleep. She's alive. Nothing else matters.

Chapter Fifty-One

Two Months Later

Izzy

My job has been to observe things. To film them. To be a voyeur of sorts looking in at other people's lives. I've never shied away from that. That's what a film-maker and a storyteller does. I've never taken it for granted either – anyone allowing you into their life is trusting you to tell their story fairly. They are trusting you with their pain and their joy and the most intimate moments of their lives.

None have ever made me feel so nervous as today does. None have ever been such a privilege as today is. And today, I don't even have a camera with me.

But I am here, with Nora Logue as she waits to see her daughter for the first time in seven years. It has been a long, painful two months for Nora – both in terms of her physical recovery but also as she was asked to be patient while counsellors worked with Daisy, now known as Isla, to explain the truth of her past, and to prepare her to meet her mother.

Nora too has been undergoing intense therapy to make sense of her memories and how they flooded back the day of the accident. She has been given a diagnosis of CPTSD, or complex post traumatic stress disorder, both in relation to her complicated childhood and to the events surrounding Daisy's disappearance. Add to that the events of two months ago – it's a wonder Nora is doing as well as she is.

And she is a remarkable woman. One who has not blamed me for my role in what happened. She has shown me incredible kindness and I am now proud to call her my friend. I'd stayed in Derry for three weeks following the accident – not because I still had a documentary to make. That's still shelved and will probably never see the light the day, even though Nora says it should. But because I wanted to help the police put together their case against The Four, and Brendan and Tom too. I wanted to make sure that no matter each of these people's motives, they paid for the damage they had caused.

Of course, the wheels of justice move slowly and they don't often make sense. Paul Bell, who it turns out was the mysterious 'neighbour' who knew my name, has been remanded in custody awaiting trial on numerous charges including kidnapping, making a threat to harm or kill, harassment, and posting malicious messages online. It's thought he will plead guilty in the hope of getting a lighter sentence. The other two members of The Four – Lucy Fields and Simon Phillips – are awaiting trial but have been released on bail.

Their names meant nothing to me when I first heard them, but I soon learned that I had interacted with both of them before. Outside of the activity of the account named The Four, both Lucy and Simon had been posting on AmateurSleuths – spewing conspiracy theories about Daisy's disappearance. Truthseeker101 and JessicaFletcherFan had both become prominent posters over the last few weeks. I even found a private message from Truthseeker101 in my inbox, telling me why I should be looking at the bigger issue of child trafficking instead of focusing on 'just one child'.

I can only assume these messages were sent to try and distract me, and to send me off in a different investigative direction. I can understand why Lucy and Simon did that. These two are the people Daisy, now Isla, has come to think of as her mother and father and they did not want to lose her. They raised Isla in a secluded farmhouse in County Armagh, cropping her hair short and giving her glasses to wear to conceal her identity. They only escaped detection for so long because they home-schooled Isla. While there are no allegations that Isla met with any of the cruelty Percy Logue's pupils did, and in fact she is deeply loved, there's no doubt her childhood has been greatly restricted by the desire to hide her true identity.

And yet, Nora has allowed Isla to maintain a level of contact with them, not wanting to distress the child by taking her away from the people she recognised as her parents for seven years. If that doesn't show a strength of character and selflessness in Nora then I don't know what would.

Both Brendan and Tom are also out on bail and for now, Brendan retains custody of Luca. While recovering, Nora has seen Luca once a week and she is dealing with her mixed feelings, and the huge guilt that came with her realisation that she had not allowed herself to love him simply because he was not Daisy. I've no doubt she will find her equilibrium with him. She does love him deeply. She just needs to allow herself to feel it.

And she needs to get through what will happen today.

'I'm so nervous, I might vomit,' she says, as we sit side by side on a small red sofa in a cream-painted room. It's designed to look like an ordinary living room but there's no hiding the institutional nature of it. This is a small room in a social services office block and any moment now, Isla will come in with her social worker and the foster mother who has been looking after her since she was found.

This is the first time Nora will get to see her daughter up close and in person. It's the first time in seven years she will be able to breathe the same air as her. To hold her. To hear her voice. To know, without a shadow of a doubt, that she is alive and well.

I can totally understand why this makes her want to throw up. This is more than she could have hoped for through all those years of horror.

'It will be okay,' I tell her. 'Just take it slowly. Go easy on yourself.'

She nods and squeezes my hand. 'You're right,' she says. 'And we've done the work.'

'You have,' I agree, thinking of the letters they have exchanged, the photos Nora has shared with Isla via her foster mother. The way they have been reintroduced to each other in small bite-size pieces. There was no immediate reunion – not least because Nora was so ill, but also because these things are delicate. They take time. Trauma sustained in childhood can run deep and last for decades. We know that all too well.

'Do you think she'll remember me? Like, really remember me? That I'll not just be a name and a picture to her?' Her voice is small and I can feel her hand shaking. My heart aches for her. She deserved none of this.

'I'm not sure,' I tell her, honestly. 'But even if she doesn't, there's time now. There's time to build new memories.'

She nods but I know she's lost in a time long ago when they sang and danced and talked about fairy houses and teddy bears' picnics.

Just as Nora opens her mouth to speak again, there is a creak as the door handle turns and she holds my hand so tightly –

the hand that is attached to the recently healed broken wrist – that I yelp. She lets go just as a little girl, her hair cut into a short bob, her eyes blue as sapphires and her tentative smile a perfect mirror of her mother's, walks into the room and stares at us both.

Holding my breath, I wait for her reaction and my heart thuds when she turns towards her foster mother and I prepare myself for her to run out of the room while I try and comfort Nora.

But Isla doesn't run from the room. She glances at her foster mother, who nods and then she lets go of her hand and runs straight to Nora who is smiling, and crying and telling her she loves her so very much and that she is the most beautiful little girl in the universe.

I can't help but cry as Isla, the little girl who was Daisy Logue, turns her head upwards to look at her mother and says softly, 'I remember you, Mammy. You were the lady who used to sing and dance with me all the time.'

Someone is watching her.
She just doesn't know it yet.

A chilling, powerful read guaranteed
to keep you up at night.

Available in all good bookshops now.

Not all secrets are meant to come out . . .

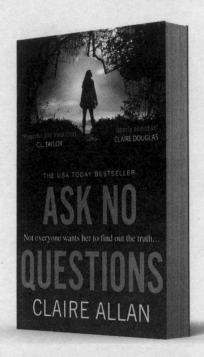

**A twisty crime thriller from the
bestselling author Claire Allan.**

Available in all good bookshops now.

I disappeared on a Tuesday afternoon.
They've never found my body . . .

An unputdownable serial killer thriller with a
breath-taking twist.

Available in all good bookshops now.

Just how far is a mother willing to go?

A gripping psychological thriller from the *USA Today* bestselling author.

Available in all good bookshops now.

You watched her die.
And her death has created a vacancy . . .

A spine-tingling psychological thriller
that will have you hooked.

Available in all good bookshops now.

Every family has its secrets . . .

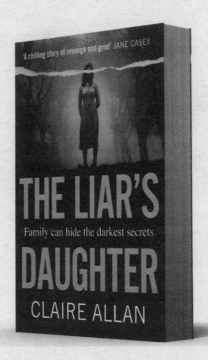

An addictive and dark suspense novel
about deadly secrets and lies.

Available in all good bookshops now.